The
Wisteria Crescent
Chronicles

Kate Forster writes books filled with love, laughter and the enchantment of everyday life. Kate, a Melbourne-based author, crafts realistic characters and touching stories that feel like you're catching up with old friends. When she is not writing, you can find her sharing glimpses of her creative life on social media, soaking up inspiration from her dynamic online community or spending time with her loving dogs, who are constantly by her side (and occasionally steal the spotlight). Kate, who is tea-fuelled and daydreaming on the beach, is all about finding joy in the little things and sharing it through her writing.

The Wisteria Crescent Chronicles

Kate Forster

ORION

First published in Great Britain in 2025 by Orion Fiction,
an imprint of The Orion Publishing Group Ltd.
Carmelite House, 50 Victoria Embankment
London EC4Y 0DZ

An Hachette UK Company

The authorised representative in the EEA is Hachette Ireland,
8 Castlecourt Centre, Dublin 15, D15 XTP3,
Ireland (email: info@hbgi.ie)

1 3 5 7 9 10 8 6 4 2

A CIP catalogue record for this book is
available from the British Library.

ISBN (Mass Market Paperback) 9781 3987 1788 6
ISBN (Ebook) 9781 3987 1789 3
ISBN (Audio) 9781 3987 1790 9

Typeset at The Spartan Press Ltd,
Lymington, Hants

Printed and bound in Great Britain by Clays Ltd,
Elcograf S.p.A.

www.orionbooks.co.uk

For all the friends I have made through my life – those who have shaped, saved, humoured, challenged and loved me. Thank you.

I

Marion

It is a truth universally acknowledged that a widowed woman in possession of a large Georgian home in Bath, but with no money to buy teabags and loo rolls, needs a solution, and one quickly. This is how Marion Gaynor, widow, mother of two and on the wrong side of seventy, found herself entertaining the idea of renting out some rooms in her lovely home, Wisteria Crescent.

If you have been to Bath, you might have seen it. It's one of the Crescent houses and is the one with wisteria at the front gate that sweeps over the front door like a glamorous updo hairstyle. Marion found it amusing that people assumed she was wealthy because of the house, but the truth was she had no actual income, which is a hard thing to admit, and an even harder thing to live on. Right now, the buds on the wisteria vines were beginning to swell, unsure whether to trust the March sunshine with freezing winds swirling about the city.

Those tourists who stood outside the house, posing while having their photos taken, pretending they were in a Jane Austen book or film, would also have conjured the inhabitants as having huge salaries. But this income was non-existent, due to circumstances out of Marion's control.

Not that Marion begrudged those posing. She understood it was a beautiful home and it gave you the feeling of better times when you saw it in person. But it had been a year of waiting for better times to arrive and Marion knew she needed to act on what she was planning. Except for one issue, her daughter, Clair, who was currently standing in the kitchen at Temple Terrace, hands on hips, just like she used to when she was five. Now forty-five, not much had evolved, especially when Clair was not in agreement with the issue at hand, like now.

'Rent rooms?' Clair was aghast. 'That's very *Bleak House*. You don't need to do that. Just sell Temple Terrace and we'll set you up in a little bungalow at the bottom of the garden.'

Marion had tried to keep her calm. She was used to Clair's overreactions to any decision Marion made since Geoffrey, Marion's husband and Clair's father, had died a year earlier. Clair had become more impatient with her, as though she blamed her mother for the position Marion found herself in. After seventy-odd years, Marion had learned that people often blame victims when terrible things happen, clinging to the belief that the world was fair and their need to have the illusion of control.

Clair believed in this world, despite everything that had happened in her life, because she needed everything to be perfect. She liked to think she would have done things differently to others who faced tough times, but her judgement was clouded by the gift of hindsight, because then she could pretend the world is fair and she could have prevented such tragedies. It's always easier, Marion reflected, to see what could have been done after the fact, when the harsh reality no longer looms so threateningly close.

'You want me to live out the back of your house in a kennel with a kettle, like an old dog you won't let inside any more because it smells and spoils the rugs?' Marion smiled as she spoke, trying to soften the message.

'Mother.' Clair shook her head. 'We just want you to be happy. It's not a punishment.'

Clair called her Mother when she wasn't happy with her, Mum when Marion was doing as she was told. Today was a 'Mother' day.

Marion was the sort of woman people trusted their children with at the park or who dogs liked to sniff and wag their tails at. She wore lovely cashmere and merino knits in winter with navy or black trousers, and in summer, sensible T-shirts or collared shirts in good-quality cotton, always with a brooch of some sort on the left-hand side of the front of her clothes. Her granddaughter, Sophie, called her brooches 'boob art', which Marion thought hilarious. She promised Sophie her extensive 'boob art' collection when she died, but right now, Marion was as fit as a fiddle and not planning on letting anything get in her way. She was chic in a tailored way, not taking any fashion risks, always appropriate in how she presented herself.

Of course, Paul and Clair wanted her to sell Temple Terrace. It would serve them well, too. Financially, they could encourage Marion to put the money towards their own home, which was altogether too big and too expensive for a family of four. And it meant they would have a live-in babysitter for their twins, Sophie and Tom.

Marion loved her grandchildren, but they were fourteen and more interested in their phones than their grandmother. They were also too old to be babysat any more. Mostly, Tom grunted at Marion when he saw her, the small boy who used to want to bake cakes with her now with earbuds in and enveloped in a cloud of heavy aftershave, despite him growing only three hairs on his chin a month. And

Sophie … well, Sophie was still lovely, but she seemed distant. Perhaps something was happening at school? Friendship drama, Marion wondered, remembering how apocalyptical everything felt as a teenager, even for her.

Clair tapped the kitchen worktop with a manicured fingernail, as though calling a court to order in the case of 'Marion's Wants versus Clair's Expectations'.

'I know Dad was irresponsible and left you high and dry financially speaking when he died, but with the cash you would make from selling the house, you could do whatever you wanted: travel, buy new clothes, perhaps a new car. Paul can invest the rest and you can live with us.'

Paul walked away and looked out of the kitchen window. He was thin, thinner than usual, and his fingernails were all gnawed. Marion hadn't realised Paul was a nail-biter, or was this a new thing? She would have asked, but Clair was too far up on her high horse at that moment to think about anyone else.

'We could go to Ikea and get some nice new things for a bungalow, so you can have a place to land between travel. Get rid of all the old stuff.'

Marion turned the mug of tea around so she could see the peacock on the china. It was a Wedgewood pattern called Fortune. It felt like a slap, since her husband had lost their fortune before he died.

'I like my old stuff. I am old stuff,' she joked to try to shift the mood, but Clair didn't acknowledge it, or perhaps she wasn't listening.

Marion remembered a quote about death revealing the truth about things but couldn't recall who said it first. But it was true. Geoffrey's decisions before he died could have ruined her, except the house was paid off.

'He wasn't irresponsible, Clair,' she said gently, trying to defend the man who had loved both her and their daughter so much. 'He had a brain tumour and it caused him to make some terrible decisions.' She paused. 'The last thing he'd want me to do is leave the house if I wasn't ready ... And I'm not ready.'

'But we never saw where he put the money, Mother. He said he put it into an investment in Africa, but where in Africa? There was nothing in the accounts. Paul never did find out, did you, dear?'

Paul shook his head. 'I've never found it. The bank and I both looked. He withdrew it, but who he gave it to is a mystery. He might have wired it to someone in Africa – older people do that more often than you would realise – but there was no record of it.'

Marion let the ageist comment go. She was an older person and she had never wired money to anyone, let alone someone in another country. She was proud of herself and how she had been managing to budget since he had died, making do as much as she could, but now, she needed a more stable solution and tenants seemed perfect.

She caught a look between Clair and Paul.

'I do think the house is too big for you now,' Paul said in a slightly apologetic tone, as though he knew there would be hell to pay if he outright disagreed with his wife. 'And you don't want renters here, smoking and having parties and doing drugs, sneaking pets in or cuckooing the place and you ending up in the garden shed.'

Clair crossed her arms and nodded. 'Exactly. Paul knows about these things.'

Marion wasn't sure how or why Paul knew about these things as a financial advisor, but she said nothing. She was used to saying nothing around her daughter and son-in-law.

Saying nothing stopped a lot of headaches and arguments, she thought, but sometimes she wished she had the strength to say something. She had let things go for so long that now that it seemed anything was acceptable in their eyes, including uprooting her and changing her life without her having any say.

If Marion was ever asked what her greatest regret in life so far was, she expected that people would assume her answer would be around trying to stop the terrible things that had happened in the past to their family. But it wasn't. It was Clair being so utterly self-absorbed and disloyal to her own mother. When had it changed? She couldn't find a date to circle on the calendar, with the note next to it announcing the day. No, it was a slow drip, until one day it had overflowed and Clair was filled with ... resentment and entitlement.

Every small grievance, every perceived slight, every moment Clair felt overlooked had accumulated over the years, hardening her heart and narrowing her vision of what led them to this moment. The girl who once brought her mother flowers and listened intently to bedtime stories about faraway trees and wishing chairs had transformed into a woman who saw the world only through the lens of her own desires.

Marion could trace the tiny moments: when Geoffrey missed her ballet recitals owing to work commitments. The conversations cut short by Marion's busy schedule entertaining Geoffrey's clients and managing two children at home when her husband was always working. The birthdays when the cake wasn't quite right according to Clair's perfectionism. The decisions made for Andy's funeral, then Geoffrey's funeral. Each worse than the next, all a drop in the bucket of Clair's discontent.

But more than that, at what stage had Clair decided to put Paul's opinion over her own? And when had she become so thoroughly unlikeable? Oh, Marion loved her daughter, that was never in question, but she didn't like her and she knew Clair didn't like her in return. Now, facing her daughter's cold indifference, Marion realised that the overflow had washed away the warmth and connection they once shared, leaving a chasm she wasn't sure how to bridge.

Clair wasn't finished. 'And the whole financial thing, well, that's never been your strong suit, has it?'

Marion stood up, took her mug and sloshed the remains of the tea into the sink. If she spoke now, she would lose her temper at Clair and she didn't want to carve the rift between them even deeper.

'Daddy always took care of the money until he was ill. You aren't familiar with the ins and outs. I mean, have you even done the figures for the lodgers to see if you will break even? Do you want Paul to look at the numbers – see if it all adds up? You have all sorts of things to consider, doesn't she, Paul?'

'Yes, there's council taxes and income tax from the renters, plus the need for savings in case something goes awry with the heating or plumbing, general repairs. What if they don't pay the rent and you have to go to a tribunal or seek legal advice?'

Marion looked out from the bay window over the double sink at the garden. It was just lawn and some pots, nothing interesting or special, mostly because Marion couldn't afford to buy new plants or get the weeds pulled in the beds. An income from some housemates would help, but she hadn't thought of everything Paul had just mentioned and fear rose in her throat.

Don't let them see you scared, she told herself.

'No, I don't need Paul to look at the figures. I did them myself and I'm fine. I have everything covered and as far as housemates, I would enjoy the company,' she said, turning to Clair.

It was true. She had thought about getting a dog, but she wanted a real connection, not just an animal waiting for a treat and a walk each day. She wanted to be a part of something again, and a humming household was where she had been happiest, just not at the back of Clair and Paul's house in a bungalow.

'That's a dig at me, because I don't come around much,' Clair almost wailed.

Marion took a deep breath. 'No, Clair, not everything is about you. I think it's a shame this big house is empty – it deserves to have people in it again.'

How could she explain to Clair the way her days were consumed by a profound sense of loneliness that made her catch her breath when she caught herself doing something for Geoffrey out of habit. Setting a place at the table for dinner on occasion, seeing something on the street she would have pointed out to him. They used to have such a nice routine before he became ill.

Up early, they would get ready and then walk to their favourite bakery. Sit and drink coffee or tea, depending on their mood, and eat a pastry. Pass the papers between them and then head home, stopping to chat to people they knew as well as friendly strangers. Geoffrey would always pat the dogs that passed and when they were home, they would do their separate activities. Geoffrey would read, Marion would read or do a sudoku, or watch interesting things on the internet. Documentaries, dances, interviews, Marion was always curious about the world and the internet made it all so much closer and accessible.

And then Geoffrey had started doing silly things, forgetting things and asking for Andy. That's when she had taken him to the doctor, then a specialist. Some scans and a week later, they had a diagnosis.

One of their phones pinged with a message, diffusing the situation. Clair picked hers up from the kitchen worktop.

'The twins are ready to be picked up from rowing,' she said to Paul.

Marion noticed he looked relieved as he grabbed the car keys.

'Want me to bring them back here?' he asked Clair.

Clair feigned a sad face. 'I would, but we have to get them home and sorted. We're off to see Coldplay in Bristol tonight and the kids are at friends for a sleepover.'

Marion started towards the front door. 'That sounds like fun. Another time, then.'

Clair gave that nervous laugh she did when she was relieved. 'Yes, another time.'

Marion opened the front door and admired some small buds coming on the wisteria as Clair passed through onto the street.

'I do wish you would think about selling.' Clair was going in for one more round. 'A nice new wardrobe, a trip to Kenya – you love Kenya! – or you could buy a lovely handbag, a luxury one. A Kelly or a Birkin.' She sounded delighted with her plans for her mother.

Marion sighed. 'I don't want a Kelly or a Birkin, and the reason I loved Kenya was because I went with your dad. I'm not about to go alone, and for the record' – she looked at Paul – 'if the jury can take note, I happen to like my clothes so don't need new ones.'

'That's not fair. I'm trying to help.' Clair pulled her thick camel-coloured coat around her thin frame.

'While I'm still capable of making my own decisions, I'll continue to do so. Unless I start wiping down the kitchen sink with a raw chicken breast, or visiting the local library asking for directions home, let's continue as normal until further notice.' She smiled as she spoke, hoping Clair would see it as a peace offering, but Clair's mouth fell open and her eyes darkened.

'Mother, please.'

Marion shook her head. 'Please stop, Clair. I know you mean well and I love you so much for caring, but I'm fine, I promise. This is a good outcome for me and for you. This way we can still have our independence and everything will be balanced between us. Why don't you all come over on Sunday for lunch? I'll make your favourite chicken pie.'

Clair scowled at her mother. 'I'm off carbs,' was all she said in return.

Paul guided Clair to the car, knowing they had lost this round.

Marion waved goodbye to them, though they didn't turn around, and with a shiver from the cold spring air, she turned and looked at the front of her beloved Temple Terrace, noticing the tangle of wisteria branches that climbed across its façade. For fifty years, she had watched the seasons change and the wisteria bloom every year, each year bringing with it a renewed sense of wonder and appreciation for the patience and perseverance of the plant. Perhaps it was a reminder for Marion not to give up or to give in to the situation in which she found herself.

There was no point in being angry about Geoffrey's poor investments when he was ill, or being angry at the brain tumour. It only mattered how she moved forwards and maintained her independence.

Marion walked back inside, where she found her iPad next to her armchair. She sat down and opened the houseshare site she had been looking at over the past week. There was no chance she could live with Clair and Paul. She would rather be homeless, she thought somewhat dramatically as she typed in her login.

Three rooms to rent – Bath proper.
Older landlady who lives on site – who uses emojis, understands TikTok and likes a neat whiskey after dinner by the fire in the winter and in the garden during summer – is opening her house in The Crescent for rent.
   Three double bedrooms, all with beds, chest of drawers, wardrobe, an armchair and ensuite available. No smoking, no pets, females preferred. Any age, I am not ageist. My grandkids tell me I'm cool, but they could just be saying so.

She stopped typing for a moment and then typed in the rent and paused.

Was it too much? It looked to be on par with other listings. In the end it was what she needed to pay the bills and have a little to live on, a nice life. She kept typing.

Two sitting rooms, a dining room, a sunroom/ conservatory, a snug and library also available for use.
   A weekly clean, change of linen and all bills (except energy – gas and electricity) are included in the rental.
The monthly rent is collected every four weeks, not by the calendar month, and it is payable in advance.

She finished and looked at the wedding photo of her and Geoffrey on the mantel.

'Needs must,' she said, using the old phrase of Geoffrey's to the photo, and uploaded the ad.

2

Felicity

Felicity Booth was twenty-three years old and without friends, money or beauty. The last one was the opinion of her grandmother, who once described Felicity as being 'as plain as a scone'. Felicity had never been able to eat a scone since, both the words and the baked goods stuck in her throat for ever.

Felicity's mother insisted that Felicity was beautiful in her own way, but Felicity had not yet found her way to that beauty her mother promised. In centuries past, Felicity might have joined a convent or become a governess, but those were not options for Felicity no matter how much she wished they still were, so she threw herself into the modern version: academia.

After a bachelor's degree in English literature and a master's in the Roman Empire from York, Felicity still didn't know what she wanted to do so decided to keep studying. She had finished school early, due to being prodigiously intelligent, according to her teachers, but since she didn't have any friends, there wasn't much else to do but study. Eventually, it felt natural she would combine the two things she knew most about and the best place she could do that was in Bath, known for Jane Austen and the Roman influence.

Sometimes when she walked the streets of Bath, she felt as though she had somehow been transported in a time machine that transitioned her from now to Roman times to the Regency era. Walking the cobbled streets, she would see the grandeur and pomp of the Roman Baths, the towering columns and intricate stonework taking her breath away. As she turned a corner, the elegance of the Georgian architecture greeted her, with its sweeping terraces and the dignified presence of men sporting the upright posture of top hats, typical of Austen's era.

And just as she thought she had finally been taken back to the times she understood more than the one she lived in now, someone bumping into her while looking at their phone, or tourists with cameras on sticks, would jolt her out of her time travel and back into the present day.

Felicity often found herself wishing she had been born in the Regency era, convinced that her fair complexion, slender figure, petite hands and feet, long straight dark hair, slightly hooked nose and bright blue eyes might have been considered attractive then. Except that she hunched herself so far over that her eyes were always on the ground, making it hard to see her face. Perhaps she might have been considered a great beauty then, but for now, according to her grandmother and her own internal critic, she was just a plain scone with no jam or cream to fancy her up.

Felicity eschewed the frivolities of the other girls at university, preferring to knit her own jumpers and cardigans in what her grandmother aptly called 'various shades of thunderstorm'. She paired these shapeless yet cosy creations with utilitarian cargo pants and sturdy work boots, giving her the look of a Victorian ghost visiting a building site to undertake a health and safety assessment.

After being in the quietude of the library for most of the day, Felicity headed towards the dormitory where she resided. This was the first time she had lived away from home and she hated it. She thought that leaving York would be exciting, away from her grandmother's house that she shared with her mother. She believed that she would finally have her own place in Bath, with no more criticisms and snide comments from her grandmother. Instead, she found she was lonely. And it was loud, the other residents wanting to party all night, despite the signs saying quiet from 10 p.m.

She climbed the stairs to her floor and walked towards her apartment, where some sort of horrific techno music was emanating from the apartment to her left. The noise inside was no better, perhaps even louder. The neighbour was a young guy who said 'cool bro' a lot and who told Felicity to bang on the wall if his music was too loud. Felicity never had, despite it being too loud all the time.

She slipped her backpack off onto the bed and sat, staring at the kitchen cupboard. Felicity had learned the description of the room by heart before she arrived at university. She was so excited to have her own space:

Your snug studio apartment cleverly combines functionality with comfort. The galley kitchen, equipped with essential appliances, seamlessly merges with the living area, where a neatly made bed beckons for relaxation. Across from the bed, a modest seating arrangement invites lounging or studying, while shelves above provide storage for personal belongings. Despite its cosy size, the apartment offers a welcoming retreat from student life.

The truth of it was that Felicity could reach into a kitchen drawer from her bed and take out a snack without having to lift her head. This was proving to be bad for her waistline and resulting in poor sleep when she rolled over onto crumbs from the crisps she had eaten earlier.

As though to prove her point, Felicity opened a drawer and took out a mini Galaxy bar and popped it into her mouth, chewing slowly as the caramel melted in her mouth. Then moans sounded on the other side of the wall opposite from Techno Cool Bro, followed by a rhythmic banging. Felicity chewed the chocolate as she watched the water in a glass on the kitchen worktop start to move in time with the wall. She knew this water-shaking moment wouldn't last long. The neighbour always seemed to have girls in his room but the main event was never epic, as it were.

By the time Felicity had gone to the bathroom, washed her hands and changed into her pyjamas, the water had stopped shaking in the glass and even the techno music had lulled. She climbed into bed, despite it being just after four in the afternoon. Then she pulled out her laptop from her backpack and opened it up. Maybe if she lived elsewhere then she would enjoy her studies more, she thought and she started to search for rooms to rent in Bath. She scrolled down, uninspired by the small digs and ugly houses and the large amount of cat scratch poles in living rooms. Felicity was allergic to cats, so this was non-negotiable.

The music started again and she took out her noise-cancelling headphones before alighting on a new house-sharing website – and then she saw it: Temple Terrace. It was exactly like the one that Sir Walter Elliot inhabited in *Persuasion*. A row of thirty houses, laid out in a crescent shape, perfectly balanced and proportioned, simple but elegant.

She clicked on the first image and held her breath. She wouldn't let it out until the end of the photos and if she could hold it for all that time, she would apply, she told herself.

The rooms were lovely, big, gracious yet unpretentious. The sitting room was painted in a soft orange, which offset the lack of light, Felicity supposed, and created a lovely rich hue, slightly sun-kissed and welcoming. This comforting palette extended to a Turkish rug, bearing the patina of time and travel, something her grandmother would have loathed. She hated anything vaguely ethnic, particularly when displayed in interiors and at mealtimes. There were two plush sofas and two large armchairs, the worn upholstery adding to its charm and proof that they had been well sat in over the decades.

The bedrooms were what Felicity was interested in most. She clicked through the images of the library and the dining room and kitchen painted in yellow until she found them. Only two on offer and each perfect, though the description had mentioned three. All Persian rugs and fireplaces with armchairs and space, so much space. The beds looked so comfortable, a four-poster in one room and a large brass one in another, both with Suzani quilts on the bed.

Oh yes, Granny would loathe this.

The little bathroom sealed the deal for Felicity. Sharing a bathroom in the university dorms was worse than the noise and the adjacency to the snacks from her bed.

Her own bathroom.

She finally let out her breath and pressed the application button. Even though Granny paid half of her rent for the dorm room, she didn't think Granny would mind if she moved to a different place if she was happier.

Felicity started to type in the application form:

Hello,

My name is Felicity Booth and I am a master's student at the University of Bath. My thesis explores the cultural and architectural influences from Roman times on the social dynamics of Bath in the Regency era.

While you might assume my application is because your house directly reflects one of the houses in Jane Austen's Persuasion, *it is not, although it certainly supports my decision to leave the university dorms where I live, because they are simply not like your home.*

University halls of residence aren't easy for someone like me. I'm twenty-three, so much older than the others, who just want to party. I prefer to read and write and knit. Yes, I am already practising for my dotage.

But I can feel I am losing myself here, and my work. The music is incessant, people laughing and yelling. Worse than anything, there is a shared bathroom. I can pay the rent you ask and I am willing to do anything you need around the house such as cleaning or bringing the bins in. I'm not much of a cook, I'm afraid. I hope you will consider my application and if you do, could you explain TikTok to me and why you like it? I thought it was just dancing.

With my best regards,
Felicity Booth

She paused, took another Galaxy bar from the drawer, popped a cube in her mouth and pressed Send. It was out of her hands now.

3

Lana

Lana Rolls had chosen to leave her marriage for several reasons. The first was that she couldn't stand the sight of her husband, Denny, and she hated every aspect of her life with him, although to others it looked like Lana had landed on her feet.

Denny was a bully. He was a bully to his staff, to his family and to those who disagreed with him. And Lana had noticed that this was starting to tip into their marriage. She read that men who abused others inevitably turned on those closest to them and now, it seemed she was next in line. Nothing was ever quite good enough for Denny – nothing she wore or cooked or said. It was so subtle, but it was, as she tried to explain to her sister, Evie, just enough to doubt yourself.

He had chosen the house they lived in even though Lana said she didn't like it. But since she wasn't earning money – Denny didn't want her to work – she didn't end up getting a choice. The house was a new build on an estate outside of Bath and it had every single 'mod con', as Denny liked to say to anyone who came to visit.

The all-white kitchen gave Lana the creeps – she felt like she was in a laboratory. The fridge had a computer installed so you could scan barcodes and when you ran out of an item, it added it to a shopping list. The oven came with a video feature that walked you through the steps so you could make anything. It even had a feature where you could watch it cook via a live stream on your phone. The night they got it, Denny watched the stream as the oven heated a frozen lasagne. It was the longest twenty minutes of Lana's life.

Denny was tight with his money, despite the technology in their house suggesting otherwise. He owned six technology stores and was opening up more, extending his 'retail footprint', as he said to all and anyone who would listen. But she also knew he hid money from her, and from HMRC, and he sold things for cash to friends and associates. He was always ducking and diving and dodging and weaving in life, and Lana had witnessed it all as a passive bystander in her own life. But she hadn't found the right time to leave yet. Security was important to Lana, but lately, she couldn't even use that as a reason to stay.

Then came the moment he ripped up her seedlings. The house was bare – minimalist, he liked to say – but the one thing she had always wanted was a garden. It reminded her of the good year when she lived with her grandmother. Denny had instructed the landscaper to create a concrete driveway and a round gravel garden with lots of hedges that had been turned into balls on sticks. There was no colour, no movement, just a very plain, uniform space outside the front of the house.

But the back was Lana's space. When Denny was away on one of his buying trips, she had brought in four raised garden beds and filled them with good compost before planting them with flowers and vegetable seedlings. She mulched the beds with straw and fertiliser, around which were gravel paths. It was to become her favourite place each morning. With a cup of coffee in hand, she would wander about the beds, seeing what was growing and whether or not the tomatoes were ready to stake or the carrots to be thinned.

Denny hadn't said much when he saw it when he came home later that week, except that she didn't need to grow vegetables because she could get them at Tesco. She ignored his comment and went outside to look at her cosmos daisies, hoping they would grow tall enough to entice bees and butterflies into their garden.

The garden was taking shape and everything had been growing well for a few weeks. Lana had even shown Denny the drawing of extra beds she was planning and perhaps some arches for growing sweet peas and runner beans. In her head, she could see an abundant, vibrant space, filled with food and flowers – everything she didn't have while growing up. What she wouldn't have done as child to be able to head to the garden and pick a cherry tomato off the vine, ripened and warmed from the sun, instead of scratching around the empty cupboards trying to find something to eat for her and her sister…

It was after she had been to see her sister that the betrayal happened. On her return, the first thing she saw was her raised beds, empty, on the verge, the iron sides caved in on two. Lana had pulled into the driveway, her heart in her throat as she ran around the back of the house and saw it was all gone. Everything. Just an empty plot of land, with a bobcat and Denny and some workmen standing around, one of whom was walking around with a can of spray paint, outlining something on the dirt.

'Denny!' she called, her voice strained, tears welling.

'Hello, trouble and strife. I thought I'd do better than the tiddly little garden you had. I've brought in a gardening team and they said they can make the back the same as the front. Don't worry – I know you love your herbs and shit, so I have had them put into some little pots around the side of the house so you can grow your mint and so on.'

'The side of the house is always in shade,' she said, feeling her voice crack and aware there were several pairs of eyes on her.

His eyes went dark and she felt the fight leave her. It was time to go. She just had to find the right time and the right reason. Because ruining her garden wasn't enough – she needed more.

Just now, Denny came up from the basement in a robe with tiny goggles on his head. He was the colour of a chicken tikka and smelled like coconut.

'Hello, trouble,' he said.

She was standing in the kitchen, trying to decide what to do about dinner. Denny was a simple man, but he did like 'chicken of the world' recipes: chicken tagine, parmigiana, schnitzels, Kievs, American-style fried and even a chicken tikka masala. His palate was more well-travelled than he was, since he had never left the UK, not even to Spain for a holiday.

Lana had tried to get him to travel, tempting him with Japan for technology or New York for networking, but he always said he was too busy. He was the king of his own little empire and nothing would ever compare.

Besides not wanting to travel, or not allowing anything older than five years in their house, what annoyed Lana about him was his insistence he was a geezer. She blamed the film director Guy Ritchie for Danny's obsession with speaking like one and learning cockney rhyming slang.

While he didn't want to travel, he did love a tan and he had his own sunbed installed at their house, with a sauna and rain shower that was so intense, Lana wondered if she was being waterboarded the first time she used it.

'What's for Jim Skinner, luv?' He moved the junk mail and envelopes that were on the kitchen worktop.

Jim Skinner meant dinner. Having an Austin Power meant shower. Going to Uncle Ned meant going to bed. Lana often wondered what cockney slang for useless git would be. Probably useless git, she thought.

'There's letters for you,' he said, tapping the pile of papers.

He looked in the saucepan that Lana was stirring. It was chicken soup, which she had bought at the deli because she couldn't be bothered cooking for him any more.

'Oh, loop the loop?' he said.

'It's chicken soup,' she said, hoping to convince him of its worth.

'I'll have it with some baby's head,' he winked. 'I'm off to get some clothes on, otherwise you won't be able to resist me,' he laughed.

Lana gave him a fake smile. It was better to go along with his rubbish than face it, because Denny could be a prick.

'Baby's head, give me a break,' Lana muttered as she looked through the mail and found the letter.

She turned it over and saw a return London postal address, an office in Mayfair. Fancy, she thought as she opened it and unfolded the letter. She turned down the soup on the burner and started to read, feeling her knees weaken. She sat down on one of the stools.

A mistress.

An affair.

Proof of paternity.

A baby.

A son.

Denial from Denny.

So, the mistress thought Lana should know what sort of man Denny is, did she?

Oh, Jesus, Lana thought. She knew he was a prick, but she also knew what a terrible father he would be to this poor kid.

They had decided no children. Lana because she had looked after her younger sister since she was eighteen and Evie was ten, and Denny because he didn't want anything to distract him from his world domination in retail. The closest they ever came to a child was a robot dog that Denny had brought back from a technology show in London. It wagged its plastic tail and gave a bark that sounded like someone was standing on its equally plastic foot. It waddled around the house and scared Lana when she was least expecting it. Eventually, it ran out of both charge and charm, and Denny relegated it to the top shelf of the linen cupboard, where it stared down at Lana whenever she changed the towels.

A child.

She fished inside the envelope once again and found a photograph of the baby. On the back was written 'Royce, born Christmas Eve'.

Royce?

'God help him,' Lana said, feeling calmer than she thought possible in a situation such as this, not that she had ever imagined one.

Lana refolded the letter and slipped it back into the envelope. Then she took the photo of the baby and taped it to the stainless steel refrigerator. Other people put their children's photos and artworks on the fridge – didn't little Royce deserve to be there, too? God knows, Denny wouldn't put him up there.

She stared at the child for a while. It was hard to see the similarities between a baby and a parent, since both looked like uncooked sausages with eyes. She was sure this was his child, but thankfully there was a paternity test to confirm the sausage likeness.

Lana slipped the letter into the pocket of her hoodie. She took out some bread, buttered four slices, cut them in half and put them on a plate. Then she poured the soup into a bowl before adding a large spoonful of cooking salt and stirring.

Just in time, Denny sauntered into the kitchen and looked at the soup, his nose slightly turned up.

'You not having any?' he asked.

'No. I'm going to shower. I'll eat later.'

She could hardly breathe from the anger welling inside her and her voice sounded foreign to her as she spoke, although it seemed Denny hadn't noticed anything different.

She heard the television turn on as she pulled four suitcases down from the wardrobe. She had bought them in the hope they would travel around the world with the two of them a few years ago. They hadn't even left the wardrobe.

Lana lined them up on the floor before picking up armfuls of clothes still on their hangers and cramming them into the cases, followed by shoes and make-up and toiletries and jewellery. She kneeled on the lids to close them tightly.

Finally she was done. She stuck her head out of the door to the bedroom. He hadn't seen the photo yet. He would need a drink with the salt she had put into the loop the loop, she thought and laughed.

One last thing, she thought. She went to the linen closet, took down the dog and put it on her side of the bed. She knew it was petty, but she also knew that Denny couldn't tell the difference between her and a robot dog any more.

Lana lifted the suitcases upright and wheeled two down the hallway to the front door before repeating the act for the last two without Denny looking around once.

She cleared her throat. 'I'm going to Evie's.'

'Baked po–tay–tah,' he said, and she took a deep breath.

Why couldn't he just say 'see you later' like a normal person? She was sure he just made up some of these stupid rhymes.

Lana opened the door and wheeled the cases towards the car, Denny watching a *Top Gear* rerun all along, still oblivious. She waited a moment and then turned and picked up her bag.

Denny stood up and walked towards the kitchen.

'That loop the loop was salty,' he complained.

She paused and heard muttering before he returned to the living room, a can of Pepsi in one hand and the photo in the other.

'Whose fucking ugly basin of gravy is this?' he said, waving the photo at her. 'You left tape marks on the fridge. That residue can leave shadows.'

'*That* is Royce,' she said, watching his face for any flicker of recognition.

'What a stupid name for a kid. Why is he on our fridge?'

'That child is on our fridge, Denny, because he's yours. That ugly basin of gravy is your son, Royce Rolls. And I agree — what a stupid fucking name it is.' She straightened her shoulders and took in the moment. 'Goodbye, Denny Rolls. You will be hearing from my lawyers.'

As she walked out, all she could think was it was time to upgrade her life to a Lana mark 2.0.

4

Marion

The doorbell at Temple Terrace had a nice melodious ring to it, slightly alto, that hummed through the house, letting the inhabitants know that company had arrived. Marion hated those loud soprano bells that screeched like a parrot. The sound of her own doorbell made her jump and she looked at the clock. It was only nine thirty in the morning and her potential renters weren't meant to be here until ten. She wasn't ready yet, she thought, slightly peeved at the inconvenience of one of them arriving early.

As she opened the door, she saw it wasn't one of the new tenants but Clair, in a fur gilet and tight leather pants, with her hair scraped back into a bun that made her wide eyes seem wider and her cheekbones even more prominent. She looked thin, like a skinned deer, thought Marion, and then corrected herself.

'Hello, darling, everything OK?'

'Hello, Mum,' said Clair, leaning in for a kiss. 'It's been a few days since I came by. I've been so busy but I thought why not pop in since I'm passing.'

Marion thought better than to bring up the fact that Clair knew very well the tenants were coming today. This was Clair's way of checking up on both her and them.

'That's lovely, sweetheart, but I'm heading out soon,' Marion said, but Clair had swept past her and was heading down the hallway towards the kitchen.

'Tulips?' Clair stopped at the hall table and looked at the vase. 'I do love flowers, but they're so expensive.'

There it was – the little barb about how Marion spent her money.

'They're a thank you from one of the new tenants.' Marion wondered why she felt compelled to explain.

Clair picked up the two key rings from the silver bowl where Marion kept her own keys.

'An F and an L,' Clair said, holding on to the little silver initials on the keys. 'Let me guess, Fiona and Laura.'

Marion was silent and Clair put the keys back in the bowl.

'Of course, I wouldn't have to guess if you had included me in this process,' Clair said and flounced into the kitchen.

Marion sighed. Once, she and Clair had been great friends, especially when the children were little. But since Geoffrey died, Marion had the distinct feeling Clair blamed her. Clair was certainly bullying her at times – or punishing? Marion wasn't sure which. Perhaps it was both ...

Clair opened the cake box on the worktop.

'Pastries also, Mum. Goodness, are these for F and L?'

'Felicity and Lana, yes.' Marion stood her ground.

'Felicity and Lana – they're pretty names, aren't they? Old-fashioned. Are they your age?'

Marion closed the lid of the box.

'No, Felicity is twenty-three and Lana is thirty-eight.'

Clair looked surprised, which pleased Marion. Everything was a power struggle at the moment and it was rare to catch Clair not getting her shot over the net.

'Pastries are a bit much, aren't they? What if they are watching their weight? Or have diabetes? It's a bit old-fashioned, don't you think? You don't want them thinking you're an old fuddy-duddy.' She gave her mother a patronising look.

Serve, forehand, backhand, drop shot and final lob to finish the rally.

Clair: one. Marion: nil.

'I might stay, then. See they're all as they say they are,' Clair said, and she picked up the kettle and started to fill it.

'Actually, they're not coming until after three now. I have some things I need to do,' Marion lied.

'But that's when I pick up the twins.' Clair was put out.

'What a shame, but no need to worry, I will call you or Paul if there is anything unsettling about them or if they bring a cat or a machete with them.'

'A machete? Don't even joke about it,' said Clair as her phone rang from her expensive handbag with the gold chain.

She took the phone from her bag and looked at the caller. Marion saw her almost wince.

'Everything OK, darling?' Marion asked, and she was sincere.

Clair could be insufferable at times, but she was also her child and she never wanted her to have a tough time.

'Oh, fine, just the builder from the renovations last year. A little issue over the bill. I'll send Paul in to sort it.'

'Good idea. Now, let me walk you out. I'm heading into town anyway, picking up some things.'

Clair looked around the kitchen. 'Everything is very clean. You must have been busy.'

Marion nodded as she guided Clair to the front of the house. 'Yes, quite, but manageable.'

There was no chance she would tell Clair that she had used some of the deposit money from the new tenants towards a cleaner.

'And you have tenant agreements?' Clair checked.

'Yes, all done.'

'And house rules?'

'Yes.'

Clair turned to her mother. 'I understand you want to do things your way, but please call me if this isn't working. I'm a bit hurt you didn't want me to review the applications, but I have to trust you made the right choice for you and the house. And make sure you understand the financial implications of this – we don't want you losing the house as well.'

Marion swallowed, touched by Clair's words. 'I know, you must feel a bit odd with strangers living in the house, but I promise I will let you know if anything doesn't work or is worrying me.'

Clair leaned over and kissed her mother on the cheek.

'Bye, Mum, speak later,' she said, and she was gone, the gold chain slipping from her thin shoulder as she walked to her car.

Clair suddenly seemed very thin – or perhaps she hadn't noticed. Marion felt terrible for not recognising it. Weight was a tricky issue with Clair, who insisted on calorie counting and reminding her own daughter, Sophie, that she should be mindful of her figure.

But the financial worry was back. Could Marion lose the house?

The truth was that Geoffrey had always looked after the finances in their home and he had done a great job until he became ill. Isn't it sad that all the good work in a life is overlooked when things go a bit pear-shaped at the end?

Marion went back to the kitchen, took the cakes from the box and placed them on a pretty Spode plate before turning on the kettle. They would be here soon.

She brushed down her grey trousers and pale blue linen shirt and adjusted her grey hair, which she kept short because she was too old to worry about styling it every morning. When she told her hairdresser she wanted to cut it off after Geoffrey had died, the hairdresser told her that women often do that after a major life event. Said that their hair absorbed the negative energy from what they had just been through and needed to be cast off. Marion just said she realised how finite life was and she didn't want to waste any of it staring at herself in the mirror every morning to do her hair in a style that pleased no one because she didn't see anyone really. She didn't have to do her hair for other's people's gaze and she could do plenty more with that time than worry about her hair.

Clair had hated the short cut. Told her mum she looked athletic, which wasn't as much of an insult as Clair had hoped. Clair also said Marion should have called her hairdresser, she would have done a better cut, and that's when Marion realised Clair was upset she hadn't been consulted on Marion's decision over her hair.

Lately, Clair seemed to question everything Marion did, which was why she had stopped telling her any of her plans until they were done. It wasn't as though she enjoyed keeping Clair out of her life – to an extent, it was self-protection. Clair made Marion feel small and she began to lose self-confidence when she was around her.

She could only hope these new tenants who would share Temple Terrace with her wouldn't let her down, because the last thing she needed was Clair saying she told her so.

5

Lana

Lana arrived at Temple Terrace in a near all-white outfit. White cashmere coat, white wool trousers, white silk shirt and a pair of cherry-red patent leather boots. Even her hair was blonde with white streaks through it. Her lipstick matched her boots, and she wore thick black eyeliner and mascara around her very bright blue eyes.

Lana looked at the climber on the front fence, all gnarled and curled around the iron. There were lots of what she thought might be flower buds on them, or maybe they were leaves. She touched one with her hand. Flowers, definitely, she thought and then went back to her task of grappling with four hard-shell suitcases – white, naturally. Her attempt to manage them wasn't as seamless as she had hoped. In the midst of her efforts, just as Marion opened the front door, one of the suitcases broke free and rolled out of the gate.

'Sorry, there are so many of them,' Lana said as she wrestled it back and took two inside the house while Marion wheeled the others in behind.

They lined them up against the wall.

'It's hard to know what you want to take when you leave a marriage,' said Lana. 'It would have been easier just to say I'm done with it all, but that's not sensible, is it?'

Marion smiled at Lana. 'Not at all, but I can imagine it's hard not to want to throw the baby out with the bathwater.'

Lana snorted. 'Too bloody right.'

'Your suitcases look like little storm troopers from *Star Wars*,' Marion said, looking at the cases.

'They do indeed. I love that you can see that,' Lana laughed.

'My son Andy used to be obsessed with *Star Wars*. My late husband dressed up as Obi-Wan Kenobi for one of his *Star Wars*-themed birthdays one year. Maybe his tenth? I can't remember.'

'You'll have to ask him – *he* will remember. I don't think kids forget those things. I once dressed up as Baby Spice for my sister's eleventh birthday. She loved it. I did, too. I do love Emma Bunton. She's always been my favourite.'

Marion didn't reply and Lana wondered if she had said something wrong. Denny said she always said the wrong thing, so much so that she stopped saying things to him after a while.

Marion's face looked startled for a moment and then slipped into a neutral expression. The warmth was still there but she seemed distant now. As though elsewhere. Lana wasn't about to ask. It wasn't her place, she knew that much.

'You got the flowers, I see,' Lana said, looking at the tulips. 'White.'

'I did and I love them, but you didn't need to do that.'

'I bloody well did. You have saved me. I've been sleeping on my sister's couch and it's pleather. I kept slipping off in the middle of the night.'

Marion burst out laughing, her energy back. 'Well that sounds terrible. You'll have a nice comfortable bed here.'

Lana was pleased she'd made Marion laugh, because she had looked sad for a moment when they were talking about birthday parties. Probably because she'd mentioned her dead husband, she thought.

Marion was exactly as she'd imagined her. Slightly rounded but in good health, with sensible trousers and a shirt. She wore a lovely gold necklace and pearl earrings. She had barely any make-up on but a slick of pink lipstick, her short grey hair in a cut that suited her.

'You look much younger than your age, unless you were telling a porky pie,' Lana said, and then hated herself for a moment for using rhyming slang. Bloody Denny.

'Oh, you can stay for ever for saying that. Now, come down to the kitchen and have a cup of tea and then we can do the tour when Felicity arrives.'

Marion's pep was back and Lana found it hard to believe Marion was in her seventies.

They walked down the long hallway, Marion pointing out the different rooms.

'This is the sitting room. I tend to sit here at night and look at things on my iPad, maybe watch a bit of telly. Be nice to have company, so please come and join me,' she said as Lana put her head in the doorway and saw a cosy, well-loved sitting room.

'I love the wall colour,' said Lana. 'It's like a sunset.'

'It is. I can't bear white walls.'

Lana sighed. 'Me, too.'

'Why choose white when there are millions of colours to choose from? But I did keep the wallpaper in the hallway, as Geoffrey and I chose it together.'

Lana touched the wallpaper as they passed by, feeling the texture of the creamy gold pattern.

'I like it,' she said.

'This is the library, or the study as I prefer to call it. Geoffrey loved to read, so I haven't been able to let go of his books yet. He read everything he could, but he particularly loved reading about Bath and its history. He also adored botany, which was odd since he worked in banking for most of his life.'

Lana looked at the room with floor-to-ceiling bookshelves with a ladder attached to a brass rail that ran along one wall. A large, imposing desk commandeered the centre of the room, demanding attention and exuding an air of knowledge. The desk's rich, dark wood gleamed in the soft light that filtered through the windows, its surface empty now, but Lana imagined it was once covered in papers and books.

Surrounding the desk, a series of Persian-style carpets lay overlapping one another, their intricate patterns and vibrant colours creating a tapestry of warmth and elegance beneath their feet. Against one wall, a large brown Chesterfield sofa beckoned invitingly. The sofa's worn, patinated leather spoke of countless hours spent in quiet contemplation or in lively discussion of important subjects, its deep-buttoned upholstery and rolled arms offering a comforting embrace to the sitter. The rich hue of the leather seemed to shift in the light, at times resembling the burnished tones of old mahogany, at others the honeyed warmth of maple wood.

'What a beautiful room,' Lana said, standing in the doorway for a moment.

'It is, but I don't come in here often. I miss Geffrey too much if I do.'

Marion stood in the hallway and Lana got the sense Marion needed to keep moving.

As they continued their tour, they passed through a formal dining room that took Lana's breath away. The walls were painted in a striking shade of turquoise, the vibrant hue a perfect complement to the rich, glossy wood of the large dining table. The table was flanked by at least ten chairs, each one with intricately carved legs and plush orange velvet seats. It wasn't a colour combination that Lana would have put together, yet it made perfect sense in this room.

'Dining room,' Marion said firmly, a hint of wistfulness in her voice. 'I never use it now. Waste of a room, really.'

They passed a closed door that led to the downstairs powder room, apparently, before finally entering the kitchen. As soon as Lana stepped inside, she couldn't help but gasp in delight.

'Blimey, this is bliss!' she exclaimed, her eyes widening as she took in the lush details. 'I saw the kitchen in the photos, but it's even better in person.'

The walls were reminiscent of a perfectly ripened lemon that had been left to bask in the sun just a little too long. The colour seemed to envelop the room in a warm, comforting embrace, instantly putting Lana at ease. The cupboards, painted in a soothing shade of pale green, stood in perfect harmony with the lemon walls, their soft hues a gentle nod to the natural world beyond the kitchen windows.

At the centre was an island fashioned from a Victorian shop counter, the old sign writing on the side reading 'Bath's Herbs and Tinctures' in beautiful faded script. One side of the worktop was covered in a dove-grey marble and the other was worn wood. Lana could imagine the pastry that had been rolled out on that surface long after it was used to mix herbal concoctions.

Lana turned and saw a worn pine dresser, its shelves crowded with an eclectic mismatch of china. The plates, bowls and cups seemed to cling to the dresser for dear life, yet Lana was sure nothing had been broken in years.

'I reckon you have a story about every piece of china on that dresser,' Lana said.

'I do. It's like a living diary of dishes,' Marion laughed.

In one corner, a small round table painted a cheerful shade of raspberry provided a cosy spot for informal dinners, and surrounding the table, four yellow chairs in the same colours of the walls brought the room together. As Lana took in every detail, from the polished brass taps of the porcelain double sink to the teapot wearing a tea cosy in the shape of a lemon, she thought this was the most beautiful, inviting home she had ever had the pleasure of setting foot inside.

Just as Lana was about to express her admiration once more, the sound of the doorbell echoed through the house, causing her to pause in her swooning. She didn't want to come across as insincere, but if Marion had seen the cold white box she had lived in with the fake plants, fake dog and fake tan, she would never leave this house again.

'That will be our other housemate,' said Marion.

Lana clapped her hands together in excitement, her gold charm bracelet jingling merrily.

Marion was already walking up the hallway. 'I'll bring her in. I'm sure she's excited to meet you, as well.'

Lana hoped so. Being with Denny meant they didn't have any friends other than work contacts, suppliers and staff. Denny seemed to dislike everyone she ever liked, so she ended up spending a lot of time with her sister. Yes, Lana was excited to make friends at Temple Terrace and she hoped to high heaven that Felicity was, too.

6

Felicity

As Felicity walked along the street where Temple Terrace was, she couldn't help but feel a sense of reverence at these iconic Georgian houses. They stood tall and proud, their Palladian architecture inspired by that of the Roman era. Felicity could write a ten-thousand-word essay on this very subject, but she could never give the reader the feeling of seeing the warm caramel Bath stone. It seemed to glow in the early March sunlight against the verdant green of the park across from the Crescent. She wondered if Jane Austen had had the same sense of marvel when she first came to Bath to live.

Felicity arrived outside Temple Terrace, wisteria winding around the iron railings. Her eyes were drawn to the large front door. It was a work of art, painted in a deep, rich navy blue with gleaming brass hardware. The knocker – a heavy, ornate piece shaped like a lion's head – seemed to beckon her forwards, inviting her to use it.

She could almost imagine the countless hands that had grasped this knocker over the years, the countless stories and secrets that had passed through this door. For a moment she wondered if Jane Austen herself had visited, but she was pretty sure everyone who lived in a Georgian house in Bath claimed that Jane Austen had once been a guest.

She knocked on the door and waited for a moment. The door opened and there was Marion. She was small but fit-looking, sort of cosy in her frame with short, thick grey hair and a happy face – that was the best way Felicity could describe her. She looked like she always had a tissue up her sleeve and Polo mints in her handbag. She was the complete antithesis of Gran and Felicity liked her immediately.

'Felicity? I'm Marion,' she said and extended her hand.

Felicity took her hand, which was cool and firm. 'Thank you so much for this. I'm so grateful.'

She looked around, immediately enveloped by the warm, welcoming atmosphere of the house. The rich, burnished tones of the polished hardwood floors glowed in the soft light that filtered through the glass in the front door. The walls were adorned with elegant wallpaper, old but timeless, she noticed, its subtle pattern and hues of cream and gold picking up the light around them. She inhaled deeply, savouring the faint, comforting scent of beeswax and lavender that seemed to permeate every corner.

'It smells amazing,' said Felicity as they walked up the hallway.

'I had a cleaner come in to get it ready for us,' said Marion, turning a little in Felicity's direction as she walked. 'She makes her own cleaning products. It does smell wonderful. I agree.'

What struck Felicity most about Temple Terrace was the way it seemed to embody the very essence of the books she loved so dearly. She could almost hear the rustling of silk gowns, the gentle clinking of teacups and the lively chatter of those who had called this house their home so many years ago.

Bubbles of excitement rose inside her as she walked past the library. Something wonderful is going to happen to me here, I just know it, she thought.

'Come through and meet Lana,' Marion said.

Felicity walked into the kitchen, her rucksack still on, and looked around the kitchen. It was like something from a painting.

'Felicity, this is Lana, she's the other housemate,' said Marion.

'So pleased to meet you,' said Lana, putting her hand out.

Felicity looked at it for a moment and frowned and then realised Lana wanted to shake it.

'Oh, forget the handshake, let's have a hug,' said Lana, and before Felicity could say anything, Lana had pulled her into a huge hug.

Felicity felt Lana's hair tickle her nose and it smelled like vanilla or caramel or maybe both.

'I thought we would have tea,' said Marion. 'And I bought some pastries. Something sweet to commemorate a great day.'

At the prospect of a sweet treat, Felicity took off her rucksack and put it under the table.

'Where were you living before here, then?' Lana asked Felicity.

'University halls.'

'You didn't like it?' Lana asked.

'It was loud and hard to sleep and study,' Felicity said with a sigh. 'It was exhausting.'

'Fair enough. I'm guessing it would be like party central there,' said Lana. 'I'd probably have loved it, but not if I was serious about my studies. I was never any good at school.'

Felicity nodded because it seemed like the appropriate response. She had never been any good at small talk – or big talk, for that matter. It was hard to make friends, especially with those at university being so much younger than her. While she had made a few friendly acquaintances at the bookstore where she worked part-time and had been invited to the pub a few times, she found it hard to insert herself into conversations. If she had to describe it, it was like being on an express train and seeing your stop whizz past and not being able to do anything about it but watch from the window.

Marion handed them good hearty mugs of strong tea and Felicity felt herself exhale. She hadn't realised she was holding her breath. There were plates and forks and an array of cakes on the table.

'Come on, come and have a little sugar. Get some strength so we can get these cases upstairs. You will have quite a trip, Lana, with your quadruple collection.'

Lana laughed. 'I'm pretty strong. I used to work in the stores moving stock and so on.' She looked at Felicity. 'My ex owns a bunch of technology stores selling computers and flash mod cons for the home. Smart TVs and the like – but sold by a stupid man. That should be his slogan.'

She sipped her tea as Felicity watched her, fascinated by her movement and accent. It was somewhere between cockney and Mancunian, with a dash of scouse.

'That's why I'm here,' Lana continued. 'I found out my ex had a baby with someone else. They sent me the paternity test in the mail and a photo of the baby.'

'Oh,' said Felicity, which seemed enough encouragement for Lana to continue her story.

'And the baby, bless his head, well, you'll never guess his name. It's a shocker.'

Marion and Felicity looked at Lana for the big reveal.

'Denny's last name is Rolls. And she named the baby Royce.'

'Royce Rolls?' Marion frowned.

'Yes!' Lana banged the table with a hand, making Felicity

jump. 'Isn't that the worst name you've ever heard? It's cruel, the poor kid.'

'My mum has a pretty bad name,' said Felicity, surprised at hearing her own voice.

'Oh?' Lana leaned forwards. 'Go on, then, what is it?'

'Ruth,' she said.

'Ruth what?'

Felicity licked a crumb from her lip. 'Booth. Ruth Booth.'

Lana paused and Felicity wished she hadn't spoken. Then Lana burst into laughter. It was a gorgeous peal of noise that made Felicity smile and chuckle to herself.

'Oh, her mum was cruel,' said Lana, wiping tears from her eyes.

Felicity was silent, looking down at her hands folded in her lap.

'Oh, I'm sorry, love. No disrespect to your gran,' Lana said, and she put her hand on Felicity's arm.

Felicity looked up at Lana and shook her head.

'No, you're right. My grandmother is cruel. She's just like Lady Catherine de Bourgh from *Pride and Prejudice* and my mother is like her daughter, Anne. A sad, sickly woman who is completely under the control of her mother. I wish it wasn't the case, but it is.'

Felicity realised the room was silent.

'Sorry, I shouldn't say that, and I've taken over the conversation.' She felt her eyes prick and she shoved half a strawberry tart into her mouth.

'Who is Lady Catherine de What's-her-name?' Lana asked.

'De Bourgh. She's a character in the book, *Pride and Prejudice*,' Felicity said. 'She's haughty and mean.'

'Never read it. I've only seen the film,' said Lana.

'She's played by Judi Dench,' Felicity said.

'Oh, she's a right twat. I remember her. I do love Judi, though.'

Marion nodded. 'Everyone loves Judi.'

Lana put her hand on Felicity's arm. 'You should say whatever you want and if your granny is an old twat like the De Bourgh character, then so be it. Say it as you see it. I always have. Anyway, she's old and will die one day.'

Lana shrugged and Felicity laughed despite herself.

'God, I hope my grandchildren don't say that about me.' Marion shuddered.

'Not bloody likely,' said Lana. 'You have a lemon-coloured kitchen and strawberry tarts. No one with that could be a bad person.'

Felicity smiled at them both.

'Do you want to take your things up to your rooms?' asked Marion.

'Yes, please,' Felicity said, needing the space to decompress.

'Do you want the room on the right or the left?' Marion asked. 'They both look out over the park.'

Lana looked to Felicity. 'I have no preference, do you?'

'None,' said Felicity.

'OK, I'll take right, you take left,' Lana said. 'Solved.'

'Let's go on up, then.' Marion got to her feet, Lana following.

Felicity sat for a moment, gathering herself.

'Come on, daughter of Ruth Booth. Come and see your new room.'

And Felicity felt for the first time since coming to Bath that she finally had a home.

7

Lana

Lana sat on the bed in her room and looked around. The past two weeks at Evie and Petey's house had been a special kind of hell. To have a bed now was a luxury after sleeping on the slippery sofa. As was not having to hear their constant bickering over anything and everything. According to Evie, everything Petey did was wrong, which it probably was, but even Lana felt sorry for the guy after being told he wasn't capable of loading a dishwasher, making coffee, vacuuming or even pegging the clothes on the line correctly. Lana never wanted to get involved, but she couldn't help standing up for hopeless Petey before she left.

'What does it matter how he does it? Surely what matters is that it gets done. Not everyone will do things the way you want them done,' she said to Evie after a blow-up over the vegetable drawer in the fridge.

'No, I like them how I like them,' said Evie, and she did that thing where she pursed her lips like a cat's bum and frowned.

When Evie was ten and their mum left them for a new life in Glasgow and a bloke she met online, Lana had seen that look many times as she had been left to parent Evie, even though she was barely an adult herself. She hadn't done too badly, she thought. Evie finished school without getting pregnant, she didn't end up on drugs and she didn't do anything too stupid besides a few pissy nights with friends. She had even studied childcare and worked as a teacher in the local school where, by all accounts – and judging by the gifts at the end of the year – she was both respected and liked.

It was more than Lana had done. Life with Denny was easy in comparison. She didn't even have to vacuum, their little robot buzzing about the house sweeping up any dust or crumbs within a minute of landing on the carpet.

When had she stopped participating in her own life?

Now, she was renting a room – albeit a lovely one – from an older woman, but she had no job, no skills and no money of her own.

The room looked cosy and comforting, but there were things that made Lana smile. She unpacked as many of her clothes as she could, but realised there were far too many of them. Most were things she would never wear again. Perhaps she could sell some, she thought as she looked at the suitcase. So many purchases just because Denny had liked them or had gifted them to her.

All those designer bags that didn't really hold enough – they seemed so garish now, looking at them through the lens of Temple Terrace, where everything was so gentle and cosy. Did she really need a white leather mini bag with gold logos all over it and a tiny gold poodle charm hanging off the side? If she were honest, she actually hated the bag, but Denny had liked it, so that was all that mattered. She should have left it for him to wear, she thought now, chuckling to herself.

After sorting them into two piles, she soon had two whole suitcases of clothes and shoes to sell, even some jewellery and bits and pieces from her life with Denny.

The fireplace was so beautiful, its marble surround a soft, pale rose pink that seemed to glow. She could only imagine how it looked when there was a fire in the grate. The fireplace itself was spotless, its hearth swept clean and its grate polished to a high shine. Beside it, a collection of kindling, pine cones and small logs sat waiting in a cane basket, ready to be called into service the minute there was a chill in the air. Lana imagined herself curled up in front of a crackling fire on a cool evening, reading a book or simply letting her mind wander as the flames danced and flickered.

On top of the mantelpiece, a small box caught Lana's eye and she lifted the lid to reveal a collection of matches and delicate tapered candles nestled in their holders. It was so specific and pretty. Perhaps the candles were meant for those cosy fires, or maybe they were a precaution against the occasional power outage. She liked knowing they were there.

Turning her attention to the furniture, the large wardrobe could have easily housed a bunch of fur coats and a portal to another world, with its intricately carved doors and brass keys with pink tassels hanging from them. Beside the wardrobe, a huge chest of drawers made of fragrant cedar wood commanded her attention. The chest was adorned with barley twist details, the intricately carved wood spiralling upwards like the tendrils of a fairy-tale beanstalk.

Denny hated 'old brown shit', as he called this sort of furniture, but Lana loved it. She ran her fingers along the cool, smooth surface of the cedar, imagining the treasures and secrets that might have been hidden within its deep drawers. Perhaps they had once held the impressive top hats of a bygone era, their depth more than ample to accommodate such fancy headwear.

Curtains hung from wooden rings, their weight and substance testament to the quality and care that had gone into every detail of the room. Unable to resist, Lana gently tugged at the curtains, pulling them back and forth, delighting in the satisfying rattle of the rings as they slid along the rod. The sound reminded her of dice shaken in a wooden cup – a playful sound that seemed to hint at the possibility of good fortune and new beginnings.

Gazing out through the window, she couldn't believe the view, the green lawn of the park stretching before her. After the monotony of the crowded housing estate, with its identical houses, driveways, fences and box hedges, the park's vibrant greenery felt like an oasis. The neatly manicured lawns seemed to go on for ever, a sea of emerald green that invited barefoot walks and lazy afternoons spent lounging in the sun.

As she watched, Lana spotted a handful of people enjoying the park. A small child, perched atop a balance bike, wobbled and weaved as their father ran alongside, offering encouragement and support. Nearby, a figure sat alone on a bench, engrossed in a book, their head down as they read. Further off, someone lay stretched out on a blanket, their face tilted towards the sun, seemingly lost in the moment, basking in the warm golden light of March. It was still fresh, but the light told her good days were coming and Lana felt an unfamiliar sense of excitement.

Perhaps, just like the playful rattle of the curtain rings, this move to Temple Terrace was a sign of good things to come, a chance to start anew and create a life of which she wanted to be a part.

There was a soft knock at the door.

'Come in,' she said, assuming it was Marion.

The door opened and she was surprised to see Felicity in the doorway.

'Hello, how's your room?' she asked. 'Can I have a peek?'

'Of course.'

'This is nice,' said Felicity, looking around the room.

'Yes, it might be simple, yet a lot of thought has gone into it.'

Felicity frowned. 'How so?'

Lana laughed. 'Come on, I'll show you.'

She led Felicity back to her own room. It was similar to Lana's except for the four-poster bed. The Persian rug was green and the curtains were a different colour but with the same thick wooden curtain rings. Lana walked over to the side of the bed.

'Those violets – I have some, too.' She pointed to the small glass vase no bigger than the length of her little finger holding a few stems with little purple buds.

She moved to the fireplace and opened the small wooden box on top of the mantle.

'Candles and matches, for the fire and just in case there is a power outage.'

Felicity nodded as Lana wandered around the room.

'Pine cones in the basket with small logs. It looks so pretty and smells so nice.'

She moved to the bed and patted it, seemingly finding the spot. She put her hand under the cover and pulled out an empty hot-water bottle with a Liberty print flannel cover.

'For your tootsies.' She smiled.

Felicity touched the item. 'That is thoughtful. I do get cold feet.'

Lana waked into the bathroom, which was similar to hers. Small but functional, with a shower, loo and basin with storage beneath. Inside the mirrored bathroom cabinet was a small selection of toiletries from a company in Bath.

'Mine smell of roses and ylang–ylang,' Lana said, picking up the small bottle of shower gel. 'Yours is orange and cedar wood.' She handed it to Felicity to smell.

'I like that,' Felicity said, surprised.

Lana shut the cabinet and then went to the bookshelf and picked up a small cloth-covered book.

'And this … is the most thoughtful thing.'

She handed it to Felicity, who opened it and read aloud.

Dear Resident of Temple Terrace,

Welcome to this beautiful home that has held my family and protected us from the storms outside for hundreds of years. Temple Terrace will always be a place to escape from what is hard or difficult outside these doors. It is also a place to celebrate your news and exciting times ahead.

I gift you this little journal so you can write down your hopes and dreams and ideas – even shopping lists if you so need. No rules for this book other than to use it for you.

I am glad you are here with me. We will all sleep more soundly at night with each other close by.

With friendship,

Marion Gaynor

Felicity looked up at Lana. 'Gosh, that's super nice, isn't it?'

Lana noticed Felicity's eyes were shining and blinking furiously. She wondered if anyone had done anything nice for her in a while. By the sounds of the grandmother, thoughtful gestures probably weren't something she was used to.

'Marion seems like a lovely person,' said Lana.

Felicity nodded.

'She hasn't really said anything about cooking or cleaning, so I think we should make sure we both help her,' Lana continued. 'I mean, she must be doing this for a reason.'

'Maybe she's lonely,' Felicity offered.

The sound of the doorbell went through the house, but they left it for Marion to answer. No one knew where Lana was, so it wouldn't be for her.

'I think it's more than that,' said Lana. 'Not that it's my business, but I don't think we should take her for granted.'

Felicity was silent.

Lana shrugged. 'I mean, you don't have to, but this is house*sharing*, not just house whatever, if that makes sense.' Maybe Felicity didn't want to pull her weight.

'I can cook,' Felicity said eventually. 'Granny didn't like my food much, but my mum did.'

'I'm sure you can cook just fine. It sounds like Granny could have breakfast, lunch and dinner made by Gordon Ramsay and it still wouldn't have been good enough for her.'

Felicity gave a little smile. 'I think you're right.'

'Let's go and see Marion and have a chat about how we can help her also since she's been so lovely to us.'

The women were walking downstairs towards the kitchen, when they heard Marion talking to someone.

'You can't just come round unannounced all the time, Clair. You're here to check on them, I know you are.'

'And you lied about going out. I parked across the way and saw them arrive. Why wouldn't you want me here to meet them?'

'Because I don't want you judging them, Clair. They need to settle in and we need to get to know each other.'

'God, Mother, they're not your friends! They're paying you money because you don't have any. It's transactional. Don't be so deluded and romanticise this situation into something it's not. I saw the one with the white suitcases. She looks like—'

'What does she look like?' Lana heard Marion say. 'Tell me what you think she looks like, Clair? I dare you, because I raised you better than that. When did you decide that your opinion on others was the be-all and end-all on the matter? You're wearing a rabbit gilet, for God's sake. I wouldn't be throwing stones.'

'That's so rude! I'm leaving.'

'See yourself out,' said Marion, and before Lana or Felicity could move out of the way, a very thin woman, with her hair pulled back tightly and who was indeed wearing some sort of rabbit waistcoat, pushed past them and out of the front door.

8

Marion

The house was silent after Clair slammed the front door. Marion sat in the kitchen, trying to get her thoughts together. Something had changed in Clair and it was getting worse. She was brittle and grabby and simply unbearable at the moment.

'You all right?'

Marion looked up and saw Lana and Felicity in the doorway.

'I'm OK. I am assuming you heard all of that?'

Lana shook her head. 'Not all of it, but the last part.'

Marion breathed out slowly. 'I'm sorry you had to hear it.'

'Families are complicated,' said Lana. 'No judgement from me. I have a sister who is hard work – I get it.'

Felicity sat down at the table with Marion.

'My granny can and has done much worse.'

'This grandmother of yours sounds formidable,' Marion said.

'We actually came down to talk to you about the house rules and how we can arrange things so the house hums along like friends, which I am sure will happen naturally, mostly because you have made us feel so welcome in our rooms.'

Lana filled the kettle, turned it on and then joined them.

Marion was quiet.

'My husband had a brain tumour,' she said out of the blue. 'And before we knew this, he made some terrible choices with our cash and savings. He lost it all – the cash, I mean. All I have now is this house and Clair thinks it's terrible I have you both here. She doesn't think I can handle the financial responsibility.'

'Oh, that's rotten,' said Lana. 'For you and for him. He must have been so confused.'

Marion shook her head. 'No, he wasn't confused. He was absolutely sure he had made astute decisions. He became very combative and difficult to reason with when challenged. That's how I knew he was unwell. Because he went from being one the wisest, kindest, gentlest men to being an absolute pain, bordering on unbearable.'

The kettle boiled and the lid popped open.

'He died fairly quickly, with no idea of the position in which I was left. So when Clair found out, I think she blamed me. She thought I should have known more about what was going on. But I never had any idea about those things. Geoffrey was the head of a bank for a long time. He was much better at those things than me.'

Lana nodded. 'I understand. So can you handle the financial responsibility?'

'I thought I could, but there are gaps in my knowledge about finances and so on, and I have no idea how to fill them. I can't really afford an accountant to walk me through it.' She sighed. 'But Clair wants me to sell up and move in with her, which sounds awful, to be honest, for her and for me. I don't want to leave here yet. I love living here and I hope you will, too.'

'And you don't need to leave. Felicity and I are thrilled to be here, aren't we, Flick?'

Felicity looked at Marion and Lana, eyes wide. 'Yes, that's right. You know, you could do a course about financial things. They hold them at the library. I gave a woman some tape to put up a poster last week advertising for one.' She pulled out her phone and tapped the screen then turned it to face Marion. 'See, Golden Years Financial Course.'

Marion made a face. 'The name is very condescending.'

Felicity nodded. 'Yes, it is a bit, but the course itself sounds like what you need.' She read aloud:

Take control of your financial future with our specially designed course for seniors. Whether you're recently retired or looking to manage your assets better, Golden Years, Golden Wisdom offers practical, easy-to-understand lessons on modern finance. From budgeting and online banking to investment strategies and estate planning, our experienced instructors will guide you through everything you need to know to secure your financial independence.

Join a supportive community of peers and discover it's never too late to become the master of your money. Don't let your golden years be tarnished by financial worries – shine bright with newfound financial confidence.

Courses run weekly for ten weeks at the Bath Community Centre. Small class sizes ensure personalised attention. No prior financial knowledge required – just bring your enthusiasm and willingness to learn to take control of your destiny.

'Gosh, that sounds like a lot of work,' said Marion. 'Do I need to know all of those things?'

'Do you want to live with Clair in a bungalow?' asked Lana, crossing her arms firmly.

Marion stood up. 'I should do something about planning dinner.'

'You're not our cook,' said Lana. 'Sit down. Think about the course, Marion. It might just be the answer.'

Marion said nothing but wondered what Clair would say if she told her she was thinking about educating herself around money. Clair would tell her Paul would take care of it all, but that defeated the purpose.

'Felicity and I were talking and we thought we would sort out a routine or roster for the cooking, shopping, cleaning and so on,' said Lana.

Marion looked up, grateful that the conversation had moved on.

'That sounds like a good idea. I hadn't thought about that yet. I wasn't sure how we would work it out. Someone online said we should have a shelf each in the refrigerator and name our food,' Marion admitted.

Lana made a face. 'I don't think that's really our style, is it? We're the ladies of Temple Terrace! We do things properly, don't we, Flick?'

Felicity winced.

'You don't like the nickname? What about Liss?'

Felicity shook her head. 'I don't mind it. I've just never been called a nickname before.'

'If you don't like it, I can stop.' Lana smiled.

'No, don't. I like it. It's just different, not bad.'

'How about we do a meal plan at the start of the week and divide the cooking for whoever is home?' Lana said.

'That's fine with me,' said Felicity. 'But I'm not a fancy cook.'

Marion smiled. 'And I'm not a fancy eater. So it's perfect.'

'We can share the grocery bills and Felicity and I can do a clean through once a week,' Lana said.

'I *can* do things,' said Marion. 'I'm not an invalid.'

'We know, but let's share the load,' said Lana. 'I need to get a job, so until then I can do as much as possible around the house. I have been so bored before now.'

The women sipped their tea, devised a rota and wrote a list of what they needed.

Marion had forgotten how much she missed both company and laughter. They had made her feel better about Clair, and as they planned the week ahead and their shopping trip to the supermarket the next day, she felt relief that she had chosen the right people to live with her.

Lana looked at her smartwatch, which was flashing green.

'Bloody Denny,' she said and pressed something on the side to stop the light from flashing.

'Is he hassling you?' asked Felicity. 'To come back?'

Lana shrugged. 'He says he wants me back, but I'm not sure he really does. He's probably forgotten where he put his nasal hair trimmer.'

Marion laughed. 'That's an image I don't want to imagine again.'

'It's worse in real life,' Lana said.

'What do you do during the day, Marion?' Felicity asked.

Marion shrugged. 'I haven't done much because of cash flow. I go for walks or I sit in the park when it's sunny. I don't really have much purpose now. Everything costs money.'

'Too right it does,' Lana agreed. 'I know Denny's going to be painful about the settlement, so I need to get a job as soon as possible.'

'Do you have a CV?' asked Felicity.

Lana shook her head. 'No, I have to do one.'

'I can help you. I did a new one when I came here to Bath. I got the job at the university bookshop with it.'

'Oh, that would be fabulous!' exclaimed Lana.

'This is just lovely,' Marion said. 'This is actually better than I thought it would be.'

'Can I ask you something?' Lana said, crossing her legs and leaning back in her chair.

'Absolutely,' Marion said.

'Why did you choose us? I would imagine there would have been a lot of applications.'

Marion nodded. 'There were – too many, in fact – but I decided I would take the first two who met the criteria and who wrote an honest letter. I needed people who needed a home and it came through loud and clear you needed a home more than a place to sleep.'

Lana looked down at her hands, twisting the gold puzzle ring on her index finger on her right hand.

'You could tell that from my letter?' she asked, finally looking up at Marion.

She nodded.

'I didn't think I needed a home, but now I'm here, I think you saw something in my letter I hadn't even seen,' Felicity said. 'But I'm not very good at always knowing what I'm feeling until after the feeling has gone.' She gave a little laugh and Marion smiled at her.

'I think you know what you need more than you know. You just have to stop second-guessing yourself. You probably have your grandmother's voice in your head a lot of the time.'

'I do. How did you know?'

'Because I have my daughter's voice in my head and it's exhausting.'

The three women sat in silence for a moment.

'The Ladies of Temple Terrace. I like that,' Felicity said.

'Me, too,' said Marion. 'Better than the Lonely Widower of Temple Terrace.'

'Or the Divorcee of Temple Terrace,' Lana said.

'Or the Spinster of Temple Terrace,' Felicity said, and the women all laughed.

Marion raised her mug of tea. 'To the Ladies of Temple Terrace. May we keep each other company, support each other's endeavours and always leave a light on for those who aren't home yet.'

9

Felicity

Felicity sat opposite her supervisor, Nigel, who kept sniffing and pushing his glasses back on his nose as he read her work. She had printed it out for him as instructed in the email when he requested a meeting at the university.

Felicity's stomach twisted as she watched his routine. Sniff. Push glasses back. Frown.

Dr Nigel Frobisher looked exactly the same as the picture his name conjured up. Thinning hair swept over his head to try to cover the balding that was occurring. Imitation tortoiseshell glasses that didn't fit his thin nose. Pale complexion, lips as thin as string and a light dusting of eczema. He wore a navy wool blazer over a checked shirt that had some sort of dried sauce or soup on it.

His long fingers ran across the papers as though reading braille, his fingernails yellowed on his right hand. A smoker.

'The problem, Felicity,' he was saying, and she returned her focus to his face instead of his tar-stained digits. 'Is that your work is uninspired.'

Felicity bit the inside of her cheek and gave a little jump as she tasted blood.

Nigel leaned back in his chair in his small office, which was surprisingly clean and organised, compared to how he presented himself.

'Are you inspired?' He tapped her work on the desk.

'Yes,' she said, but as she spoke, she knew she was lying to herself. 'But I've just moved house and I've been busy.'

'I don't need excuses, Fe-li-ci-ty.' He sounded out each syllable. 'You're in Bath, the home of the Romans and one of Jane Austen's favourite places in Britain, and you write as though you are looking at a set of photographs. It's so distant – disconnected, in a way.'

Nigel was right, but Felicity wouldn't let herself get upset in front of him.

He shrugged. 'You either love your topic or you don't, but if you don't, you won't get your master's. You have to want to know the answers.' He picked up some of the pages. 'This reads like a guidebook, not the work of someone who is trying to explore the social tapestry of Bath in Austen's times versus Roman times.' He gestured around him. 'Bath was a social playground – all the class issues and money and the rules, gentry and so forth. I see nothing in here exploring that theme.'

He turned some of the pages.

'Both societies were very complex and yet you skim over it as though it means nothing.'

Felicity was silent. He was right and she knew it.

'Bath was the place for love, conquest, power, in both times,' he continued. 'Everyone trying to work out who was who and if they were good enough. This should be a delight not only to research, but also to write *and* to read.'

He gathered the papers and ordered them, then handed them to her over the desk.

'You need to go out into the world more,' he said. 'Imagine you are a young woman during both of those times. Go and find out about them. Make up names, characters. Live their lives in your head and then start to find the similarities. This is a creative exercise first, then the rest will come.'

Felicity took the pages and stood up. 'Thank you.' She walked to his office door, hearing her voice break a little.

She had to be honest with herself – she wasn't working hard enough, she wasn't inspired by her own work, and nothing had changed since she had moved to Temple Terrace.

'Miss Booth,' she heard, and she turned to her supervisor.

'This is a master's in *history* above all else. The Jane Austen link was your idea. I went along with it only because you were so highly recommended by Professor Leslie at Bristol, but if this doesn't improve, I will be suggesting you step back from the task for a while. Not everyone can finish a master's.'

Felicity felt tears sting as she nodded and left his office. She stood in the hallway, trying to find an exit. It wasn't the halls of residence that was interrupting her work, it was her that was getting in her own way. She made her way down the stairs and out into the sunlight.

The sound of her phone pierced her thoughts and she saw her grandmother's name on the screen. It had been a week since she had moved into Temple Terrace and she still hadn't told either her grandmother or her mother. All she had done was pay Marion instead of the university with the money her grandmother gave her.

Felicity looked at the phone and then slipped it back into her tote bag with her laptop and bits and pieces and walked towards the café. She needed a coffee and she needed to think.

For twenty-three years, Felicity had stood on the sidelines of life. It was more than being chosen last for sports and games or not receiving invitations to birthday parties. For that matter, she hadn't even being asked to parties as a teenager. She was sidelined because she didn't fit in, and she knew it. No matter how hard she tried, she usually said the wrong thing, wore the wrong thing, did the wrong thing.

Felicity ordered a coffee, convinced she was ordering incorrectly and that the entire café was laughing at her. Her phone rang again and she saw Granny's name once more. Panic seized her and she darted outside, taking deep breaths, trying not to sob and pull her hair. She had done a lot of therapy to stop that and she didn't want to start again now.

She closed her eyes, letting her breath out slowly, feeling the pieces of her mind settle back into place.

'Excuse me?'

She heard a male voice and opened her eyes to see a man in front of her, holding a takeaway cup out to her.

'You left without your coffee.'

He smiled, his teeth perfect and white against his dark skin, she noticed. He had tight curls and wore a green T-shirt with a film character on the front. A superhero of some sort.

'Thank you,' she said, and reached out to take it from him, her hand shaking.

'How about we sit for a minute?' he said, and he carried the coffee to a table with two seats. 'Come on, you look like you need to take stock.'

Felicity sat down and sighed. 'Sorry, I think I was having a panic attack.'

'You should probably be having tea instead of coffee.'

'Probably, but I love coffee,' she said, and she lifted the cup to her lips and took a sip.

'Gabriel,' he said, 'but everyone calls me Gabe.'

'Felicity. Felicity Booth.'

'You studying here?'

'Hmm, but not very well, according to my supervisor.'

'PhD?'

'Master's, in Jane Austen's literature. It was a long bow I was trying to draw, but I think I'm failing before I've even started.'

'It's early days yet. Don't give up so quickly.'

He smiled and she felt herself smile back.

'Are you studying here?' she asked.

'I am. Drama. But I also work in the coffee shop and have a few other jobs to keep myself in cash while studying.'

'You work here. In the café, I mean?' she asked, startled. 'Goodness, I'm keeping you from your job. Sorry. I'm OK.' She looked around to see if anyone was calling for him.

'I'm on a break,' he said and tapped his fingers on the table as if warming up his fingers to play the piano. 'You mentioned Austen — you're a fan of her work?'

'More of an admirer. I'm not an Austen fanatic, but I like her ability to write about society and class and love. She really gets into the female psyche without belittling her fellow sisterhood.'

'So what's your master's topic?'

'It explores the cultural and architectural influences from Roman times on the social dynamics of Bath in the Regency era.'

'You sound like you're reciting a multiplication table,' he laughed, but not meanly.

'It feels more like an unsolvable problem, to be honest.'

'Why?'

'Because my supervisor said I'm not into the research enough. I'm not living it, experiencing it. I mean I moved to Bath, didn't I? How much more can I experience?'

'Gabe?' she heard, and saw a girl in an apron waving at him.

'I have to go,' he said as he stood up. 'Meet me on Sunday afternoon, at midday, at Abbey Churchyard. I'll show you something that'll help your work. See you Sunday,' he called behind him as he jogged off, leaving Felicity to wonder if what he said was a compliment or an insult and whether she would even consider going on Sunday.

She drained her coffee and then walked over to the bin, glancing inside the store. Gabe was making coffees and laughing and talking animatedly to everyone and no one in particular. No, she wouldn't go on Sunday. He was just being nice because she had been a fool in the café. She knew she shouldn't have gone there. People always knew she wasn't right, she heard her grandmother say. She turned away and walked towards Temple Terrace.

10

Marion

'Of course you're bloody going,' Lana said as she peeled potatoes while Felicity sat at the kitchen table, her chin resting on her hands.

'I've never really gone out with someone like him before,' said Felicity.

'Like who? A man?' asked Lana.

'Do you mean because he's black?' asked Marion, moving around behind Lana.

Lana gasped. 'No! You're not racist, are you?'

'No, I'm not, but my granny is,' Felicity said.

'Well then she doesn't have to go out with him.' Lana sniffed as she spoke.

'What I mean is that I haven't really gone out with *anyone* before,' Felicity said.

Lana put down the potato and peeler and placed her hands on the worktop as though steadying herself.

'You have never been out with anyone before?'

Felicity shrugged.

Lana turned to Marion, who was sipping from a glass of white wine. Felicity had refused anything to drink, stating she wasn't sure she liked wine.

'Can you believe this?' Lana asked, and she turned back to

Felicity. 'You're twenty-three years old. How have you never been out with anyone?'

'I was never asked,' Felicity said, her voice rising.

'OK, maybe that is too personal,' said Marion to Lana, who picked up the potato and peeler again.

'I know, but she's so beautiful and clever. I thought blokes would be lining up.'

Marion looked at Felicity and saw her frowning.

'What's wrong?' Marion asked.

'I'm not beautiful,' Felicity said, shaking her head in denial.

'You bloody are,' said Lana. 'You're like a girl out of those books you read. You know, the one they always do a make-over on and she comes out and surprises the ball.'

'Please don't do a makeover on me,' begged Felicity.

'You can do one on me,' said Marion, putting her hand up to her head like a model and doing a twirl.

Lana giggled. 'Don't tempt me. Do you not think you're lovely?' she asked Felicity.

Felicity picked at her fingernails, her dark hair like a curtain over her face.

'No, I'm plain. My granny always said it was good that I was smart instead of being pretty.'

Lana gave Marion a poke in the leg with her foot at mention of the grandmother.

'This granny of yours has a lot to say about you,' Marion said gently. 'But you must remember, not everything us grandparents say is true. Or relevant, for that matter. Some of us fall behind in the times.'

Felicity looked up at Marion. 'I wish you were my granny,' she said, perhaps more serious than Marion expected.

'Oh, sweetheart—' Marion began, when the doorbell rang. 'Let me get this and we can chat. Are you all right to check the chicken?' she asked Lana, who waved her away.

Lana saw Marion pick up a few tulip petals that had fallen on the table on her way past, opening the front door to find Clair standing there.

'Hello,' Lana heard Marion say. 'Come in.'

Clair leaned in and kissed her mother's cheek.

'You've been drinking,' Clair stated.

'Yes, would you like a glass? The girls and I are making dinner. Lana opened a bottle for us.' Marion stood back to let Clair inside. 'Come on, then. I know you're keen to meet everyone.'

Clair walked down the hallway, Marion following, silently making a pact she wouldn't rise to anything that Clair did or said. She had to give her daughter the benefit of the doubt.

'Lana, Felicity, this is my daughter, Clair,' Marion said cheerfully.

Clair gave a thin-lipped smile at the women.

'Oh, yes. You left in such a hurry the other day, we didn't get to meet you properly,' said Lana.

Marion grimaced. If she had to put a bet on who would win an argument between Lana and Clair, her money would have to go on Lana, even though Clair was the queen of the well-placed cut.

'Yes, I was in a rush, but it's nice to meet you properly now.'

Clair was being gracious at least, Marion thought.

'Glass of wine, darling?' asked Marion.

'Just a small one.'

Marion poured one and handed it to her.

Clair took a sip and made a face. It was the tiniest muscle movement, but Marion knew Clair didn't like the wine. Probably not fancy or French enough for her. When had Marion gone wrong with her daughter?

'So, Lana, you're looking for a job, my mother tells me,' Clair said.

Lana smiled at her, but Marion noticed there was no warmth there. She could understand why. She wished Clair would be more like herself, but that person had slowly faded since she had married Paul.

Marion could have blamed it all on Paul, but the truth was, Clair was complicit in the snobbery. In fact, she seemed to be worse than Paul now. She needed the best of the best in everything in life, as though she were trying to prove something to someone, but who that someone was, Marion didn't know.

'I am, but I haven't got much experience in anything, so I will have to take whatever I can get.'

Clair gave a little sniff of the wine. 'Perhaps a wine merchant? You would benefit from learning a lot about wine.'

Marion felt her jaw drop at Clair's rudeness, but Lana simply laughed.

'I know – it does taste a bit like "how did you get the cat to balance on the bottle?" But I don't have much money to spend yet as I'm waiting for my settlement from Denny, so I bought what I could afford.'

Lana's candour was a slap to Clair and she lost her footing and leaned against the kitchen island. For a moment she was back to herself again, back before pretention overtook her life. The Clair who used to tell Marion that she wanted to be a nurse and look after sick babies and who always wanted to give her pocket money to the needy.

'That's smart,' conceded Clair, and she turned her attention to Felicity. 'And you're doing a master's in Austen, I hear?'

Felicity looked up as though surprised to be included in the exchange.

'History, actually. Connecting Roman and Regency society and manners.'

'Wow, that will be a shoo-in to find work when you finish up,' Clair said and laughed a little too loudly.

'Clair, please join me in the sitting room,' Marion said firmly.

'No, Mother, I'm here to get to know the girls, as you call them.'

'No, you're being rude and I don't know why,' said Marion, standing her ground. 'You either talk to me in the other room or you leave. Why come if you're going to be so rude?'

'She's trying to make it uncomfortable for us,' Lana said, checking the chicken roasting in the oven. She turned to Clair. 'Aren't you, love?' She looked at Marion. 'She thinks if she makes it awkward for us then we will leave, I assume.'

Clair was silent, her hands on her skinny hips.

'And then I will have no housemates and I will have to sell the house.' Marion spoke slowly, trying to grapple with Clair's motives.

'Don't be so ridiculous, Mother. I'm simply concerned for you. This is too much for you – the house, the money, the organising.'

'Well, I'm about to start a financial literacy class, so I will soon be able to look after myself and be less of a burden on you, because if this is the way you act when you're con-cerned for me, then it's not worth this stress for either of us.'

Clair stared at her mother. 'A course?'

'Yes, Felicity found it for me. She wants me to control my own future, not be controlled.'

'Aren't you a clever little thing, Fe-li-ci-ty! Who would have guessed? Not me!' Clair almost snarled at Felicity, who stepped back from Clair's venom.

Marion had had enough.

'Clair, you need to go. Please don't come back until you have apologised to Felicity and Lana and to me.'

Clair stood her ground, but Lana stepped forwards. 'I'll see you out.'

After Clair had left the room, Marion stood in the middle of the kitchen trying to manage her anger. Eventually, she looked at Felicity.

'She would never have been like this to Geoffrey if he was in the same position.'

'Do you think so?' Felicity said.

'I do. The two of them were always great mates. She wouldn't be like that to him.'

'Would he have sold the house for her?' asked Felicity.

Marion paused. 'I think he would have, to keep her happy.' She sat down at the table, twisting her sapphire engagement ring before glancing up the hallway.

'She's gone,' Lana said.

'I'm so sorry. She's clearly not herself,' Marion said.

Lana topped up the wine. 'More cat piss, anyone?'

'Marion, you mentioned you had a son. Why can't you talk to him about Clair's behaviour? He is her brother.'

Marion took a sip of wine and then looked at the women who shared her home. It was time to share the truth.

'My son died twenty years ago in a motorcycle accident. Clair changed when he died. She was twenty-two, he twenty-four – it broke her. They were such good friends as children and remained close as adults. She married Paul only six months after Andy's funeral. She wanted security, safety. Paul's very controlling. He said he would shield her from any pain ever again ...' Marion paused, thinking.

'But that's impossible,' she continued. 'Life is filled with pain. We can't avoid it. I guess that's what makes me so aware of the beauty and good times. I think she's been so protected and controlled by Paul that she's forgotten to see these wonderful things. She can't even grab at them. They seem to pass her by.'

Lana took Marion's hand. 'I'm sorry for your loss.'

Marion noticed Lana's eyes were bright with tears.

'Thank you.' She squeezed Lana's hand. 'But I think there is something happening with Clair and if she keeps ignoring it, it will just get bigger until it explodes or implodes. I don't know what to do, but I do know I can't push her to tell me until she's ready. Meanwhile, I'd better look up this course, because if I don't do it now, I will never hear the end of it.'

I I

Lana

Lana opened her emails and saw three job rejections and one from Denny asking her where she had hidden the remote control for the outdoor lights along the side of the house. She ignored his email because she hadn't hidden it – he was just terrible at remembering where he put things. It was just his way of trying to start a conversation with her. As far as she was concerned, he could stay in the dark, she thought as she opened her resumé and reread it.

She really didn't have any skills that an employer might want or need, for that matter. For a moment she felt a wave of shame wash over her for letting herself become reliant on Denny, even when she was betraying herself and what she felt. Clearly, Denny was the one who had been betraying her if he had gone off with someone else. They had both been in denial. Thank goodness little Royce Rolls had showed them the truth.

Lana's phone rang and she saw it was Evie.

'Hey,' she said.

'How's the granny house?' Evie asked.

'Don't be rude, and it's great, actually.'

'You could have stayed with us longer.'

Evie sounded put out yet was sulky when Lana was staying there with them. She could never win with her sister.

'I need to start out again on my own. I can afford this for a while until I get a job and the settlement from Denny comes through.'

'Actually, speaking of Denny...'

Evie's voice had that weird tone she used when she was trying to make something less of a deal than it was, which meant it was a huge deal.

'Y-e-e-e-s?' Lana dragged the word out slowly, like exhaling smoke.

'He's offered Petey a job at the new store.'

'Has he now?'

Lana didn't mention that Denny called Petey a loser whenever they saw him, which wasn't untrue but then again, Lana was probably considered a loser at the moment, by all appearances.

'Yeah, said he will train him up to manage the store,' Evie said.

There was a pause. Lana knew why Denny was doing it, but that was for them to find out. No warning would help Evie or Petey. Denny was a born salesman, and Petey and Evie had just bought into his rubbish.

'I hope it works out for Petey,' she said with a sigh, shaking her head, though Evie couldn't see it.

'Is that it? I thought you'd be mad. You're shaking your head, aren't you?'

Lana gave a hollow laugh.

'Evie, you're an adult and so is Petey. If you think he can work for Denny, knowing what he's like and how he's treated people in the past, not to mention his lies to me, then that's on you.'

Evie was silent for a moment.

'It's just Petey's finding it hard to get a job,' Evie said eventually.

'I know.' And she did know. All the job rejections in her own inbox was testament to that. 'Just tell Petey to be careful. Don't buy into his sales pitch too much.'

'I will. Thanks, Lana.'

Evie sounded relieved.

Lana put down the phone and looked around her room. She couldn't stay here all day, she thought. She found Marion in the kitchen watering a houseplant.

'I'm sure you said you were going to take me to the bakery,' she winked conspiratorially.

Marion smiled. 'I'd love to. I need a walk to clear my mind.'

Lana sighed. 'Me, too.'

'Something troubling you?'

'Get your things and we can walk and talk.' Lana pulled on a white blazer over her white T-shirt with gold sequins on the front spelling out Foxy.

Soon they were on the street outside Temple Terrace. Marion locked the door while Lana looked at the wisteria, touching the silvery green buds.

'There will be a lovely show this year, looking at the amount of buds,' said Marion.

'What's the flower bud and what's the leaf bud?'

Marion pointed out each.

Lana peered at the difference. 'How old do you think the plant is?'

Marion slipped the keys into her pocket.

'It was here when we bought the house in the seventies, but not as lush. Maybe planted in the sixties. Geoffrey did nurture it like another child, though. I'm not sure I have quite the same skills as him, although I could look it up on my iPad or read one of his many gardening tomes in the library.'

They started to walk along the Crescent.

'The little garden out the back was beautiful at one point, but once he became sick, it was forgotten. There was too much else to do and to be honest, I don't have the money to bring someone in to bring it back to life.'

Lana dug her hands in her pockets against the cool air, thinking about the little garden and then her own garden that Denny had destroyed. The longer she was away from Denny, the more she saw he was abusive. Everything he did was about control. She had once wished for someone to make the decisions for her. She had thought there were so many back then, when their mother left. She supposed this made her complicit back then. Now, though, she realised she couldn't do it any longer.

It was easier to explain to people that Denny had had a child with someone else while they were still married than tell them that he had ripped up her precious vegetable garden. Easier than saying he had paid landscapers thousands to turn it into the sort of garden you found surrounding a mausoleum.

'Would you mind if I pottered in your garden while I'm looking for a job?' Lana said eventually.

'Not at all. Be my guest. There are plenty of things in the little potting shed to the side of the garden. At the back, there is a door to the lane, so you can get rid of any cuttings and so on.' Marion led the way.

Lana missed walking like this. She looked around. The grand No. 1 Royal Crescent stood proudly as an icon of the area. Around them, people strolled past, seemingly in no rush, as though Bath were asking them to slow down and be in the moment.

'Let's pop in here for a second,' said Marion, stepping through a doorway in an old wall.

They emerged onto gravel, which made a pleasing sound under Lana's trainers.

'Have you been here before?' Marion asked.

Lana looked around the space. It was a formal garden, with round beds in the middle, surrounded by hedges and what looked to be rose bushes. They were in early bud, tiny leaves making their way into the sunshine. More beds surrounded on three sides, with smaller hedges to match and bigger shrubs and trees behind it, all in a lovely green.

'This is a Georgian garden. This is what Temple Terrace would have looked like once, I believe. It was Geoffrey's dream to turn it back into something of its time, but he never got round to it in the end.'

Lana looked around. 'It's very formal.'

'Apparently, that was because the garden was designed to be looked at from above.' Marion turned and looked up at the terrace house. 'It's all symmetry and flow. I'm sure Felicity could tell you more.'

'I can just picture the girls in their gowns swanning about, picking a rose or something,' Lana said as she walked around the space.

Marion smiled. 'Yes, I can, too.'

Lana took out her phone and took a few photos. Then she came to Marion's side and lifted the phone up, putting her head next to Marion's.

'Smile for a selfie,' Lana said, beaming, and took the photo. 'We look great,' said Lana, sending it over to Marion.

Marion took her phone out of her bag and peered at the image. Lana's glamorous blonde hair cascaded over the shoulders of her white blazer, a hint of the gold sequins catching the morning sunlight. In contrast, Marion's shorter grey hair framed her mature features, her navy quilted coat the opposite of Lana's sparkles, yet the pair looked happy.

Behind them, a light orb hovered, its ethereal glow casting a soft otherworldly luminescence over the image.

'You know, they say when light orbs appear in photographs, it's actually someone you loved who has passed,' Lana said, smiling at Marion.

'Maybe it's Geoffrey,' Marion half joked. 'He would more likely be here than at home. He loved this place.'

'Morning, Geoffrey,' called Lana into the day.

Marion smiled and put her arm through Lana's for a moment, squeezing her tight.

'You're so much fun,' Marion said. 'You remind me to have fun.'

'I wasn't fun for a while. Being around you makes me feel like things are going to be OK.'

'Because they are going to be OK,' Marion said firmly, and she looked back at the image on Lana's phone. 'I look old,' she complained. 'I don't feel that old.'

'But a good old, like someone who enjoys life,' Lana said, looking at the photo. 'Look at your eyes – they're sparkling. And your skin is great. You have a gorgeous haircut and that pink lippie really suits you.'

Marion laughed. 'Gosh, you do have a way of making someone feel better. You're a balm, Lana.'

'A balm?'

'Soothing, healing.'

'I've been called many things, but never that. Not that it's bad, a balm,' she repeated as she sat on the small bench and looked around.

Marion looked enchanted by the tranquillity of the space in a busy place like Bath. The hedges were perfectly uniform, matching the buildings of the time.

'The gardens are an unspoiled example of Georgian architecture,' said Marion. 'Geoffrey was a big supporter and came down when they were doing the architectural dig here. We used to come here early in the morning before the tourists gathered.'

Lana looked at the meticulously manicured lawns, precise geometric patterns and carefully trimmed hedges. 'It's so perfect.'

The garden was laid out in a series of terraces, each a few steps lower than the last, creating a sense of grandeur and providing a perfect vantage point from which to admire the intricate design. The uppermost terrace boasted a long, straight gravel path, flanked on either side by low, perfectly clipped boxwood hedges. They almost looked like green velvet ribbons, stretching towards the horizon.

On either side of the path, the lawn was divided into a series of small square beds, each filled with a variety of shrubs that hadn't started to flower yet. From the buds, Lana guessed they were roses. At the centre of each bed stood a carefully pruned topiary, shaped into a perfect sphere or pyramid.

'Come and explore,' said Marion.

Lana got up and followed her landlady to the lower terraces, where they discovered even more delights. A small, bubbling fountain occupied the centre of one terrace, its sparkling water catching the sunlight, casting a mesmerising shimmer across the nearby flower beds.

'God, this is stunning,' Lana said.

Benches were arranged in a circular fashion around the fountain, inviting visitors to sit and enjoy the tranquil atmosphere.

'It's usually crowded,' said Marion. 'Geoffrey must have spooked them away this morning so we could have it to ourselves.'

Marion laughed and moved to the lowest terrace, which was home to a charming orangery, its tall windows allowing sunlight to stream in and nurture the citrus trees inside. The heady scent of orange blossoms drifted out into the garden, adding another layer to the already intoxicating sensory experience.

'This is the new part,' said Marion. 'They were fundraising for this when Geoffrey was ill. I wondered if my husband had donated to this cause when he was ill. There again, they never dedicated it to him or called it the Gaynor Orangery, so I suppose he didn't.' She took a leaf, splitting it and then sniffing the orange oil.

Looking back up at the terraces, Lana could appreciate the overall design, with its symmetrical layout and carefully planned vistas, but she felt like something was missing. It was so formal it felt as though it were holding its breath, which Lana could relate to. She had felt like this when she lived with Denny. Everything perfect and no personality.

But she couldn't deny the sense of peace that surrounded her now. Was it this garden that gave her that feeling or being in a garden in general?

Lana sat on the bench, revelling in the peace and quiet. The only sounds were the chirping of birds, the gentle rustling of leaves and the distant, soothing gurgle of a fountain. A sense of calm washed over her, as though the garden were as much a balm for her soul as she was for Marion.

'You can come back whenever you want. It's free entry, but come early or late to avoid the crowds,' Marion said.

Lana stood up. 'Righto, let's go to the bakery. They have an almond croissant with my name on it. Thank you for showing me that, Marion. It felt special.'

'Good, I'm glad you can appreciate it.'

They walked along the beautiful streets, Lana admiring the houses from up close.

'Since I moved in with you, I keep getting the feeling that I'm getting closer to something. I don't know what it is, just that it's getting close. It's not a bad feeling, just different.'

Marion smiled. 'Well I'm glad. Just stay with it and see where it takes you. Perhaps you're leading yourself there.'

'Perhaps,' said Lana, but she wasn't so sure.

12

Felicity

Felicity stood at the kitchen sink watching Lana move plant pots around outside and brush down the uneven brickwork. It was her new project, she'd told Felicity over dinner a few days ago, and she was hoping to find her calling whenever she lifted the bricks and laid down gravel. It sounded like a punishment to Felicity, but she said nothing. No one needed her opinion on things.

She felt her phone ringing in her pocket but ignored it as Marion came into the kitchen holding a wicker basket of washing.

'Don't you have you meeting with that man from the café today?' she asked as she put it down on the table.

'I don't think I'm going to go,' said Felicity, helping Marion to fold the towels.

'Why not?'

'I don't know. I mean, why would he ask *me* to go, anyway?'

Felicity had been mulling over the invitation for the past three days and the more she mulled, the more unlikely her attendance became.

'What were you planning to do instead?' Marion asked.

'Read, work on my thesis.' Felicity sounded unconvinced even to herself.

'Go and meet your new friend. And remember, he said

he had something to help you with your work. We should always say yes to adventures,' Marion insisted.

Felicity thought about staying upstairs in her room and thinking about the thesis, trying to read, trying to concentrate, but another fruitless day beckoned. She pulled her phone from her pocket and saw three missed calls from her grandmother and one from her mother. She still hadn't told them she had left the university residence halls. She wasn't sure why, but she was sure her granny wouldn't like it.

She saw she had twenty minutes to get to where Gabe had said to meet, at Abbey Churchyard.

'OK, I'll go,' she sighed.

Marion opened the back door and called to Lana, 'She's going.'

Lana stood up from where she was crouching over some bricks and clapped.

'Yay! Go and meet your Angel Gabriel who rescued you from the panic attack.'

Felicity frowned. 'I don't think he's my angel. I don't believe in angels.'

'I do,' Lana said. 'Marion is my angel.'

Marion laughed. 'I think some would say I'm more of a devil.'

Felicity looked at her phone and saw another missed call. She sighed.

'OK, I'm off,' Felicity said.

If she was busy, then she had an excuse not to talk to them for a while longer.

'Good girl,' said Marion, wiping her hands on her trousers as Lana came to her side. 'I'm thinking we should get a take-away tonight. It is Sunday, after all, and I don't like cooking on a Sunday. We can hear all about your afternoon, if you're keen to share.'

'Good idea. I'm in. Indian? Chinese?' Lana asked.

Felicity smiled. 'That sounds nice, thank you.'

Felicity went upstairs to fetch her tote bag. At the last minute, she grabbed her hairbrush and brushed out her long hair. Then she clutched her keys in her hands and bounced down the stairs and out of the front door.

It was the sort of weather that made Felicity happier than she liked to admit. People assumed she was the morose sort who like rain and drizzle and wintery storms, but she actually liked summer days just as much. The quietude of a park somewhere with a book to read and an iced coffee. She could lie on the grass and dream all day if she was allowed.

She walked in the direction of the Abbey Churchyard, along the Crescent and down a side street and onto the Circus, where a few tourists were taking photos and looking at guidebooks before glancing up at the circular buildings. She headed to Milsom Street and then down to the Abbey Churchyard. She hadn't wanted to admit she hadn't been there yet, knowing it was an important part of Roman history in the city, never mind mentioned in Austen's books. Sometimes she wondered if everything she knew was on the page rather than experienced in person.

The square was busy with tourists, looking at their phones and maps and chatting among themselves, surrounded by historic architecture. She looked around for Gabriel but couldn't see him. He hadn't specified where exactly they would meet and there were so many people. A busker was playing 'La Vie en Rose' on a violin while some American tourists were calling out for Mr Darcy after the character in *Pride and Prejudice* and laughing loudly.

Felicity looked in her bag for her headphones and then remembered they were on the floor next to her bed, where she had plugged them in to charge. It was too loud and she was also regretting the woollen cardigan and the cotton turtleneck she was wearing.

Turning to leave, she felt a hand on her shoulder. She spun round and there was Gabe, in a top hat with a cravat in a rich cream and a tailored Regency jacket in royal blue and what looked to be riding boots.

'Oh my,' said Felicity. 'Why are you dressed up?'

He looked incredibly handsome, his close proximity unnerving.

'Because I'm at work, and I'm taking you along with me,' he said, smiling broadly.

It was the biggest smile she had ever seen on a man in her presence.

'Work?'

She looked around and saw a group people with backpacks, some wearing lanyards. They were gathered around a middle-aged woman in a Regency dress and bonnet. She was wearing a headset underneath the hat, curls springing out and sticking to her warm face. She seemed at her wits' end.

'I'm part of the Jane Austen Bath Walk Tour,' he said, and he gave an elegant bow. 'And I will give you a free tour of Bath and its connection to Miss Austen, including the walks she used to take when she was living here. Our feet will touch the ground she once walked on – that's pretty cool, isn't it?'

Well, she was here now, she reasoned. She could at least listen, especially since Gabe was inviting her to explore for free. She moved to join the group milling around the woman in the bonnet.

Gabe stood on a step and removed his hat in a flamboyant manner.

'Greetings and welcome to Bath's Abbey Churchyard – a serene oasis nestled in the heart of our fair city.'

He gestured around him and the group watched him with wide-eyed interest.

'Once a sacred burial ground, now a peaceful haven where visitors gather to admire the abbey's grandeur and reflect on its rich history,' he continued. 'Let us embrace the tranquillity of this historic square as we explore Bath together!'

He jumped down off the step and smiled at Felicity.

'Let's go and see what this place has to offer you,' he said.

The woman in the bonnet was called Denise, who also worked at the Jane Austen high-tea experience at a teashop, and the Jane Austen Centre, she told the group as they walked.

Gabe came up to her. 'I'm glad you stayed.'

He was carrying a walking cane with a silver top. It was silly and perfect at the same time.

'Denise must know a lot about Austen, considering all of her jobs are involved in some way. I'd love to pick her brain about the books set here.'

Gabe laughed.

'What? Why wouldn't she want to talk to me?' Felicity asked, slighted.

'Oh, she'll talk to you all right about stories set in Bath, but she's never read the books. She's seen the films and TV shows, but she never tells them she hasn't read the books. There would be outrage. I think she's sort of tired of it, to be honest.'

'She shouldn't lie.'

Gabe snorted. 'Why? It's just a job. It's not her life's purpose. People love her. She knows a lot – a lot more than you would think. She's surrounded by Austen fanatics who talk to her about it in a way it's impossible not to learn from. We glean lots from them, but at the end of the day, Denise and I are just doing a job. We don't have to be an expert or perfect in everything to enjoy it and do it well.'

She felt like a bucket of cold water had been tipped over her. This went against everything she had been told growing up and at school, even university.

'You have to do better than the rest of the class or you will be held back,' they'd said.

'If you don't work harder then you will fall behind.'

'No one wants a failure.'

The mottos of her childhood were ingrained in her soul, dovetailed with a deep fear of being held back, rejected in life, not getting ahead. But how had that worked out for her so far? She didn't have any friends, was failing her degree and no one wanted her. Except Gabe.

And Denise – despite being more of a Keira Knightley fan than of Jane Austen's writing – was happy. Popular, it seemed. She realised this was a Felicity issue more than anything and she had to undo all she had learned before.

They were now at the thermal springs and Gabe moved to the front of the group.

'Welcome to the thermal springs of Bath, where the Celtic goddess Sulis reigns supreme.'

Gabe's voice was rich and resonant and he held the group in the palm of his hand as he spoke.

'While she's known for her healing powers, Sulis was also believed to wield the ability to curse those who dared to disrespect her sacred waters. As the guardian deity of the springs, her curses were seen as a form of divine justice, striking fear into the hearts of those who crossed her.'

He gave a flourish with his cane and the group gasped. Felicity smiled.

'So, as you enjoy the soothing waters, remember to show respect to Sulis and her sanctuaries, or risk facing her wrath.'

His eye caught Felicity's and he gave her a wink. For the first time in her twenty-three years, she swooned.

13

Marion

After Felicity had left, Marion sat outside on a wrought-iron chair enjoying the sunshine in the back garden. When the weather was warm, she used to sit out here with Geoffrey and chat, or when the children were little they would play out here. She could still remember Clair and Andy playing badminton, or Andy trying to convince Geoffrey to build a skateboard ramp. It seemed so long ago and yet like yesterday.

Lana was oblivious, huffing and puffing as she moved the pots to one side of the garden, lining them up in order of size, like a descending terracotta staircase for little garden gnomes.

'I haven't sat out here for a long time – too long,' Marion said.

She looked around at the roses that lined the walls around them, heavy with buds and a few early blooms already open. Hopeful bees busied themselves, darting in and out, encouraging the petals to open for their benefit.

'Why not? It's lovely.'

Lana stood up from where she was crouching over a plant pot and stretched. She was wearing jeans and boots she had bought from a charity shop and an old pink T-shirt that used to be her gym top. Marion had noticed she was wearing different clothes since she had moved into Temple Terrace.

She had stopped wearing white all the time and was much more relaxed, casual – more herself, Marion guessed.

'I think I felt guilty that I couldn't do more, as in the gardening and cleaning up, so I avoided it. Sometimes I used to pull the blind down so I didn't have to see it when I rinsed the dishes at the sink,' Marion admitted.

But she didn't mention that she had also pulled the blinds down on the memories made in the garden. That was far too intimate for such a new connection with someone.

Lana laughed. 'Well, I will do what I can with what's here. It really needs a tidy first and then we can decide what to do next.'

Marion looked at the garden bed along the north wall. 'There are so many suckers on those roses. I should really get the secateurs from the kitchen and cut them back.'

Lana reached into the back pocket of her jeans and pulled out some secateurs. 'Already on it.'

'I didn't think you knew much about gardening,' said Marion as she watched Lana cut off the lanky suckers.

Lana proceeded to cut them into smaller pieces and placed them in a plastic bucket she had found.

'I'm not a complete novice,' she said. 'Growing up, my nan had a lovely garden and I spent a lot of time in it with her. Mum used to leave me there when she was off with whoever her latest boyfriend was. Nan would show me the difference between a pelargonium and a geranium and how to cut back the pansies to encourage new flowers in summer.'

'You know more than me. I did see the wisteria was out this morning, which means the tourists will be lining up to have their photos taken.'

'Do they do that?'

'Oh yes. If I charged for the privilege, then I wouldn't have to rent rooms out. But then I wouldn't know you, so it's all meant to be.'

Lana smiled. 'It's nice out here. I've been trying to see where my mind wanders while I clear it out, like you said, but all I think about is how much I like being out here.' She held her hands out to look at her nails and then held them up to Marion. 'Look at these ... Chipped, shorter, dirt underneath them, even a few scratches. I'm getting gardeners' hands,' she said proudly.

'Is your nan still around?'

Lana shook her head and pushed her hair back with the back of her forearm.

'She died when I was fourteen and Evie was six. Then it became a downhill shitshow with Janice, our mother. I had four years of her coming and going, until one day she didn't come back. It was a relief, really.'

Marion watched as Lana pulled some weeds from the beds with deft hands.

'You're a natural at this,' Marion said. 'Maybe this is what you're meant to be doing. Since your mind isn't wandering, it's just staying here.'

'Pulling weeds isn't going to pay the bills,' she laughed. 'I'll get something from my divorce, but it won't be enough other than to buy something small. I'll still have to work.'

'What if you learned how to do this for a living?'

'Pulling weeds? Nan used to pay me 5p a bucket. I don't think the wages have improved much since then, so I'd have to pull a lot of weeds.'

'No – gardening. Think about it. If it makes you happy, you should consider it. You could go to university to study horticulture.'

Lana gave a dismissive snort. 'You can't lead a whore to culture and make her think.' She laughed loudly.

Marion joined in but then shook her finger at Lana. 'That's a terrible yet very clever saying, but don't call yourself names.'

'I'm only joking, but seriously, thirty-eight and studying? God help me.' Lana snorted again, then picked up a broom and started to sweep.

'It's never too late to do anything,' Marion said firmly and walked back inside the house.

If she had her time again, what wouldn't she have done, she thought as she turned on the kettle. Not that life with Geoffrey had been bad – it hadn't. It was a lovely life. But at some stage, Marion realised she had been left behind. She didn't know the details of their bank accounts when he became sick, so learning the money had gone was a shock. He had withdrawn it all in cash over several weeks and what happened after that she had no idea.

She wasn't good at anything technology-minded until her granddaughter, Sophie, showed her how to use an iPad and her phone properly, but she still didn't get some of the features and still didn't understand how to use Siri. At least she could work the laptop Geoffrey had left. Perhaps she should take it with her to the finance class now she had booked in online.

Once, she had challenged Sophie and Tom to research something using their grandfather's extensive library, but they had laughed at her. They weren't being mean. It was just that in their eyes, she may as well have been suggesting they write a letter with a quill and ink.

She headed for the library. Geoffrey's interests were eclectic, so they used to tell people he was interested in evolution and revolutions, but it was more than that. Art, design, poetry ... God, how she missed him. No one had warned her on the day she walked up the aisle in her silk dress and veil, holding a bunch of white roses, that she would also have to bear the loneliness after he had gone.

Do you, Marion Anne, take this man for better or for worse, in sickness and in health, and then commit to living without him, where you miss him every day. Where you seek him out to talk about the simple things: the weather forecast, if he wants lamb cutlets or salmon for dinner – or to discuss what was happening with Clair and what could they do.

Her eye was caught by a book on Medici garden design and she pulled it off the shelf and placed it on the table. There was another about the landscaper André Le Nôtre at Versailles, and another on espaliering trees, of course. There were books on gardens in Italy, on bonsai and on royal gardens of the world. Soon, Marion had three piles of books on the table and she stood back to look at them. There was a slight vapour of dust in the air, so she opened the window and smiled, then walked outside into the garden.

'Can I grab those secateurs?' she asked Lana, who was wrestling with a dead plant in a pot.

Lana handed them to her.

Marion picked a few roses and then handed them back. 'Come inside. I have something for you.'

Lana followed her inside. Marion placed the roses in a little silver vase with some water and then went into the library and placed them on Geoffrey's desk.

'All of these books are on gardens. These are the ones I have found so far, but I am sure there are more if you search. I'm not climbing that ladder at my age.'

Lana looked at the pile of books. 'And what do you want me to do with them?' She looked confused.

'Read them. Immerse yourself in them. If you are interested, keep reading. If it doesn't pique your interest, combined with the pottering you're doing outside, then perhaps gardening isn't for you. But you have to learn from the past to make a future.'

Lana picked up a book on edible gardens and flicked through it.

'I'm not really a book reader, so thank God there's pictures.' She laughed but started to sift through the pile and then looked at Marion. 'I have always loved gardens … I–I started a garden at home, but Denny tore it down.'

'He what?' Marion's voice was almost a screech.

Lana nodded and then told Marion what happened.

'That is appalling, truly terrible.' Marion slapped her own knees in protest. 'He should be charged.'

'With what? Being a total prick?' Lana snorted.

'Yes, why not?' Marion shook her head in disbelief. 'Well, then you must pursue it now. Denny might have pruned your interests, as it were – well, more like tore them apart – but if it made you happy, then you will adore it even more now you're away from him. It could be good for your spirit.'

Lana picked a dead leaf off the rose bush.

'I used to think I wanted to work in a garden, or as a florist when I was a child, but you know … life got in the way. Too late now.'

A shadow of wistful sadness passed over Lana's face and then she shrugged it away, like an old overcoat.

'Too late? Why?' Marion asked.

'Because I need a job. I don't have time to look into a course or anything.'

'Maybe just get into the garden first and then see what comes up while you're working. You need time to think to make space for the new ideas to pop their little heads up.'

She thought for a moment. 'I think Geoffrey planted some grape hyacinths in the beds at the back, so they should be showing their little heads very soon, too.'

But Lana was lost in the past again.

'Having a career wasn't really a thing for me as a kid. It was just about having a job, enough to put food on the table. I worked from the moment I turned twelve, delivering papers, then I got a job in a nursing home handing out meals, and then in shops and so on. By that time, Denny said I didn't need to work any more. I was ready to stop. I was tired. I haven't given thought to what I *want* to do right now, just what I *have* to do.'

Marion sat down at the table and wiped some dust specks from the glossy wood.

'That's because it's a privilege to be able to pursue what makes you happy. Most don't have the luxury to chase what they are interested in, what makes their hearts sing.'

Lana sat down and opened a book, turning the pages slowly.

'What would you chase?' Lana asked.

'What do you mean?'

A light breeze blew through the window. Not cool, not hot, just a gentle caress, bringing with it a thistledown seed head that landed gently on the table near Lana. It was so graceful, Marion was reminded of ballerinas in 'La Sylphide'. She picked it up and held it on the palm of her hand.

'What is the one thing you always wanted to do? To learn more about, explore. The thing that makes you lose time when you're doing it.' Lana looked up at Marion and smiled.

Marion sat and thought for a moment. 'You know – and I don't want to sound like a sad old woman, because I'm not – but I have never been asked that before.'

'Never?'

Marion shook her head. 'No, never. I was a corporate wife. I was a mother. It was never even considered that I would work. And now, I suppose it's a bit late for that.'

Lana frowned, the dandelion seed head still semi-floating on the palm of her hand.

'It's never too late for anything, you told me not ten minutes ago,' Lana said, raising her eyebrows at Marion. 'Drink your own medicine, Mrs Gaynor.'

Marion laughed. 'You are a tonic, Lana, honestly.'

'So, if you could do anything right now, what would you do?' Lana persisted.

Marion shook her head. 'I honestly don't know. It feels like I am trying to find an answer in a much-neglected part of my mind. The part I don't use any more.'

'What part?'

'The part where I think about possibilities for my future,' Marion admitted. 'Being older means I think about how not to be a burden to anyone. But I haven't thought about what might be possible for me in the future for so long, perhaps not in fifty years.'

Lana put her hand out towards Marion with the thistledown head in her palm.

'The key is still inside this. Pull it out and make a wish.'

Marion took the seed head. 'We used to call these fairies when I was small.' She stood up and went to the window.

'Make a wish,' Lana called from behind her.

Marion pulled the seed from the centre and then blew it out of the window, closing her eyes and making a wish.

14

Lana

The solicitor looked at the papers on the desk, shuffled through them and then pulled one out, running her finger along the sentences. She turned to her computer, typed something on the keyboard and then finally looked at Lana.

'He's offering you half,' she said with a tone that spoke volumes.

'Half of what?' Denny was a lying piece of work, so half of anything could be half a stale doughnut, as far as she was concerned.

'Half of the house.'

Lana thought for a moment.

'What about the business? I worked on that with him for years.'

The solicitor shook her head. 'He said you didn't help at all, that you were a stay-at-home wife.'

She gasped. 'That's a lie.'

The solicitor nodded. 'It always is. I see this all the time with spouses of men with careers and businesses.'

Lana put her hands up in anger. 'All those ideas, the advice, the research I did for the stores and the locations and the products. He said there was no future in robot vacuums, but there was. I wish it had sucked him up and out of my life.'

The solicitor gave a little laugh.

'And I listened to his bullshit and helped him to grow the business. I even managed the staffing issues. He's a total dick to his staff. People don't stay because he's such a prick.' Fury ran through her and the more she thought about the business, the angrier she became.

'Do you have any emails or texts confirming that?' asked the solicitor.

'I do. I have so many.'

'Good, send them over to me. The more evidence we have that you were a part of the business, the more we can negotiate.'

Lana paused for a moment. 'I don't want you to think I'm greedy or a gold digger or anything.'

The solicitor shook her head. 'I don't, and even if you were, I wouldn't care. You know what you're worth, and you know what you did to help the business. Why shouldn't you be recompensed? You gave him your time and ideas and support. He can pay you for it now.'

Lana felt her shoulders drop. 'Thank you, I needed to hear that.'

'Go and collect all the information. Put it in a folder somewhere safe and share it with me when you can.'

'I will.'

After Lana left the office, she went to her car and sat in it for a moment. Denny was always going to make this difficult and it would be worse now Evie's boyfriend was working for him. She wouldn't be able to tell Evie anything because it would get back to Denny, no matter how much she made Evie promise not to gossip.

Half the house would be fine, but she knew Denny had more than that and the fact he was trying to gaslight her over the business made her furious. She had a choice to make: she could take the money from the house and leave, ignoring the fact she was being taken advantage of, or she could stay and fight for the work she had done alongside him.

As she drove towards home, she passed a garden centre she hadn't been to before, only seen from outside. She suddenly felt a need to look at plants and flowers and seedlings, all the possibilities for a beautiful garden in one place. She didn't even want to buy anything. She just needed to see plants and be reminded by their resilience.

She parked up and climbed out, her anxiety easing as the scent of damp earth and fresh greenery enveloped her. She meandered through the aisles, her fingers brushing the leaves of potted herbs and trailing over the rims of terracotta pots.

In the bedding section, trays of colourful pansies and cheerful marigolds caught her eye. Their vibrant petals seemed to nod encouragingly in the gentle breeze from a nearby fan. Lana paused, drinking in their simple beauty, remembering the marigolds she had planted to keep the bugs away from her little vegetable seedlings.

Damn you, Denny, she thought as she turned and found herself in an aisle of larger shrubs and saplings. A particularly handsome rhododendron, its red buds tightly furled and full of promise, made her smile. She imagined how glorious it would look in full bloom, its flowers a riot of pink against dark green leaves. God, how she wished she could have a garden like this one day.

The vegetable patch display was a marvel of neat rows and tidy labels. Lana chuckled at the determinedly upright runner bean plants, their fragile tendrils already seeking something to climb.

'I get it,' she whispered as she helped one to find its way to the stake.

She walked towards the greenhouse and as she entered, she was struck by the warm, moist air and the lush abundance of foliage. Ferns unfurled their fronds in graceful arcs, while exotic orchids perched regally in their pots. A tray of tiny succulents, each one a perfect miniature garden, made her heart swell with unexpected joy.

As she wandered, she felt the tension in her shoulders ease. The steady, quiet growth of the plants around her reminded her of patience and perseverance. Change and growth takes time, she thought.

By the time she reached the herb section, Lana felt renewed. She inhaled the pungent scent of rosemary and the sweet aroma of basil. This is why she loved plants so much. They reminded her of the cycles of growth and rest, of dormancy and flourishing. She smiled at the thought of feeling bonsaied by Denny, but now she was free to grow.

'Can I help you?'

She turned and saw a woman in cargo pants and a top bearing the name of the nursery.

'I was just looking. I love plants.'

'You're a gardener, are you?' she asked.

'Trying to be, but I'm only a novice. Sort of teaching myself, I suppose. I guess I'll have to read some books or something before I start anything too ambitious.'

The woman nodded. 'We hold a short course here for beginners, if you're interested. All the basics and a bit more. It's run by the owner. It's very good. Covers everything you need to know to get started: composting, soil testing, what likes sun and shade and so on.'

'How long is the course?'

'It's held over four weeks, one night a week, but you get a pretty hefty discount on the plants and seeds.' She smiled. 'There's a brochure on the front counter if you want to have a read.' The woman went off in the direction of a phone ringing.

Lana plucked a leaf and rubbed it between her fingers, bringing it up to her face to inhale the scent. She read the label: lemon balm. It was apt. She was a balm for Marion and this place was a balm for her. On her way out, she picked up the pamphlet on the course and headed back to Temple Terrace.

Later, when they had finished dinner, Lana handed Marion the course brochure as they sat in front of the television in the sitting room. Felicity had gone upstairs to write and was being studious since she had joined the Jane Austen tour with Gabriel. Not that she had talked about it much, but she was certainly more motivated than she had been a week ago.

'What's this?' asked Marion, taking the brochure from Lana and reading the front. 'Are you thinking about signing up?'

Lana shook her head. 'Hmm ... Maybe. I mean, it's only a few weeks and it's not expensive. Might be good for me to do something I like and learn something in the process. Would be a good distraction to stop me from worrying about Denny and getting a job.'

'I think that's an excellent idea. Put your little toe in the water without any pressure other than it being something new.' Marion looked at the front of the brochure and read aloud: 'Grow your skills. Blossom with Bath Gardening School!'

'It will probably be a bunch of old fuddy-duddies wanting to learn which way to pop their bulbs in, but I'm willing to learn.'

Marion laughed. 'Old fuddy-duddies like me, you mean?'

Lana shook her head. 'You're not old to me. You're like a girlfriend. A smart girlfriend, though, the sensible one.'

'I'm glad. Thank you, Lana.' She paused. 'Now tell me, which way up do I plant the tulip bulb?'

'Oh, get away with you.'

'There's a new *Vera* on the TV now if you want to watch Brenda Blethyn solve a mystery. She's smarter than any man in the room.'

'Sounds right up my alley. Let's watch Vera fix the world.'

Lana picked up her fine china mug and sipped her tea, taking a bite of the shortbread Felicity had bought. In that moment, she doubted there was a house cat as content as her.

15

Marion

Marion adjusted her silk scarf around her neck for the umpteenth time as she approached Bath Central Library. The grand Georgian building, usually a source of comfort with its promise of quiet corners and well-worn books, now loomed before her like an intimidating fortress of financial knowledge about to punish her for not knowing her stocks from her bonds.

She watched as a group of silver-haired individuals made their way inside, chatting amiably. Were they heading to the same class? Marion's stomach did a little flip. What if one of her friends saw her? What would they think?

She had managed to keep her financial troubles quiet from her social groups, but it became harder to connect when friends wanted to go to the theatre or lunch or even shopping trips and she couldn't participate. She hadn't said she was skint, just that she was a bit depressed and wouldn't be good company, which was partly true, but seeing a show or having a nice lunch would have been lovely. The invitations had slowed over the past six months and when she saw some friends on a trip to London that she hadn't been invited to, she knew she was now excluded.

She watched two women chatting as they walked past her, one wearing a very nice coat that Marion knew was expensive by the cut and the quality of the fabric. What if she was the only one who had experienced financial upheaval? What if they were all well off and just learning how to make more money from investments and the like?

Don't be daft, she told herself, squaring her shoulders. You raised two children and ran a household for decades. You can handle a bit of mathematics. You were quite good at school. With a deep breath that did little to calm her nerves, Marion pushed open the heavy wooden door and stepped inside.

The familiar scent of old books and polish did nothing to soothe her, either, as she followed the signs to Community Room 3. She hesitated at the door, taking in the scene. A dozen or so people, all around her age, were settling into chairs in a semicircle. At the front stood a smart board and a petite woman with a stylish grey bun and green glasses. She was arranging papers on a desk.

'Come in, come in!' the woman called out cheerily. 'Don't be shy. We're all friends here.'

Marion managed a wobbly smile and chose a seat near the back. A gentleman with an impressive moustache nodded in greeting.

'Right, then,' the instructor said, clapping her hands together. 'Welcome to "Golden Years, Golden Wisdom". I'm Meera Collins and I'll be your guide through the wild world of finance in your senior years. Now, who's ready to become a budgeting billionaire?'

A nervous titter ran through the room. Marion clutched her handbag tighter as though she were about to make a run for it at any moment.

'Let's start with introductions, shall we? Tell us your name and why you're here. Who wants to go first?'

Marion's heart raced. She should have sat in the middle. Now she'd have to wait, listening to everyone else's surely more legitimate reasons for being here.

One by one, her classmates introduced themselves. There was Arthur, recently widowed. He realised too late he'd left all the finances to his late wife and now didn't know his gas bill from his telephone bill. Gladys, who was determined to stop her grandson from 'borrowing' her pension. Apparently, he seemed bent on setting a system she couldn't follow. Then there was Howard, who'd lost a bundle in a pyramid scheme and was determined not to be fooled again. His daughter had sent him here to give him some financial confidence and knowledge.

All too soon, it was Marion's turn. She stood, her knees giving slightly.

'I'm Marion,' she began, her voice barely above a whisper. She cleared her throat and tried again. 'Marion Gaynor. I'm here because ...' She paused, considering her words carefully. 'Because I've realised that being a good wife and mother didn't prepare me for managing my own finances. And it's about time I learned.'

There. She'd said it.

Marion sat down quickly, her cheeks burning. She didn't want to go into the illness of Geoffrey and the lost fortune, or the pressure from Clair. Instead, she kept it simple, but it was true.

'Hear hear,' called out Gladys from across the room. 'It's never too late to take control, love.'

Meera beamed. 'Exactly right, Gladys. Now, let's dive in, shall we?'

The next hour passed in a blur of terms Marion had heard before but never truly understood. Assets, liabilities, net worth. Her head spun as she tried to jot down notes in the notebook Lana had given her with a gold hummingbird on the front, her usually neat handwriting growing increasingly spidery.

'Don't worry if it all seems a bit much,' Meera said, noticing Marion's furrowed brow. 'Rome wasn't built in a day, and neither is financial literacy. Now, for next week, I'd like you all to create a personal balance sheet. List everything you own and everything you owe. Then write down any financial goals and we'll go through them together.'

As the class filed out, Marion lingered, staring at her notepad covered in question marks and half-finished sentences.

'All right there, Marion?'

It was Arthur, the moustachioed gentleman from earlier.

'Oh, yes, fine,' she said, stuffing her notes into her bag. 'Just a lot to take in.'

Arthur nodded sympathetically. 'That it is. But we'll muddle through together, eh? Same time next week?'

Marion managed a genuine smile. 'Same time next week,' she agreed.

It wasn't as bad as she thought and it was nice to see her brain was still sharp. She had done quite well at school, had even entertained the idea of going to university and studying something to do with numbers, maybe bookkeeping, but then she had got married instead.

The walk home to Temple Terrace was a quiet one, Marion's mind buzzing with new information and old worries. The wisteria-covered façade of her beloved home came into view and with it a fresh wave of determination.

Inside, she headed straight for Geoffrey's old study. The room still held a faint trace of his spirit and for a moment Marion allowed herself to miss him fiercely. Then, squaring her shoulders, she sat at the imposing oak desk and pulled out her course materials and Geoffrey's old laptop, where he used to manage their accounts.

'Right, then, Geoffrey,' she said to the empty room. 'Let's see what mess you've left me to sort out, shall we?'

As Marion began to list their assets and liabilities, a strange feeling washed over her. It wasn't exactly confidence – not yet – but something close to it. Hope, perhaps. Or the first stirrings of empowerment. Whatever it was, Marion decided she rather liked it.

16

Felicity

In the week since Felicity had been on the Jane Austen tour with Gabriel leading the way, she had been in a dream, as though she had spent her life waiting for that moment. After the tour he had taken her to the pub for a drink and they chatted about nothing and everything. Even though all she'd had was a pint and some chips, she was floating on her way home afterwards. She hadn't even told Marion or Lana how she was feeling, because deep down, she knew it was silly. It was crazy to think that anyone could fall in love the first time they met someone.

If Felicity were honest, she lived life through books. Her greatest adventures were in these pages, her first love was a character on a page and her best self was mirrored in the heroines she read about. It was hard being introverted, having so much to say and yet being unsure of the right time to speak. She'd watched the girls at school and university glide effortlessly through life in terms of both conversation and connections while she herself felt as though she was always standing on the outside.

And then there was Gabe. That one chance meeting in the café and then the afternoon spent traipsing after him in his top hat and cane. It was as though the curtains had been pulled back and Felicity had been pushed onstage. When he smiled at her or made a joke, it was like a warm spotlight was on her and there was no one else but the two of them.

The tour through Bath had made the place come alive. She could feel the energy of the dances that would have been held at the Assembly Rooms, feel the expectations of society judging the women in Roman times when they were at the baths in the afternoon – the only time they were allowed to attend. All that gossip and intrigue, all that snobbery, it was that that stopped people from being free or living their own independent lives. It was certainly something she understood and could identify with. Gabe threw himself into his role and she could tell he loved being a part of everything.

Learning about Bath and its history hands-on – or rather feet-on, in her case – had enabled her to view the city through a new lens. It was impossible not to fall in love with the city once you wandered the beautiful streets and understood its history.

And now she felt like she was hiding in her room, writing away on something that wasn't her dissertation. The idea came when she couldn't sleep, which was common when she was overwhelmed and anxious. The only way she knew to escape the feelings that came with these emotions was to dive into her imagination. She would come up with various scenarios and play them out in her mind in minute detail. Fantasies and dreams turned over and over in her mind until she felt she had played them out accurately. From love affairs to showdowns with her grandmother, she re-enacted and pieced together everything she was afraid of in her real life.

But tonight she went into a different time, imagining herself in Regency times and what her life would have been like. She would be different to how she was now, though. Empowered and brave, funny and charming. All the things she wished for now. The fantasy evolved into meeting a man — a nameless, faceless man who declared she was the most sparkling of all women in Bath. But in her fantasy she was far too busy writing the greatest novel of her time to bother with a man. He would have to work harder than he ever had before to woo her away from her writing.

Whenever she played these scenes in her mind, it made her smile, keeping her awake at night until she could bear it no longer. At which point she climbed out of bed, pulled a shawl around her shoulders that she had knitted herself and went to the desk. Then she'd sit and write until she got the scenario out of her head and onto the page.

And then everything changed. Once she had the first scene down on paper, she could sleep. The next day she worked during the day and then lay down at night and imagined the next part of the story. Each time she had it clear in her mind, she moved it to the page. Sleep came easily once she had cleared her mind.

Every day since, she would wake and head downstairs, where she'd make coffee and toast before heading back up-stairs to her desk. If she wasn't at her desk, she was working a few shifts at the university bookstore. But the hours were fewer since term was underway and now books were largely in digital form.

She could hear Lana and Marion leaving for their daily walk to the bakery, where they would get something for Felicity to have for morning or afternoon tea. They had stopped asking her to join them, as she would only decline, stating she had writing to do.

She had given Gabe her phone number but she hadn't heard from him and she wasn't about to text him. What would she say? He was a busy drama student, he had a job and friends and a life. She was just a bit of a gooseberry, she thought, as she looked at the pile of reference books from the library and the eBook reader on her bedside table filled with fiction to read. She had a choice – write her paper for the university professor or continue getting this idea of hers down on paper about the nameless man. She wasn't even sure it was any good.

Felicity sipped her coffee and looked at the text on the screen. She didn't want to reread it yet, she just knew she had to keep writing. On a good day she could push 4,000 words out, sometimes even 5,000. She was exhausted afterwards, her mind having played out what she was seeing. Sometimes her mind whirred so fast, her fingers could barely keep up when typing.

Her phone ringing made her jump and she saw her mum's name on the screen. She couldn't avoid her mother and grandmother forever, she knew this, but still, life was so much more peaceful without them sometimes. It didn't stop her from feeling guilty for thinking it, though.

'Hi, Mum,' she said.

'Felicity, where have you been? We have been so worried.' Her mother was almost panting in her anxiety.

'I'm fine, Mum. I've been busy, that's all.'

'We even called the university residence and they said you moved out. Are you homeless? Are you living on the streets?'

Her mother's voice was taking on the pitch that Felicity knew was in the danger zone. Soon she would be hysterical, then her grandmother would get on the line and that would be it. Everything would be thrown up in the air and Felicity would have to deal with the fallout. When she lived at home, that used to mean putting her mother to bed with some sort of homeopathic remedy her grandmother recommended, the blinds drawn. The older Felicity became, the more she came to understand that her mother needed mental health support, not a tincture of St John's wort and a dark room.

'No, Mum, I've moved. I'm sorry I haven't told you, but I have been busy.' Felicity was regretting not telling her mum now, because she had the feeling this was about to blow up.

'Moved! Where?'

There was a rustling on the line and then a change of voice.

'Felicity Booth, what are you up to?' came her grandmother's voice.

'Hello, Gran. I've moved, that's all. I didn't like living on campus. It was too noisy and small.'

'Did you not think to call me to discuss this, since I pay the fees?'

'No, I didn't,' lied Felicity. 'But I should have. I'm sorry.'

'Yes, you should. I read your emails from university and I saw you are behind in your work. Since your meeting with your supervisor ten days ago, I see you haven't attended any lectures or submitted new work for him to review. What have you been doing for the past ten days? Are you on drugs?'

Why did old people always assume someone young was on drugs when they weren't doing what they wanted them to do? Or was that just her grandmother?

'Why are you reading my emails?' Mental note: change university email password.

'Because I'm paying for you to be there.'

The tone was clear. Felicity knew if she changed her password, her grandmother would cut off her finances.

'I'm not on drugs, Gran, and you shouldn't have read my emails.' The anger and betrayal stuck in Felicity's throat, her words static as she spoke.

'You are taking my money to do this silly degree and I tell you, unless the work improves and you go back to the halls, I will not be funding you.'

Felicity was silent, thinking about Lana and her bravery at leaving Denny, of Marion opening up her house to strangers. What had Felicity ever done that was brave?

She looked at the words on the screen in front of her. Was she wasting her time doing what she was doing? Whatever this was, it gave her more happiness than her degree and whatever happened next, at least she could say she'd tried.

But to do it she would have to be braver than she had ever been in her life.

'That's fine, then. Don't pay. Because I'm not going back to the university halls and I am not finishing my degree. I'm deferring it. Put my mother back on the phone, please.'

Felicity could hear the gasps and angry words exchanged from her grandmother as her mother said a timid hello.

'Mum, if you want to speak to me any time, you can, but I don't want to speak to Granny. And I want you to realise something. She's abusing you and controlling you. Worse – she's stopped you from living your own life. But she won't stop me from living mine.'

Her mother said nothing as Felicity continued.

'If you want to come to Bath to see me, you can, but I do *not* want you telling her where I am. I will be OK. I will send you the address so you can think about it, but not her. Do you promise me?' Felicity was shaking as she spoke, but she had never been surer of her words.

'I promise,' her mother almost whispered and then the call ended.

Felicity was still shaking as she put down the phone. She stared at the screen. For ten days, she had been writing solid. Ten days of non-stop ideas and dreams, playing out the life of a woman much stronger and smarter than her. A woman who had fallen in love and who was living the life Felicity wanted more than anything else in the world.

Her grandmother would think writing a novel was even more foolish than this degree. But if she were truthful with herself, she enjoyed writing about love and dresses. She enjoyed tales of men and women with passion in their hearts and bodies.

Tears formed and she felt them drop onto her desk as she wondered what on earth she would do now. The job at the bookshop wasn't enough to live on and pay the rent at Temple Terrace. Perhaps she would have to live under a bridge, but it would be better than being controlled by her grandmother.

Her phone rang and she checked to see it wasn't her grandmother. It was an unknown number.

'Hello?' she said tentatively.

'Felicity? It's Gabe. Sorry I've been MIA,' he said in his beautiful rich voice.

'Oh, hey,' she said.

'You OK? You sound like you're a bit congested.'

'I'm fine. Maybe a little sniffly.'

'Listen, I still want to catch up with you properly as friends, but I have a question and if you say no, I get it, but I don't know who else to ask.'

She paused. 'O–K ...' she said slowly.

'Denise has done her knee in – slipped on a cucumber sandwich at an afternoon tea.'

'Oh no.'

'Yeah, not good. She needs surgery and will be out of action for at least twelve weeks. We need someone to do the tour with me on Sundays. There's also a position with a fellow named Colin on Tuesdays and Thursdays. He's great. He's not at university, but he's also an actor, like Denise.'

'But I'm not an actor.'

'No, I know, but Colin can do all the performing and you can talk about the historical stuff. You'll be great.'

'Denise was great. I'm not a performer.'

'Treat it like you're teaching a class. I mean, you'll do that anyway when you finish your degree, I guess.'

Felicity was silent.

'And the pay is great, because the tour is so popular. There are always people wanting to join. And it's double on Sundays.'

She ran the numbers through her head. That plus her shifts at the bookstore meant she might just be able to manage.

'And sometimes we run extra tours in the holidays, so you and I could do some more shifts together.'

That was it.

'OK,' she said, not believing her own ears. 'I'll do it,' she heard herself saying. 'But I'm not wearing that stupid bonnet.'

The sound of Gabe laughing was almost as great as the idea that she was no longer under her grandmother's thumb.

17

Marion

When Marion had blown the seed head out the study window, she had wished that Clair would find her way back – not to Marion but to herself. It was an important distinction, because Marion was sure Clair had lost her way long ago.

Perhaps Marion blamed too much on Paul for the way Clair was now, because after everything was said and done, Clair was complicit in the way Paul controlled Clair and the family. It was a shame the twins weren't younger, because then Marion would have an excuse to go to their house and see what was really going on behind closed doors.

And then as luck would have it, Sophie texted:

Do you have any vintage clothes I can look at and maybe borrow?

Marion had texted back quickly:

There are some things of your mum's still here from the 90s, if you want to go through them. They're upstairs.

Sophie told her she would be over after school and Marion informed her there would be cake. Sophie sent her a kiss and that was that.

It was nice to have something to look forward to, Marion decided as she put her plate from lunch in the dishwasher. Felicity was always studying these days and Lana had her head in books trying to read up before her gardening course started the next week.

She didn't want to interrupt them from their work, but she could do with the distraction. There wasn't always much for her to do and Sophie coming over to rifle through her mum's old things would be a laugh.

Just before four, the doorbell rang and Marion opened it to see Sophie and a group of tourists taking photos of the house. The wisteria was growing now and leaves were replacing the flowers. The bees didn't seem to mind, as they were still buzzing about happily, not annoying the tourists and not feasting on anything but the pollen.

'Hello, sweetheart, come in.' Marion ushered her granddaughter down to the kitchen, where Lana was making tea. 'Sophie, this is Lana, who is living here and who is about to start a course to be a gardener. And Lana, this is Sophie, my favourite granddaughter and a clever clogs at all she does.'

'I'm her *only* granddaughter.' Sophie rolled her eyes at Lana.

'But the best one, I'm sure,' Lana smiled.

'Cake first or after?' asked Marion.

'After,' Sophie decided.

'Then let's go and find these old things of your mum's. I don't know if anything will be your taste, but I suppose everything comes around in fashion again.'

They went up the flights of stairs, Sophie slowing for Marion, who poked her in the bum with her finger to hurry on.

'Don't wait for me. You run ahead and open the window, it will be musty in there.'

Sophie did as she was told and by the time Marion entered the room, Sophie was pulling things out of vacuum-sealed bags.

'What are you after, exactly?' asked Marion as she sat on the bed and picked up a checked party dress that she remembered Clair wearing to her fifteenth birthday.

'I don't know, but I'll know it when I see it.' She pulled out armfuls of scarves and made a face. 'What's with the scarves?'

'It was a thing back then,' said Marion, pausing for a moment. 'How's things at home?' she asked lightly.

Sophie sniffed. 'Annoying. Tom and Dad are fighting, and Dad and Mum are fighting. I try to hide in my room.'

'Wise idea,' said Marion, pausing once again. Never go in too quickly with teenagers, she had learned. 'What are Tom and Dad fighting about?'

'Tom doesn't want to go to our school. He wants to change. He hates it.'

'Do you like it?'

Sophie shrugged and held a tie-dye windcheater up against herself.

'I don't care, really. I mean it's fine, I have friends, but you know, Tom really hates it and he detests rowing. He wants to stop.'

Tom was the stroke in the junior eights in rowing and was being trained for bigger things. Him giving it up would upset Paul, mostly because Paul never got to do the things Tom did. Misplaced ambition, Geoffrey always said about Paul.

'Oh, that's no good at all. I like that top against you.' She nodded towards the windcheater.

'Yeah, me too,' Sophie said, putting it aside.

'And what about Dad and Mum, what are they fighting about?'

Sophie shrugged. 'I don't know, really. Money, I think. And Dad said she should get a job.'

Marion tried not to react. Ever since Clair and Paul were married, he'd said she didn't have to work, she could be at home and he would take care of things, so suggesting she get a job was something extraordinary.

'Does Mum want to work?'

Sophie shook her head and took out a singlet top with a beaded butterfly on the front.

'I can't work out if this is ugly or cool.' She held it up to her body. 'It depends what I wear it with,' she said, deciding to keep it and put it with the tie-dye top.

Marion sighed inwardly. Sophie was not going to give too much away and rightly so – her loyalty should be to her parents – but since Clair was being so difficult, Marion wondered if Sophie might have said something more.

Sophie kept rummaging through the clothes and pulled out a T-shirt with the *Star Wars* logo on the front.

'Oh, this is cool,' she said, and Marion almost snatched it from her.

'Sorry, that shouldn't be in there.'

Sophie frowned. 'I don't think it will suit you, Granny.'

Marion held it close. 'It was Andy's.' She buried her face in it, hoping she might capture something of his scent or spirit, but they were long gone.

Sophie stared at the floor. 'Sorry, I didn't realise.'

'You don't have to say sorry.' Marion shook her head and smiled at Sophie. She held it up to look at it one more time and put it on the pile on the bed. 'You know, it's silly to keep it. He would want you to wear it. I was being sentimental.'

Sophie sat down next to Marion. 'I don't have to have it. I mean, if it's something special of his ...' Her voice trailed off.

'It's not, because he's not here any more, and if he was, it wouldn't fit him anyway.' Marion patted Sophie's hand. 'It's important to be sensible about these things.'

Sophie looked down at her hands, twisting the ring on her thumb. 'Mum doesn't talk about him at all.'

Marion nodded.

'What was he like?' Sophie asked.

All this time and neither of the grandchildren had really asked about Andy. Of course it would be Sophie who asked first, though, as she was the most like him.

'He was a lot like you, actually.' Marion smiled at her granddaughter.

'How?'

Marion remembered the need as a teenager to understand herself and her granddaughter, Sophie, was no different.

'Smart, kind, aware of those around him. Not wanting to be like everyone else, not really caring what their mother insisted they should do.' She raised her eyebrows at Sophie, who laughed.

'Yeah, Mum wasn't happy about me going through her old clothes. Couldn't understand why you even kept them.'

Marion laughed. 'I happen to know she kept all of your knitted clothes from when you and Tom were babies, so I don't think she can say too much about this.' She gestured to the mess strewn everywhere.

'Do you have anything else of Uncle Andy's?'

Marion shook her head. 'I don't. Your grandpa got rid of it all. He said it would make me sad, which it would have, but that's part of the grieving, I think. I was so cross with him – still am.'

Sophie picked up the T-shirt. 'I honestly don't need it.'

'I don't, either, so wear it with his blessing.' She smiled and stood up. 'I'm going downstairs to make us some tea. You come down when you're ready.'

She walked to the door and was about to leave, when Sophie spoke.

'Gran?'

Marion turned.

'Things are a bit shit at home. Can I stay here tonight?'

Marion paused. 'You can always stay with me, but you would have to sleep in here. It's a bit dusty and musty.'

Sophie shrugged. 'It's better than being at home, to be honest.'

'That bad?'

She nodded.

'Let your mum know,' Marion said with a smile, her heart sinking at the sad look on Sophie's face.

Things were clearly worse than she had imagined, but how she would get Clair to share that with her, she didn't yet know. One thing she did know was that eventually, things boiled over if you didn't attend to them. If Clair wasn't careful, she could end up burned.

18

Lana

The shed at the garden nursery where Lana attended her class was the stuff of Denny's nightmares, which only made Lana love it more. It was messy, with plants and pots scattered around the wooden benches, mismatched chairs and dirt on the ground. But there was also lush foliage in every corner, with potted plants hanging from the beams in the old space in vibrant shades of emerald and jade.

She looked at one of the labels. Begonia, it read. She admired its spotted leaves and heavy head of flowers.

'She's gorgeous, isn't she?'

Lana turned to see a man next to her looking up at the basket.

'I've never seen one before, I don't think. It's incredible. I hope I can grow something like that one day,' she said.

'You will, I'm sure,' he said confidently. 'You can grow anything if you know how.'

'I hope I can learn as much as I can. I'm a novice, but I love being in the garden, don't you? You know how men go down the pub for their mental health? Well, I like being in the garden.

'My nan used to pay me to collect a bucket of snails from her cabbages when I was kid and I used to take my time, so I could spend more time in the garden. I never told anyone this, but I used to throw the snails over the fence into the neighbour's garden so they would be back the next day, just so I could do it all over again.'

He laughed. 'I'm sure your nan knew. She probably just liked you being out there in her garden.'

His face was open, she thought. He looked like a good sort, as her grandmother would have said. He had very green eyes, proper green, she noticed – not the usual sort of green but hazel. He wasn't craggy but had more the face of a man who spent time outdoors. He was taller than her and had broad shoulders. Not a gym physique as such, but that of a man who was fit. How long had it been since she had been able to talk to a man without Denny homing in on them and pushing his way into every conversation? His jealousy was one thing, but his need to be the centre of attention all the time was bigger.

Others were milling about, chatting, and she wondered if everyone knew everyone or was it simply that they didn't know her?

'I'm a bit nervous, actually,' she confided.

'Why?'

He looked around the space and she noticed his jawline. She wondered, just for a brief moment, what it would be like to kiss under there, along his jaw and to his mouth. A shudder went through her body. Get it together, Lana. He's probably married. Control yourself, girl.

'I haven't been to school since I was a teen and I left before I could do anything like exams and so on. I just wonder if I can keep up.' She looked around at the others in the room, all of them older than her. 'I wasn't very good at school. I used to play up to get out of stuff because things were a bit shite at home. That way, they would just think I

126

was a brat instead. No one thought to ask what was happening outside of school.'

God, why was she talking so much? She must be super nervous, she thought. Stop talking, Lana, she told herself. But it was too late now. Anyone would think she was a teenager who'd had their first ever alcoholic drink.

'Oh, it's not like school, I don't think. It's more just hands-on learning. No tests or anything.'

Lana leaned in closer. 'I can hear some posh accents,' she whispered. 'I mean I'm not posh, but you know, these people probably all have fancy gardens to look after.' She gave a nervous laugh. 'Sorry, I'm talking too much.'

'Not at all. You're interesting.'

'Oh?' She wasn't sure if he was making fun of her or not.

'Yes. So far we have discussed begonias, your catch-and-release programme when it came to snails, your time spent meditating in the garden, your shit time at school and what sounds like an even worse home life. It's interesting. I like people who are honest from the outset.'

Lana felt her nerves subside. She wasn't sure what was worse: butterflies from nerves or the flutters of excitement in her stomach.

'Do you have a garden?' he asked.

'We have a small one where I am renting. The landlady said I can do anything to it, but I don't know where to start. I love being out there. I mean, I would like to learn – maybe do something one day. It's where I feel most at home, you know?

'I just walked out on my marriage and am trying to get a job, but it's hard. I haven't worked for such a long time. My landlady, Marion, said I should do a course in something I like, so here I am, but ...' – she glanced around – 'I think I might be out of my tax bracket.'

The man smiled. His face was kind, she noticed, and he looked to be in his mid-forties.

'I wouldn't worry about that. Plants don't. You can have all the money in the world, but if your maidenhair fern hates you, there's nothing you can do about it.'

Lana laughed and looked around.

'Gosh, this is nice, though, isn't it?'

Large windows lined one wall, allowing ample natural light to flood the room and nourish the plants. In the early evening a few late sunbeams danced through the glass, casting dappled patterns of light and shadow across the floor. On each of the benches was an array of gardening tools and supplies — from trowels and pruners to bags and packets of seeds tied with string, little notes welcoming them to the course.

In one corner of the room, a cosy seating area beckoned, with old armchairs and cushions, inviting students to relax and unwind. The small table was piled high with gardening books and magazines, full of inspiration and advice for aspiring green fingers. Above, a series of wooden beams criss-crossed the ceiling, adding a rustic charm to the space, providing support for climbing vines and trailing plants that cascaded from above them.

'This is my new favourite place,' she said to the man. 'I'm Lana, by the way.'

'Alex,' he said with a smile. 'Excuse me, I have to do something.'

Lana nodded, wondering why he was here. He was probably escaping her incessant chatter right now, she thought as she sat down at one of the benches. There were about fifteen people now and Lana watched them chatting. Perhaps this was a silly idea, she thought. Why on earth would she think she could learn at this age?

She picked up her bag, ready to make a dash, when she heard someone clap for attention and begin to speak.

'Hello, everyone, welcome to Bath Gardening School. I'm your teacher and the owner of the school, Alex Hayes. I'm very much looking forward to teaching you everything I know to help you on your journey to understanding gardening.'

Lana's hand stilled on her handbag and she felt his eyes meet hers.

'Whatever your journey as to why you're here and where you want to go, please know I'm here to help you get your hands dirty and to support you in any way I can.'

Lana's hand loosened its grip and he smiled at her.

'Now, let's all introduce ourselves. I'll start with Lana, whom I've just met. Lana, why don't you tell us what you love about gardening and why you're here?'

Her hand moved from the bag to her lap. She looked around the room and all she saw were smiles and encouraging nods from the other students. She looked at Alex and gave a little laugh.

'Hello, I'm Lana,' she said, and she felt a warmth in her stomach she hadn't felt for a long time. She was in the right place with the right people.

19

Marion

Marion arrived at the library for her second class with a spring in her step and a folder full of meticulously completed homework. She had also brought Geoffrey's laptop with some basic accounting software on it that Meera had recommended in an email. She had spent the better part of the week poring over bank statements and old financial documents, piecing together a picture of her fiscal life that was illuminating and terrifying in equal measure.

As she entered the classroom, she spotted Arthur, the moustachioed gentleman from last week, frowning at a crumpled piece of paper.

'Hullo, Marion,' he greeted, his bushy eyebrows furrowing. 'Tell me, does this balance sheet malarkey make any sense to you? I've got more questions than answers, I'm afraid.'

Marion smiled sympathetically as she took the seat next to him. 'Oh, I know the feeling. I must have started mine over a dozen times. But I think I've got the hang of it now. Would you like me to take a look?'

Arthur's relief was palpable as he handed over his work.

'Would you? That would be marvellous. I'm beginning to think I should have paid more attention when Carol handled our accounts.'

As Marion gently pointed out a few errors in Arthur's calculations, Meera swept into the room, her colourful pink silk shirt a bright contrast to the library's muted tones.

'Good morning, class!' she chirped. 'I hope you're all feeling a bit richer today – in knowledge, if not in pounds and pence. Now, who's brave enough to share their balance sheet with us?'

A hush fell over the room. Marion felt her newfound confidence waver. Sharing her financial situation with strangers seemed akin to dancing naked in the town square. But then Arthur gave her a gentle nudge.

'Go on,' he whispered. 'You've got a better grasp of it than any of us.'

Before she could second-guess herself, Marion's hand was in the air.

'Wonderful, Marion!' Meera beamed. 'Come on up to the board, if you would.'

As Marion wrote out her figures, she could feel her classmates' eyes on her back. But when she turned to face them, she saw only encouragement and recognition. These people understood. They were all in the same boat, trying to navigate choppy financial waters.

'Very good, Marion,' Meera said, examining the board. 'Now, class, let's look at how we might improve Marion's financial position. Any suggestions?'

What followed was a lively discussion that left Marion's head spinning with ideas. By the time she left two hours later, her notebook was filled with potential strategies for reducing expenses and increasing income at Temple Terrace.

'Same time next week, partner?' Arthur asked as they exited the building.

Marion nodded, realising she'd made her first friend. 'Wouldn't miss it for the world.'

Back at Temple Terrace, Marion settled into Geoffrey's old study, spreading her notes across the desk. She began to go through the household accounts with fresh eyes, looking for areas where she could apply her new knowledge.

The electricity bill caught her attention first. 'Good heavens,' she muttered, 'we must be lighting this place up like Blackpool Illuminations.' She made a note to speak to Lana and Felicity about energy-saving measures.

Next, she turned her attention to the garden. It was a source of joy, certainly, but also a significant expense. Perhaps Lana's budding interest in horticulture could be put to practical use. Marion jotted down the idea of a small vegetable patch to offset their grocery bills.

As the afternoon wore on, Marion found herself growing excited by the possibilities. She was no longer just the caretaker of Temple Terrace – she was its financial manager, its strategist.

A knock at the study door startled her from her calculations. It was Felicity, a concerned look on her face.

'Everything all right, Marion? You've been in here for hours.'

Marion glanced at the clock, surprised to see how much time had passed.

'Oh my, I didn't realise. Yes, everything's fine, dear. Better than fine, actually. I think I've found a way to make Temple Terrace work for us, rather than the other way around.'

Felicity's eyebrows rose in seeming surprise. 'That's wonderful! You are getting something from the class, then?'

'I am. It's very helpful and I wish I had done it sooner. I mean Geoffrey was fine with money. but I think there are things I could have done back then that would have made a difference to our lifestyle. Thank you for recommending it, Felicity, it's so helpful.'

'I'm glad. Thank you for taking it onboard. Many people your age refuse to learn new things.'

Marion laughed. 'Sometimes we have to be dragged there, but it has certainly made me see things with new eyes. Money seemed so frightening before this course, but two lessons in and I can see it needs to be handled confidently. With the right knowledge, I can make my life a little easier.'

Felicity nodded, her face proud. 'I love this for you!'

As Felicity left the study, Marion turned back to her notes. There was still much to learn, but for the first time in a long while, she felt truly in control of both her life and her home.

'Well, Geoffrey,' she said softly to the empty room, 'I think you'd be proud. Temple Terrace is in good hands, and they're mine.'

With a satisfied smile, Marion closed her notebook and the laptop. Tomorrow would bring new challenges, but she was ready to face them, armed with knowledge, determination and a growing sense of her own capabilities. The golden years, it seemed, still held plenty of sparkle.

20

Felicity

The dim light of the desk lamp cast a soft glow across the room as Felicity sat hunched over her laptop. Her fingers danced across the keys, weaving together the threads of her imagination into a tapestry on the page. If the thesis was hard to write, then this was deceptively easy. She could have written all day and night if her body didn't insist on sleep.

It was late, far past midnight, but she couldn't tear herself away from the story that had taken root in her mind. She had started to write after her meeting with Dr Nigel. She was anxious to begin with, and when she was anxious, she needed a form of escape. Some people used drugs and alcohol, Felicity went to other worlds, and now she couldn't stop.

The gentle hum of the laptop and the soft clicking of the keys formed a soothing soundtrack to her late-night writing session. Felicity's eyes remained fixed on the screen, her gaze intent and focused, as if she were peering through a portal into another world. The characters she had birthed from her imagination took on a life of their own, their voices clear and distinct in her mind. She could see their faces, feel their emotions and understand their motivations with a clarity that both surprised and delighted her.

As she wove together the threads of her story, she felt a sense of exhilaration and purpose she hadn't felt before.

If only Dr Nigel Frobisher could see her now – would he think she was passionate enough?

Hours passed, unnoticed and uncounted, as Felicity lost herself in the world she had created. Her whole childhood she had escaped into other worlds in her daydreaming. Complex and intricate stories that helped her to escape from her grandmother's criticism.

Even as her body began to protest against the long hours spent hunched over her laptop, Felicity found herself reluctant to tear herself away from her work. The story had taken on a life of its own, begging to be told, the characters demanding her attention when she wasn't transcribing their movements and conversations. Whatever happened now, she felt an unwavering commitment to seeing it through to its conclusion. She knew that sleep would eventually claim her, forcing her to rest and recharge, but for now, she was content to let the words pour out of her, to let the story unfold in all its messy, beautiful glory.

In the dim light of her desk lamp, surrounded by the quiet stillness of the night, Felicity had found her true calling, whether she realised it now or not. She had discovered the reason for the bubbles of excitement that started to fizz when she first stood outside Temple Terrace.

With a sigh of satisfaction, Felicity finally finished the chapter she had been working on and leaned back in her chair, stretching her cramped muscles. Glancing at the clock, she realised with a start that it was close to one in the morning – she had been writing for hours without a break. This novel was her passion project, her secret dream that she had been nurturing in the quiet corners of her mind for years. And now, with each word she penned, it was slowly but surely coming to life.

As she saved her work and shut down her laptop, Felicity felt a surge of excitement coursing through her veins. She hadn't told a soul she was writing this, but somewhere deep inside she knew it was turning into something special. It wasn't just something for her eyes only. She wanted someone to read it, someone with no expectations of her, someone who was smart and had taste.

What if she shared a glimpse of her work with someone else? Just a few pages. Nothing too revealing, but enough to pique their curiosity and maybe determine if she was delusional about what she was doing.

She opened her laptop again, looked at the first pages and then pressed Print. Her little home printer spat out the first two chapters. Slipping them into a document envelope, she wrote on the front:

Marion,

Could you please read this and tell me if I am kidding myself? Be honest.

Felicity

She sealed the envelope and padded down the stairs and into the living room, where she left it on Marion's chair. Would she be intrigued by the story? Impressed by Felicity's writing skills? Or would she dismiss it, as she was sure her grandmother would, as the fanciful ramblings of a young woman with a vivid imagination and no real direction in life?

Whatever Marion thought, it would help Felicity to decide, she thought as she went back upstairs to try to sleep. She was meeting Gabe at Denise's house the next day to choose a costume for the tour and Denise would be testing her on her knowledge of Jane Austen. Gabe insisted she would be great. In fact, he told her she would be great at everything, which wasn't true but it was a nice thing to hear anyway.

She turned her pillow over and closed her eyes.

'Please let Marion like my story,' she asked whatever magical force was out there and then added an extra wish or two. 'And please let me not be rubbish at the tour. And please let me not have to wear a bonnet.'

She felt her body relax as sleep came over her. One more wish can't hurt, she thought.

'And please let Gabe fall in love with me.'

Felicity's phone ringtone woke her up. She checked the screen and saw it was Gabe.

'Hey,' she said, trying to sound awake.

'You coming?'

She looked at the time on her phone.

'Oh, yes, sorry, I'm so sorry,' she said, jumping out of bed and running to the bathroom.

She was supposed to be at Denise's house going through the safety procedures and other administration that she didn't know was part of the job until she had accepted the position. Gabe told her it wasn't much, but she still had to know all the ins and outs. She had remained firm in not wearing a worn bonnet with a faded pansy on the side of the rain-spotted velvet.

Showered and dressed in an oversized cotton fisherman's jumper with some black trousers and a pair of boots, Felicity ran down the stairs and towards the front door.

'Felicity? Is that you?' she heard Marion call from up the hallway.

'Yes, but I'm late.' Oh, God, she thought, remembering the pages she had left for Marion on her chair. 'I'll be back soon. I have to go and try on a costume for the tour.'

Marion came to the doorway at the end of the hall.

'Can we talk when you come back?' she asked, her expression not giving anything away, not that Felicity was always great at reading people.

She nodded, feeling her stomach drop.

Marion would tell her if it was a waste of time and just to go back to reading the classics, not to try to write one, surely.

Felicity closed the door behind her and walked outside, where she noticed the wisteria was out, hanging down like a waterfall. She touched it gently and then ran towards the bus stop. She didn't want to lose the job before she even started.

The trip to Denise's was easy enough and didn't take too long, but Felicity couldn't stop thinking about Marion wanting to talk to her. It wasn't going to be good, she was sure of it.

By the time she had walked to Denise's little house and rung the bell, she had worked through the scenario that Marion had read the pages, called her grandmother to confer about how rubbish her writing was, and then showed her advisor and the vice chancellor of the university. She would have to move out today and return to Bristol to live with her mum and grandmother again, where she would be forced to scrub floors and eat scraps for the rest of her grandmother's life.

The door opened, jolting Felicity from her desperate catastrophising and into the present.

Gabe frowned. 'You need coffee,' he said, but she could tell he wasn't mad at her for being late.

'Please,' she said.

'Denise is in the kitchen. Come on, sleepyhead. How come you slept in? Have a big night out on the town?'

She snorted and he turned to her. She realised he was serious. He assumed she had been out late the night before, doing what he would do – drinking, dancing, partying.

She laughed. 'Not quite.'

They found Denise sitting in an armchair, her leg propped up on another chair with a cushion under her knee.

'Hi,' Felicity said.

Should she mention the leg, or would it upset her? Felicity was never sure if she should mention these things or not, as her grandmother always told her she said the wrong thing at the wrong time.

'This is a bloody shit thing, isn't it?' Denise pointed at her leg with a knitting needle, gesticulating wildly with the implement. 'I could feel something pop when I fell. I tell you, it was like I had been shot in the knee. Not that I've ever been shot in the knee, but if I had, I would imagine it felt like that.'

Felicity stepped backwards, away from the needle. 'I'm sorry to hear about the injury. Sounds terrible.'

'You're a lifesaver for doing this,' said Denise. 'The tour operators weren't happy when they heard, but Gabe was straight up with the recommendation of you, good lad.'

Felicity turned to Gabe and smiled.

'Except she won't wear that bonnet of yours,' Gabe said.

'Fair enough. It's a bit worn out – like me, it seems,' Denise laughed. 'I have a whole Regency selection in the spare room. I do the costumes for the Bath Am Dram Society – they love doing Austen adaptations – so you can wear whatever you want, if it fits. But I wouldn't recommend the evening dresses – too much polyester lace.' She scratched her neck with the knitting needle. 'Scratchy.'

Gabe headed towards the stairs. 'Come on, then. Let's find you something to wear. Are you feeling like a Lizzie or an Emma?'

Felicity laughed. 'My gran says I'm more of a Mary Bennet.'

'Mary?' Gabe said. 'Isn't she the boring, plain one who is always correcting people in *Pride and Prejudice*?'

Felicity said nothing. She had always loathed Mary and her grandmother telling her of the supposed resemblance always stung.

'No, that won't do. You will have to choose a different character,' Gabe laughed as they climbed the stairs.

He opened the door to a room of rails of clothes. There were dresses, jackets, waistcoats and open shelving housing hats, bonnets and extravagant hair pieces and wigs. She stood in the doorway as Gabe stepped inside first and did a theatrical twirl.

'So, choose your outfit, Miss Felicity, because you're about to become the heroine of your own story.'

21

Lana

Lana's heart was still warm from the encouraging and supportive atmosphere of those on the gardening course as she entered the quiet sanctuary of Temple Terrace. The house seemed to welcome her home with its peaceful stillness, a stark contrast to the lively energy of the class. The smell of beeswax here was in stark comparison to the fertiliser of earlier. She couldn't help but smile as she recalled Alex's kind words and the camaraderie among the students, all older than her but all eager to include her and learn together.

Lana tried to be quiet as she padded about the kitchen. No doubt Felicity was buried deep in her studies and Marion, the heart of their little household, was likely already fast asleep. Marion liked to go to bed early and be up early, always dressed before the rest of the house.

She opened the refrigerator to see fresh ham. She could have it with sourdough bread from the bakery. Perfect, she thought, adding extra butter and some pickle.

The soft glow of the small lamp Marion always left on cast a comforting warmth over the kitchen, making Lana feel safe and cared for. It was a small gesture but one that spoke volumes about the sort of woman Marion was and the home she ran so beautifully.

Settling down at the table with her supper and a glass of crisp apple juice, Lana's eye was drawn to a stack of papers spread out before her. She began to read as she ate.

From the very first sentence, she found herself captivated by the story unfolding on the pages. A tale of forbidden love between a young duke and a woman deemed unworthy by society's rigid standards. With each bite of her sandwich and sip of juice, Lana delved deeper into their world, her heart aching for the star-crossed lovers. Whoever wrote this was smart, she thought as she turned the page.

Time seemed to stand still as Lana lost herself in the narrative, the quiet house fading as she became fully immersed, carefully setting each page aside as she finished, treating the manuscript with respect.

Before she knew it, her sandwich was gone and only a few drops of juice remained in her glass, but the story continued to grip her heart. As she placed her dishes in the dishwasher, her mind raced with questions, desperate to know the fate of the young lovers. With a sigh, Lana realised that she would have to wait to discover the rest of the tale.

Had Marion written it? Or Sophie? Maybe it was Felicity. But she was so busy with her degree, surely she wouldn't have time to write this, she thought as she went upstairs.

As Lana went to bed, she closed her eyes and thought about her life now. Her head was swimming, what with the house, the garden, Alex, the story she had just read and the warm feeling it left of only good things, which was a lovely change for once.

In the morning, Lana went downstairs in her robe and saw Marion fully dressed at the kitchen table.

'You always put me to shame the way you're dressed and ready in the morning,' Lana said as she turned on the kettle.

'I'm not sure what I'm ready for,' laughed Marion. 'I haven't had much to be ready for since Geoffrey died.'

Lana looked down at Marion's cup and saw it was nearly empty. 'More tea?' she asked, noticing the pages she had read next to Marion.

'Oh yes, I read that last night. I couldn't put it down. Is there any more of it? I got up to the duke pretending to be the stable boy and Mabel meeting him at the racetrack.'

Marion was about to say something, when Felicity walked into the kitchen.

'Have you read it?' asked Felicity.

'Did *you* write that?' Lana smacked the bench with her hand. 'Bloody hell, I loved it! I need more of it. Can I read the rest? I couldn't put it down. And I tell you, I've never read a book in my life. Then I picked that up while having a butty and I was suddenly swept away to those times. God, it was hard, wasn't it? Not being the same social class and all that. Is this for your degree?'

Felicity looked at Marion. 'I said they were for *you* to read.'

'I'm sorry, Felicity, I left them out on the table. I wanted to talk to you about them. But what a review from Lana. And I feel the same way. It's wonderful. You have a natural talent for storytelling.'

Lana looked at Felicity, who was standing very still in a white nightgown and dark blue robe with bare feet. She could be a heroine in her own stories, Lana thought.

'You didn't hate it?' she asked Marion slowly, as though coming to terms with the review.

'Not in the slightest. The characters were real and rounded and the settings were as though I were watching it on film. Just marvellous.'

'Oh, I agree, all those streets with horse shit on them. You know, you don't think about that, do you, when you watch those costume dramas on the telly? Imagine your shoes? No wonder they got carriages everywhere.' Lana laughed.

Felicity came to the table and sat down.

'I want to leave university and write,' she said.

Felicity's look of surprise told Lana that this was news to Felicity, too. Perhaps it was the first time she had voiced it aloud.

Lana set about making more tea while looking to Marion for her response. She wasn't offended Felicity hadn't asked her to read the pages. She would also have gone to Marion first. Marion had such a calm energy and life experience behind her.

Marion nodded at Felicity. 'You're not happy with the course?'

Felicity shook her head and sat on one of the yellow chairs.

'I hate it. I hate my advisor. I hate it all.'

Lana made tea for them all and brought it to the table along with a plate of delicious-looking raspberry pastries from yesterday.

'If you're not happy then leave, love, it's not worth it.'

'And do what, though?'

'Write,' said Marion. 'It's clear you have a talent and you know your subject. You have passion and humour and wonderful pacing – write!'

Felicity sighed. 'Do you know how many people want to be writers? It's embarrassing to put myself into that crowd.'

Lana snorted. 'Wanting to be a writer and being a writer are very different.'

'I agree, Lana, good point,' Marion said.

'What do you mean?' Felicity asked.

146

'Everyone wants to be famous – a singer, an actor, a writer, an influencer, good at something. I think people look at sitting down and writing something as easy, but I know it's not. I couldn't do it and there are enough crappy books out there to prove that not everyone should.'

Marion laughed and Felicity smiled.

'You would tell me if you thought it was rubbish?'

'Of course I would,' said Marion. 'I mean, I wouldn't say this is rubbish ...' She tapped the manuscript. 'But I would perhaps direct you to a new path.'

Felicity smiled.

'I told my grandmother I'm deferring my degree and she said she has cut me off.'

Marion and Lana were silent.

'But I have my job with Gabe on the tour and my job in the bookstore, plus I can do the cleaning here so we don't have to pay someone, if that helps? I can meet the rent, just.'

Marion shook her head. 'You do not need to do the cleaning and you pay what you can.'

But Felicity put her hand up. 'I would rather do this than feel obligated. I've lived with that long enough.'

Lana reached out and took Felicity's cold hand in her warm one.

'I'm happy for you, darling, I am, but I have to ask ...' She paused, all eyes on her, Felicity in particular looking nervous. 'When the hell will I get the next chapters in the book? I need to know what happens.'

Felicity gave a joyful sound of laughter and squeezed Lana's hand.

'You know, I will write it just for you, I promise. I don't have an excuse now – I have to finish.'

Lana nodded and gave her a cheeky smile. 'Yes, you do, so get writing, woman.'

22

Marion

Sophie was back at Temple Terrace. It was clear something wasn't right at home if the teen was over twice in a week, but Marion knew not to pry. She wanted to give her granddaughter a safe place if she didn't feel she could be at home right now. When they were little, they used to stay all the time, but it had been years since Sophie had stayed over and now she was here again. Something was definitely up at home.

Marion had introduced Paul to Lana when he came to drop Sophie off and he'd been polite but awkward. She had reached to kiss him goodbye, but he was already walking towards his car. In seconds, he was gone.

'Dad OK?' Marion asked.

Marion couldn't help herself. He was usually unfailingly polite. He was always confident, assured – with a strong sense of self, Geoffrey used to say. Marion said it was ego, and too much of it. But she had noticed he looked paler than usual, and thin, but not in an athletic way. He had always watched his weight. There again, he had also watched Clair's weight – and the twins – to the point of being controlling. He was forever commenting on what they could eat, frowning at the twins if they reached for another piece of cake. These days, he looked drawn and impatient.

'Shitstorm at the old HG,' said Sophie with a sigh and she walked into the house. 'I'm going to make cupcakes, that OK?'

'Of course,' she said and gave the girl's arm a quick squeeze of support as she walked past.

'Shitshow, eh?' Lana remarked to Marion when Sophie was out of earshot.

'Yes, something is off, but I can't call Clair and ask because she will shut down completely and I don't want to betray Sophie's confidence.'

'Fair enough,' said Lana as she snipped at the plant that was throwing out new leaves and tendrils faster than Marion had seen in a long time.

Marion knew wisterias lived for hundreds of years, but the last two seasons it had seemed to be struggling, not flowering for long or as abundantly.

'What about Tom?' asked Lana. 'You haven't heard from him?'

'No, but Sophie says he and Paul are fighting a lot because he wants to give up rowing.'

Lana shook her head. 'I don't know that that's worth getting upset about. If your kid doesn't want to row then he shouldn't have to row.'

'You and I know that, but Paul is very particular about those things. You know, it's very important to him that the children are sent to the right school, holiday in the right places, have the right sort of friends, do the right sort of sports and so on.'

Lana laughed and brushed her hair out of her eyes. 'Is there a wrong sort of sport? I mean, I hated any sort of sport at school and so did my sister, Evie. It must be genetic.'

'You should invite Evie over. It would be nice to meet her.'

Lana cut another runner from the wisteria.

'I could, but she would bring her droopy boyfriend and then they would go back and tell Denny about me. To be honest, I kind of want to keep my life private at the moment. It's so nice here, I don't want anyone saying anything or disapproving of what I'm doing when I haven't been able to make my own choices for so long.'

Marion gave a knowing laugh. 'I understand that.'

'How does Clair feel about Sophie being here?'

Marion looked at the house and gave a large sigh. 'I don't have any idea, but I might call her and tell her Sophie is here and have a chat, keep it light.'

'Light is good,' said Lana and she pulled her phone from her pocket. 'I have to go – I have a potting soil class.'

'You back for dinner?'

'Absolutely,' said Lana and they walked into the house.

Marion could hear music playing from the kitchen and she smiled. 'I cannot tell you how nice it is to hear life in this house again.'

'You deserve life around you, Marion,' Lana said fondly. 'You're one of the good ones.' She gave Marion's shoulder a quick pat and then ran upstairs to get ready for her class.

Sophie was in the kitchen, cracking eggs and singing as she cooked.

'What sort of cupcakes will they be?'

'Chocolate, I think, or maybe vanilla. Maybe even red velvet. Perhaps all of them.'

Marion chuckled and then made her way to the front sitting room, settling down to call Clair.

'Hi, Mum, Sophie OK?' asked Clair, and Marion noticed she sounded tired.

'She's fine. Making cupcakes.'

'Oh, lovely.'

'How are things, darling?' Marion kept her voice light as she asked such a loaded question.

'Fine. You know, busy.'

'Always is when you're in the thick of it.'

'What do you mean, "In the thick of it"?' Clair's voice was immediately defensive.

'I just meant being a busy mum of two with lots of school and social commitments.'

'Oh, yes, fine, we're all fine. Getting on with it.'

Marion knew that phrase. She'd said it often herself after Andy died. Clair had probably picked it up from her.

'How is Paul? He seemed busy today. Didn't have time to stop for a chat.'

There was a beat. A pause that was long enough for Marion to know that things weren't good. At such times, Clair would always fill in the space with endless chat. Social nothingness, Marion called it – something else Clair had learned from her mother, Marion having been the good corporate wife for so long.

Marion could hold a conversation with anyone about absolutely nothing, moving seamlessly from the weather to the price of salmon with skin on versus skin off. Nothing too controversial or confrontational, and definitely nothing that offered an opinion that might upset other parties. It was all about keeping a steady face to the world.

'Paul? He's fine. Busy.'

It was now that Marion realised she had created this exact same relationship with her own daughter.

Marion took a deep breath. If she didn't say anything, she would regret it, but if she did, she could risk her already tenuous connection with Clair.

'He looked stressed. Is he OK?' she said.

There was that pause again.

'He's fine, Mother. Listen, I need to go. Tell Sophie I will fetch her in the morning. I'll text her from the front, as I won't have time to come inside.'

Marion sighed. She had taken a risk and it had failed. At least for now.

'You know, you can talk to me about anything, Clair. Anything.'

'I know, and I will if I need to, but I don't. I have to run. Speak soon.'

And the line went dead.

Marion was alone again.

'Gran, can I watch *The Bachelor* after dinner?' Sophie called from the kitchen as Lana came running down the stairs.

'Oh, yes please, can we?' Lana asked as she put her bag over her shoulder.

Marion laughed at the two faces looking at her hopefully.

'Of course,' said Marion. 'I don't care what we watch. I just love your company.'

'Save me a cupcake,' called Lana and she was gone, the door closing with a satisfied click behind her.

23

Felicity

Felicity looked at herself in the mirror. For her costume, she had chosen a dress made of fine lightweight cotton in a soft shade of pale blue with tiny sprigs of white flowers scattered about it. It was a perfect summer dress if she was back in 1795. The dress was actually quite flattering for her figure, featuring a high waistline, just below the bust, which showed off her height and her svelte frame. The bodice was fitted, with a square neckline trimmed with delicate white lace, and the skirt fell gracefully, flowing down to her ankles.

Denise had suggested a few different dresses, but this one had stolen Felicity's heart. There were tiny daisies embroidered along the hem in white thread with little yellow centres and it made her happy to know they were there, even if no one else noticed them.

Over her dress, she wore a pelisse coat in a slightly darker shade of blue, as Denise said it could get cold, especially when they were in the older parts of Bath surrounded by damp stone and cold air. The pelisse was made of fine wool and was trimmed with ornate frogging in a pale butter yellow and a high collar that showed off Felicity's long neck. The final accessory, much to her disappointment, was a blue bonnet trimmed with a blue ribbon and a cluster of yellow artificial flowers on one side.

'No lady would go out without her bonnet, and you know it,' Denise told her when Felicity had come downstairs with everything but the offending item.

Felicity had stomped back upstairs, returning with said hat. 'Gloves?' Denise had asked.

Felicity had waved them at her as proof. And that was it. A small bag was provided for the tour, although Felicity doubted it would be big enough. And she had already been cautioned by Denise to wear sturdy flats, as the stone could be slippery.

'Righto, I'm here to do the curls,' Lana said as she came into the room and looked at Felicity. 'Oh, wow,' she gasped, circling Felicity. 'You look straight out of a movie. You were born in the wrong era. This is so you.'

'Do I need curls? I can just pull it into a bun.'

Felicity saw Marion in the doorway.

'She needs curls, doesn't she, Marion?'

'Curls would be nice,' Marion agreed, and Felicity sighed. 'You look marvellous. The dress is gorgeous.'

'Denise made it,' said Felicity. 'She has a whole room of them.'

Lana sat her down in the chair at the desk and opened a large box of hairstyling equipment.

'God, you're like a professional.' Felicity made a face at Marion. 'This seems a bit much, doesn't it?'

'No, it's your first day of a new job. You need to look like Jane Austen herself styled you,' Lana said as she brushed Felicity's hair and sprayed something in it that smelled like coconut.

'I have all the latest hair tools from Denny, but you know, I have stopped using them since I've moved in here. I don't really care about how I look as much and I don't think I need to have my hair straightened to weed the garden.'

Felicity felt her wind her hair around a curling iron and hold it for a few seconds.

'I don't even wear the clothes I brought with me,' Lana said. 'I seem to want to wear colour now. It's weird.'

'You were probably dressing like someone you thought you were supposed to be,' Marion said. 'That's the great thing about getting old – you dress for comfort and choose clothes that don't need ironing.'

Lana snorted. 'I must be getting old, then, because I just go to charity shops and buy old gardening T-shirts and jeans. I might get some cargo pants like you, Felicity. They look sensible.'

'You can borrow some of mine,' Felicity said. 'I have lots of pairs in black and blue.'

'Like a bruise,' said Lana with a laugh.

'I know, I need to wear colour, too,' Felicity said.

'You don't need to do anything you don't want to,' Lana said. 'But I have to ask you about what's going to happen next in the book. I can't wait till the next chapter.'

'You will have to wait, because I haven't written it yet,' said Felicity. 'I've been studying for the tour.'

'Oh, poo,' said Lana as she opened a tin of hairpins and started to pin the curls around the base of Felicity's neck, She then created two curls on either side of her face.

'God, I will look like King Charles the First with these hanging down,' Felicity complained.

'Stop whingeing. You will look gorgeous.'

Lana stepped back.

'Can I do a bit of make-up? It's just that the bonnet will cast a shadow and I want to make sure everyone can see your sparkling eyes.'

Felicity threw up her hands in surrender. 'Do what you will, I'm all yours.'

'You know, you'll be all Gabe's when he sees you dressed in this Pemberley fantasy ensemble.'

Felicity gasped and Lana pushed her chin up to close her mouth.

'Now, let me finish my masterpiece.'

She pulled out a make-up kit that would have made up a chorus of showgirls *and* their mothers.

Felicity looked at Marion and mouthed the word 'help', but Marion only laughed and walked out of the room with the words, 'I'm staying out of it.'

Lana dropped Felicity at the designated start spot, where she would be meeting Gabe. She felt eyes looking at her as she passed, people smiling and some taking photos of her as she walked to the Abbey Churchyard. She felt foolish standing in the costume and for a moment, she wished she had said no to Gabriel about joining the tour as his assistant, but then she wouldn't have seen him and she needed the job. This was the price she had to pay.

'Felicity, you look amazing,' she heard, and she turned to see Gabe in his top hat and costume.

'Oh, thank you. It's Denise's dress, really. It does wonders for me.'

Gabriel shook his head. 'No, it's perfect for you. Really.' He took his hat off and bowed to her, his brown eyes sparkling with mischief and his teeth gleaming as he smiled.

'You're such an actor,' she laughed at him.

'And you look beautiful, I mean that,' he said, and Felicity knew she was blushing. 'You ready for the tour?' he asked as he looked around.

'I think so. I've been studying.'

'Studying? You should know all of this.' He fished out an iPad from his bag and checked the numbers for the tour.

'I think I do, but I like to be prepared.'

'I think these people are for us.'

Felicity looked up and saw some tourists coming their way. Nerves fluttered in her stomach and she grabbed Gabe's hand.

'God, I feel sick,' she said. 'They will know I'm faking this, that I'm not really a Regency woman.'

Gabe laughed. 'Felicity, we are all faking it and if you were a Regency woman, you would be in the wrong century. All you have to do is share your knowledge and make them feel as if they are back in those times. You're super smart, so just remember – have fun. You're with me, remember? We're born to do this.'

Felicity felt him squeeze her hand and the nerves in her stomach transformed into butterflies.

'OK, we can do this,' she said, more to herself than to Gabe.

24

Lana

Lana picked at the soil under her fingernails, the very same ones that she used to have manicured and gelled every two weeks in silver and pale pink with little diamantés and pearls glued on them. She would get a large iced coffee and sit in the salon, scrolling on her phone, looking at other people's full lives on social media and wondering why hers felt so empty.

Now, she was standing at a potting bench, her hands in the soil as Alex explained about peat moss, compost, pine bark, worm castings, perlite, loam and fertilisers. Alex was walking around the room with a container of soil, asking people to sniff and tell him what they could smell. The students were laughing, saying they smelled either nothing or dirt, but then Alex was at Lana's bench, holding the container towards her.

'Tell me what you can smell, Lana?'

She smiled at him. He was looking extra gardener-ish today, she thought, in cargo pants and boots and a cotton shirt with the sleeves rolled up, showing strong forearms. Focus, Lana.

She leaned forwards and inhaled before looking up at him. 'It smells like a fresh morning.'

He gave her a quizzical look. 'What do you mean?'

She took another sniff and smiled. 'It smells sweet – like possibility, you know? Like in the morning when you get up and go outside and you think, something good might happen today.'

Alex paused. 'You're right,' he said, not taking his eyes off hers. 'It smells like sweetness, like a place to grow. It's the best-quality soil from my own garden.'

She nodded. 'I'd love to see your garden. I'm trying to fix up the garden where I live at the moment. It would be great to have some inspiration.'

Lana, she thought, what sort of forwardness is this? You know nothing about this man. He could be married with seven children and you're inviting yourself round to see his garden.

But somewhere inside her she knew he wasn't married. Nor did he have seven children. She also knew he was as curious about her as she was about him. Perhaps she was kidding herself, but she'd noticed the way he paid attention to her, made jokes with her, looked at her when he thought she wasn't looking. Mind you, she was the only woman in the class who wasn't over sixty.

He looked surprised at her request but then nodded. 'Why don't I come and see your garden first? Then I can give you some ideas and check the soil with my testing kit.'

'That would be great,' she said and as he walked away, she felt the woman next to her come close.

'Oh, he likes you. Me and the other ladies were talking about it earlier.'

Lana looked around and saw some of the women grinning at her. 'You were?' She gave a small laugh. 'I don't know how I feel about being talked about.'

'Oh, it's nothing bad. Everyone thinks you're lovely.' The woman looked at Alex. 'And every woman I've spoken to thinks he's gorgeous. He would do well to go out with someone like you after all he's been through.'

Lana bit her lip as she watched him talking to an older man about the soil.

'What's he been through?' she asked the woman, who seemed to know everything about him.

But before the woman could answer, Alex shouted, 'Now, it's time we finished up, but if you want to talk more about soil, I will be here for a bit.'

He looked at Lana and held her eye. She swallowed and wondered why she felt like a teenager. She turned to the woman to find out more, but she was chatting with some of the other ladies. The last thing she wanted was to be seen gossiping about him with them, because then she knew she would be the next one gossiped about.

Instead, she walked up to Alex and wrote down her number on the back of a scrap of paper.

'This is my number. Call me if you want to come and see my garden.' She blushed, wondering why it felt rude to say that.

Get a life, Lana, she told herself.

'Thank you. I'll message you,' he said, taking the paper and putting it in the breast pocket of his shirt.

'Excuse me, Alex, a question about compost,' she heard and saw a man standing expectantly next to her.

'I'll leave you to it,' she said and she left the nursery, avoiding the looks of the women who had seen her handing the piece of paper over.

Lana walked out to her car and was digging out her keys from her bag, when she heard a familiar voice.

''ello, Treacle.'

She took a deep breath. 'Denny,' she said and turned to see him coming up beside her.

He was wearing a white tracksuit with red trim and red-rimmed sunglasses that made him look like he had raided Elton John's closet.

'Why are you here? You're not following me or anything, are you?' she asked.

'I'm not, actually. I saw your car and waited. I wanted to see how you are.'

She shifted her weight to one foot and crossed her arms.

'I'm fine, Denny, but I don't know why you're here. We're supposed to talk through lawyers.'

'I know, but you see, I wanted to make you an offer off the record. Do you want to have a drink somewhere? There's a pub down the road.'

Lana shook her head. 'I don't want to have a drink and I don't want to hear about your offer, Denny. You know what you owe me and I'm being very reasonable. Nothing outrageous.'

Denny shuffled his feet. He was wearing new designer trainers.

'You see, things have been a bit slow lately and I just think we need to reassess the settlement.'

'Those Gucci trainers would tell me otherwise, Denny,' she said, and she turned and opened the car door. 'Go through my lawyer, please.'

Denny walked up to her. He was too close now and she was pressed against the car.

'I gave that turnip Petey a job because of you. If you don't settle, I'll sack him.'

'Are you threatening me? Step away from me now.'

He stepped even closer, almost touching her now.

'Denny, whatever you're doing right now, stop.'

Denny's eyes were steely. She'd seen him intimidate people like he was doing to her now. She supposed this was how

164

it was always going to end. He'd always had it in him and she should have known that eventually, it would be directed towards her.

'Lana.'

She heard her name called from across the street and she turned to see Alex striding towards her.

'You OK?' He turned to Denny. 'Who are you, mate?' he asked, moving closer to him.

'I'm her husband,' Denny said, looking Alex up and down.

Alex looked at Lana.

'My *ex*-husband,' Lana corrected. 'And he's just leaving, aren't you, Denny?'

Denny took a step back. 'Yeah, I am, but you know what I'm gonna do, Lana.'

'You do what you have to do, Denny, but go through my lawyer and if I ever see you anywhere near me again, I'm going to the police.'

Denny took a moment and then turned and walked away to his BMW, taking off with a roar of the engine.

25

Felicity

Felicity undid the bonnet and pulled it off her head, taking about three hairpins and some of the curls with it. She flopped on the bench next to Gabriel.

'That was exhausting,' she said.

'It's only your second tour,' he said, turning to her with a laugh.

'I know, but there's so much to tell people and they have so many questions, too.'

'Well, you do tell them a lot. They ask way more questions with you than they do with Denise, but you know all the juicy stuff. You're so smart, it's crazy.'

Felicity clasped her gloved hands. 'I'm not that smart, I just know a lot about this one topic. I don't know much about other things.'

'What sort of things?'

People passed them and smiled at the young couple in Regency dress sitting and chatting outside the Assembly Rooms.

Felicity stared ahead. 'Well, I haven't been to many parties. I didn't get asked much when I was at school or university.'

'That's not good,' said Gabe, and he elbowed her arm. 'I'm going to one tomorrow night. Do you want to come?'

'What sort of party is it?' she asked warily.

'I don't know – a normal one? Like you would have been to before.'

Felicity snorted. 'I'm not really the party sort.'

'What? You don't like them?'

'No, like I'm not invited to them and if I was, my gran wouldn't let me go when I was at school. And at uni ... well, I got a bit nervous of them, I suppose. I know it's stupid. I think my grandmother scared me too much, always telling me people would be trying to get me drunk or forcing drugs on me.'

Gabe shook his head. 'It's not stupid. You're just not party experienced. Come to mine and you can stay as long as you want. I can't deny – there might be things your grandmother doesn't like there, but you don't have to do anything you don't want to. View it as research into the current culture of the Bath university party scene versus the old.'

Felicity pondered for a moment. 'OK, I'll come. What do I have to wear?'

Gabe got to his feet, grabbed her hands and pulled her to her feet.

'Whatever you want! It's not formal. Just come and have a dance, talk to some of my friends, have a laugh. It'll be great, I promise.'

'OK, I might come for a bit.'

'Great, now come on. I have to go home and practise a monologue for next week's Shakespeare class and it's my turn to clean the bathroom.'

'What monologue are you doing?'

'*Hamlet*.'

'Bo-o-oring.'

'You're saying a monologue from *Hamlet* is boring?' He feigned shock and clutched his chest.

'No, I'm just saying they've been done too much. I think there are much better monologues by Shakespeare that are criminally underrated.'

'Don't tell me – you're also an expert on Shakespeare?' he said mischievously.

'Not an expert, but I know the plays well. When I was a child, my grandmother had a complete works of Shakespeare. It was huge – a tome – and I used to sit under the dining room table and read it. I liked the way the words sounded as I spoke them. Eventually, I looked up the plays and read them all. So now I have my favourites.

'Every other guy in your class will be doing a monologue from *Hamlet* or something from *King Lear*. You should do something that is right for you. Something you would be cast in now, given the chance.'

'Like what?' Gabe asked.

Felicity stopped walking and Gabe stopped also. She looked at him.

'*Timon of Athens*,' she said.

'I don't know that one.'

'No one does unless you're a Shakespeare nerd.' She laughed.

'What's that one about?'

Felicity started to walk again, swinging her bonnet from her hand.

'So, there's this rich guy in Athens named Timon. He's super generous and throws these lavish parties for his friends, giving them expensive gifts and all that. He's what you would be if you won the lottery tomorrow night.'

Gabe laughed. 'You know I would. Go on.'

'So he's got this philosopher friend, Apemantus, who warns him not to be so generous with his money. Timon doesn't listen and keeps spending until he's totally broke.'

'That's very on brand for me,' Gabe agreed with a grin.

They came to the bus stop and Felicity continued while they waited.

'So when Timon realises he's out of cash, he goes to his friends for help, but they all turn their backs on him. He's furious and disappointed that his generosity isn't reciprocated. He leaves Athens and goes to live in the wilderness, thinking that animals are more loyal and kinder than people.'

'He's not wrong, though, is he?'

'But wait, here's the crazy part. While he's out there in the forest or wilderness or whatever it is, he finds buried treasure. Instead of using the gold to get his life back on track, he decides to give it to bandits and prostitutes, hoping they'll use it to cause chaos and trouble in Athens as a way to get back at the city that betrayed him. Anyway, it's a wild story about friendship, betrayal and the consequences of being too generous without thinking about the future.'

'Why don't I know about this play?'

'Because he wrote it with someone called Thomas Middleton and it's often overlooked as a problem play, but I like it. There's a great monologue in it. Look it up,' she said as her bus came towards them, the doors hissing as they opened. She climbed onto the bus and smiled. 'Act Four, scene three.'

'Oh, I love you for this, thank you!' he called as the doors closed.

Felicity remained standing on the bus, watching a waving Gabe becoming smaller in the distance.

26

Lana

After Denny had driven away in what could only be described as a macho tantrum, Lana let out a big sigh.

'He seems nice,' Alex said sarcastically, and Lana burst into laughter.

'I don't know why I'm laughing. I think it's nervous energy,' she said, tightening her jacket around her closely as though it would protect her from what just happened. 'I've never seen him like that. Well, I have, but not towards me.'

Alex closed her car door, preventing her from entering.

'Come inside and wait for me in my office. You can't drive anywhere right now. Let me make you some tea and we can chat.'

He had such a sense of calmness about him after Denny's chaotic energy that she felt herself relax a little.

'OK,' she said and followed him into the little office behind the counter.

'You sit here and let me finish with the students. I'll be back.'

Lana stepped into the office at the back of the nursery, her eyes widening in delight as she took in the cosy, inviting atmosphere. The sage green walls and the warm natural light filtering through the large window at the back gave her a sense that she was in a secret garden hideaway. It wasn't a normal office, though, compared to what she had seen at Denny's work.

The round wooden table in the centre of the room was adorned with gardening tools, little rocks and stones and a half-made antique terrarium. A vintage globe sat on top of a bookshelf groaning with gardening books and pinned to the walls were some drawings by a child. 'Dad and Rosie', one was titled, written in a young hand.

She turned and saw a cosy reading nook to the left of the desk. The deep armchair looked so inviting that she almost couldn't resist the urge to sink into its arms, imagining herself curled up with a book about gardens. She wondered if Alex sat here with Rosie, reading stories and chatting.

There was a small table on the other wall, with a battered electric kettle and some mismatched mugs, a jar with teabags and another with sugar. Not a coffee drinker, she noted.

Between these cornerstones of the room were potted plants and hanging baskets, with more terrariums scattered about the office, creating a living, breathing space that made Lana never want to leave. It was as though she had yearned for this room her whole life and didn't know it until now.

'Sorry about my messy office,' she heard, and saw Alex standing in the doorway.

She shook her head. 'Don't apologise. It's the most gorgeous office I've ever seen.'

He laughed. 'Really? My ex-wife used to tell me I was a hoarder and needed to throw things out.'

'Don't, it's lovely,' she said as she looked around. 'Who is Rosie?'

Alex looked at the drawings. 'She's my daughter. She was only six when she did those. She's fourteen now and hates me every other day.'

Lana laughed. 'She will get over it. It's all hormones and drama for teenagers. Don't you remember?'

'You have one yourself, then?'

He moved to the seat at his desk and gestured for her to sit in the lovely armchair that had been beckoning earlier.

'I pretty much raised my sister when she was ten and I was eighteen,' she said. 'It's not easy, but then I don't think I was any prize through my teenage years, either.'

Alex laughed. 'I was pretty bad myself. It's not an easy time, is it?'

She smiled.

'Let me make us tea,' he said.

'You don't have any coffee?' she said cheekily.

'I don't, but I can get some from the staffroom.'

'No, no, it's fine, I can have tea.'

'Nope, I'm getting coffee,' he said, and was gone and back in a moment with a jar of instant and a pack of custard tarts. 'Righto, how do you have it?'

'White with one.'

'The old café standard, eh?' He boiled the kettle and started sorting out the mugs and sugar.

'Is that right?'

'Yep, I used to work in a café and that's what people always ordered.'

'What a shame I'm not original, then,' she laughed.

He turned to her. 'I think you're very original.'

'Do you?' She felt those butterflies come back to visit and she crossed her legs.

'Yes, there's something about you. You seem to understand what I'm talking about more than the others. Like today with the soil, you got it, and when we were talking about pruning the other night, you were so respectful of the rose.

173

You were working with it, not trying to control it into something you wanted it to do. Only bonsai artists can do that and it takes years, if not centuries, to be able to work with plants at that visceral level.'

Lana wasn't sure what he was going on about. All she knew was she had never wanted to kiss anyone as much as she did at this moment. She felt like she was a teenager again and also, he was her teacher and she was his student, and that would never be a good idea.

It had been a long time since she had wanted anyone. She and Denny had stopped having sex years ago and she had sort of turned off her desires. Maybe it was all the fertiliser and compost that was going to her brain, she thought.

Alex placed a coffee down next to her and opened the custard tarts. 'Help yourself.'

'So, your ex, why was he outside? Was he waiting for you?'

Lana sighed. 'He said he saw my car, but I don't think that's true. I think he probably did follow me. I told my sister where I was living and she would have told her boyfriend who works for him.'

Alex made a face. 'Nice to have family loyalty.'

Lana sipped her coffee. 'I know, and I knew Denny was only giving my sister's boyfriend the job to keep tabs on me, but he's threatening to fire him now since I won't agree to a settlement without lawyers.'

'He's charming, isn't he?'

Alex took a large bite of custard tart.

'I know. He's got a baby now with another woman. That's why I left. Well, sort of. I wanted to leave anyway, but the baby made it easier. I think he's panicking about paying me out and having to support a child.'

Alex chewed and then swallowed the tart.

'If he confronts you in the street again, or comes here or goes to your house and does what he did, you have to go to the police. You call me and I'll take you myself. OK?'

Lana nodded. Those damn butterflies were back.

He pushed the tarts towards her. 'Go on, get one into you.'

Lana took one and smiled.

'Do you counsel all of your students like this? And ply them with custard tarts?'

She laughed, aware she didn't want him to say yes. She wanted to be special, to be singled out. Damn it, Lana, she thought, you want to be the teacher's pet.

'Not really,' he said. 'I'll always have a chat with anyone, but I haven't seen ex-partners come and intimidate them in the street before.'

'You know, I never thought he would do anything like that. I've seen him be heavy on people who owed the business money or with people he didn't like, but I never thought it would end up directed at me.'

'It's inevitable.'

Lana nodded. 'I worked that out when he was breathing down my neck.'

'Are you safe where you live?' he asked, concerned.

'I'm fine, I promise.'

He leaned back in his chair and brushed some crumbs from his trousers.

'I need to come and see your garden that you're working on,' he said all businesslike.

Lana felt her energy deflate.

'Sure, anytime,' she said, putting down her cup of coffee. 'I should go. I'm keeping you from work.

She stood up and Alex did the same.

'I'll walk you out,' he said, and they strolled onto the street and to Lana's car. 'So, how about Sunday, about six thirty?'

'Oh, OK, after you finish work, sure,' Lana said, thinking out loud.

'Well, yes, but then we can do dinner afterwards, if you like?'

Lana almost fell backwards.

'I would like that very much,' she said, and she wondered why her life felt like it was suddenly in technicolour.

27

Marion

Marion burst into the kitchen, her eyes bright with excitement. The scent of freshly baked lemon cake, courtesy of Lana, filled the space, and an air of contentment was in the house. Felicity was typing on her laptop at the raspberry-painted table in the kitchen, while Lana was sitting in the worn armchair by the window, reading her gardening magazine. The late afternoon sun streamed through the lace curtains, casting a warm glow over the lemon-yellow walls and pale green cupboards.

'Ladies, I've had the most brilliant idea from Meera's finance class!' Marion exclaimed, settling herself at the Victorian shop counter that served as the kitchen island.

Lana looked up from her gardening magazine, grinning. 'Go on, then, what's our savvy landlady come up with now?'

Felicity paused from her typing, the gentle clacking of keys giving way to expectant silence. She swivelled in one of the yellow chairs to give Marion her full attention.

'Yes, do tell. What new financial strategy has Meera imparted this time?'

Marion beamed at their enthusiasm. Ever since she'd confessed to taking the course, Lana and Felicity had been her biggest cheerleaders. She spread out a stack of pamphlets on the dove-grey marble work surface.

'Well,' Marion began, 'Meera's been teaching us about household economics and I've been looking into our energy usage. I think we can cut our electricity bill by at least 20 per cent with a few simple changes.'

As she outlined her plan for energy-efficient bulbs and better insulation, Lana and Felicity listened attentively, offering their own suggestions.

'We could start a compost for the garden,' Lana said, her eyes lighting up. She gestured with the magazine towards the small backyard visible through the window. 'There's a great how-to article in this. We can collect food scraps and so on. It will be great for the garden and then we can grow veg if we want.'

'That's a fab idea,' said Felicity, her fingers hovering over her keyboard. 'I'm actually very good at budgeting and finding the cheapest things online, so give me the grocery list each week and I can get the most from the least. I have a spreadsheet I can use.'

'That's super dorky,' said Lana with a laugh. 'I'm impressed.'

Marion noticed Felicity blush. The young girl was blossoming in this warm, inviting space, surrounded by the comfort of the old and the excitement of the new. As they continued to brainstorm ideas, the kitchen seemed to come alive with their shared enthusiasm.

There was an energy in the house that had been missing for years, Marion thought as she absent-mindedly traced the faded 'Bath's Herbs and Tinctures' script engraved into the island. It was beautiful and healing, a perfect blend of past and present, much like the kitchen itself. As the sun began to set, casting long shadows across the warm room, Marion knew that while things would never be the same, they could still be wonderful in their own unique way.

★

Later that week, as Marion was pruning the wisteria whips that were reaching out onto the street, she spotted a familiar figure ambling down the street. It was Arthur, looking rather lost.

'Arthur!' she called. 'Are you all right?'

He looked up, relief washing over his face. 'Oh, Marion! Thank goodness. I'm afraid I've got myself a bit turned around. Was trying to find that new café everyone's been talking about.' He looked up at the house, 'She's a grand old dame, isn't she?'

'The house isn't bad, either,' joked Marion.

Arthur burst into peals of laughter. 'You're good fun, Marion.'

Marion came out onto the street. 'Thank you. I forgot that I have a sense of humour under the weight of financial pressure, but things seem to be looking up a little lately.'

'Good! Me also. Now, would you happen to know of The Lavender Tearooms? I read about it and they have wonderful cakes, apparently, but I can't seem to find it. I wanted to buy something for my son and his wife who are coming for dinner this evening. I have a nice chicken pie and salad prepared, but I don't do well with baking.'

Marion nodded. 'It's just around the corner. I was thinking of popping in myself sometime. Would you like some company?'

Arthur clapped his hands. 'Excellent news. Let's go. I'll buy you a cup of something.'

Soon, they were settled at a cosy table, chatting over steaming cups of Earl Grey.

'I must say, Marion,' Arthur said, stirring a second sugar into his tea, 'you seem to have really grasped those budgeting concepts from Meera's class. Any secrets you'd care to share with a struggling classmate?'

Marion chuckled. 'No secrets, I'm afraid. Just a lot of late nights and two very patient housemates who don't mind me muttering about compound interest at odd hours.'

Arthur's eyes twinkled. 'Ah, yes, your famous lodgers. You know, the way you talk about them, they sound more like family than tenants.'

Marion smiled warmly. 'They've become that, in a way. We're quite the team now, especially since I started Meera's course. They've been incredibly supportive.'

'That's wonderful,' Arthur said sincerely. 'You know, I was thinking... perhaps we could make our study sessions a regular thing. Meet up before class to go over Meera's homework.'

Marion hesitated. She was happy to make a new friend but didn't want anything more. Nor did she want to assume so.

'Just as friends, of course,' Arthur said, as though reading her mind. 'My Carol was my one love, so I'm not asking you to be anything more than that, if that eases your pause for thought.'

Marion gave him a rueful smile. 'You read my mind, Arthur, but yes, I am never too old for a new friend and I would love to work with you before classes. I think we could be a great support for each other.'

28

Felicity

Tourists lined up to have their name ticked off the list by Gabe as Felicity paced back and forth trying to remember her content for the tour.

'I don't know how you do this acting thing,' she said to Gabriel. 'How you have to remember lines and be in character, it's exhausting.'

Gabe shrugged. 'I can't explain it. There is nothing like the feeling when I'm acting onstage. It feels like everything is in the flow. I'm where I'm supposed to be. There is a story to tell and I'm the right one to tell it in that moment.'

Felicity could understand that much, she thought. 'I get that feeling when I'm writing,' she said as they waited for the final tour members to arrive.

'Your degree?' he asked, adjusting his top hat.

She paused. 'No, I'm writing a book, actually, outside of my uni work.' She didn't admit it was instead of her work, but that was for her to know and no one else but the other women at this point.

'A book? I am impressed. What's it about?'

'It's about an affair between a duke and a lady's maid, but they can't be together because she's not from his social class.'

'Good trope – always popular.'

'Yes, but the difference with my story is that my heroine makes a lot of money gambling on racehorses because her brother grooms them at the stables, so in theory she is able to marry the duke. But the construct of class means they are still divided because her money is considered new money and that's bad.'

Gabe laughed. 'I think that is fantastic. So it's a comment on social class, financial independence and the class systems that keep marginalised people down.'

Felicity nodded.

'Is there also lots of desire and lustful looks and brushing of skin with ungloved hands?' he teased, and Felicity blushed.

'Yes,' she admitted.

'Then it's a bestseller already. My mum would love to read that. She's got all those books with men on the front with their ruffled shirts open at the neck. I was obsessed with those covers as a kid.'

Felicity thought about her mother's reaction if she found out what Felicity was writing. It wouldn't be praise, she thought. Shock and horror would be more in order and, well, as for her grandmother, it wasn't worth thinking how badly she would take it.

'OK, everyone is here,' said Gabriel.

Felicity looked out at those before her. She gasped and then bit her lip. There was Marion and Lana, smiling and waving at the back of the group. Felicity didn't know if she wanted to hug them or tell them to go home, so instead she decided to ignore them and get on with the tour.

'You can start,' said Gabe. 'I have to sign these last two stragglers in.'

They're my stragglers, thought Felicity as she glared at them. Lana poked her tongue out as if in reply.

Felicity cleared her throat. 'Welcome to the lovely city of Bath! My name is Felicity and this is Gabriel. We will be your guides on this fascinating walking tour, where we will learn about the life and times of one of England's most beloved authors, Jane Austen, and her time spent living here. Bath held a special place in Austen's heart, as she lived here for several years and used the city as a setting in some of her novels.'

She looked at Gabe, who nodded for her to continue.

'Now let's make our way to the Jane Austen Centre on Gay Street. This charming museum is dedicated to the life and works of Jane Austen, offering a snapshot of what life was like during the Regency era.'

The tour group started to follow her.

'Did you know that Jane Austen lived in Bath from 1801 to 1806? In fact, she lived at number 25 Gay Street for a time, finding a place to rest between assemblies and balls and social visits.'

The tour moved on, stopping occasionally to take photos as Felicity fell to the back with Marion and Lana.

'What are you two doing here?' she asked, flipping her reticule at them.

'We wanted to see you at work,' said Marion. 'You're so good.'

'And we wanted to lay our eyes on your Angel Gabriel,' teased Lana. 'He's lovely.'

Felicity looked back at Gabriel, who was talking to some tourists.

'He's handsome, isn't he?' said Felicity, watching him.

He looked very debonair in his Regency costume and judging from the giggles of some of the younger female tourists, she wasn't the only one who thought so. She shook herself mentally.

'I haven't done anything yet,' Felicity scoffed.

'You have a sense of great knowledge about you,' said Marion. 'I feel like I'm in safe hands.'

Felicity laughed. 'You're just trying to boost me up.'

'Yes, we are, but also, you are very clever and I can't wait to learn from you,' said Marion.

'You know, I've never been on this tour,' said Lana.

'Me neither,' admitted Marion. 'I'm a bad Bath resident.'

'I like it. It's like being on holiday,' Lana replied, looking around the Abbey Churchyard.

'Well, you can redeem yourself today under my guidance,' said Felicity.

The others laughed, suddenly realising she had made a joke. Oh well, she would take a laugh with them, not against her, anytime.

They arrived at Gay Street and Felicity led the way as they toured the museum. She found herself starting to feel a little pride at the way the tourists nodded and asked questions for which she knew the answers.

'You should go on *Mastermind*,' said Lana. 'Your topic could be Jane Austen. You would win it for sure.'

'I don't know ... I always seem to say the wrong thing at the best of times, so I would do it on telly for sure.'

'Who said you say the wrong thing?' Marion frowned as they made their way to the Thermae Bath Spa.

'My gran. She says I don't think before I speak, but I swear I just say it as I see it and then she tells me I'm rude and inappropriate.'

This had always confounded Felicity. She knew she was a bit different growing up. Other children made fun of her for not knowing enough about some things and knowing too much about others. Some teachers wanted her tested, but her grandmother wouldn't hear of it, saying there was nothing wrong with Felicity, she was just unthinking and impulsive.

Felicity had gone to the big dictionary in the sitting room and looked those words up.

What adults fail to realise is that children become what you tell them they are, because they have such a need to please and to fit into the world around them. Felicity heard the words from her grandmother so often that she actually came to believe she was unthinking, impulsive, rude, arrogant, unsociable and mean. Even though her mother would whisper in her ear later that Gran didn't mean it and that she was just an old, crotchety woman, Felicity noticed her mother never corrected her in person when she spoke harshly to Felicity.

'I think your gran might be a bit old-fashioned,' said Marion. 'If she thinks *you're* rude, she'd best not meet my grandchildren. They say it as they see it, I'll tell you that right now.' She laughed to herself.

'I have to go,' said Felicity, moving towards the front of the tour group.

'Welcome to the Thermae Bath Spa,' Felicity said. 'While this modern spa complex wasn't around during Jane Austen's time, it's a fascinating example of how Bath has evolved while still paying homage to its rich history.' She paused for breath and then continued, 'The Thermae Bath Spa is located in the heart of the city, just a stone's throw away from the ancient Roman Baths.

'The spa's modern facilities are fed by the same natural hot springs that have been drawing visitors to Bath for centuries. One of the most iconic features of the Thermae Bath Spa is the open-air rooftop pool.' Felicity pointed upwards. 'From here, you can enjoy stunning panoramic views of the city skyline while soaking in the warm, mineral-rich waters. It's a truly unique experience that blends the best of Bath's past and present.'

She recited the lines she had learned from Denise by heart, but she could hear her own voice droning on. She caught Lana and Marion's eye. They were nodding politely but a few of the attendees' eyes were drifting away. Her material was boring. And safe. What she really wanted was to tell everyone what she knew and why it was interesting to her.

'So, let's talk about the Romans and their love of a good soak. Now, I know what you're thinking – the Georgians were a sophisticated bunch, but when it came to bath time, the Romans were way ahead of them.

'You see, the Romans knew that taking a bath was more than just functional for getting clean. It was a time to relax, socialise and even get a good sweat on.'

The group turned their attention back to her.

'The Georgians thought sponge-washing was the way to go, but the Romans were much more advanced. They built these incredible structures around the hot baths, which, by the way, are heated by the Earth's core. Yes,' she said, seeing eyes widen at this information. 'They even invented concrete floors to keep the water clean from Bath's regular flooding. And they invented underfloor heating. So if you have that in your house, you can thank a Roman for it.'

There were a few laughs from the crowd. Emboldened, she went on.

'Now, I know what you're thinking – the Romans were perfect. Well, not quite.' She paused for effect, the way she had seen Gabriel do before. 'Famous athletes of the time actually had servants who would scratch off their grimy sweat and bottle it to sell to their fans. I mean, that's a lot, isn't it?'

People laughed and made faces. She paused once more for them to settle, saving the best for last.

'And the Romans didn't know everything. They used their own urine as mouthwash. So I guess any argument about Roman society being perfect just went down the drain with that one.'

Everyone laughed loudly and chatted about this fact between themselves. Gabriel turned to her.

'If your book is as entertaining as that trivia was, then I think you're on to something,' he said.

Felicity bit her lip, trying not to smile too much.

29

Lana

'I hate everything I own. I hate it all,' Lana said to Marion, who was sitting in Lana's bedroom, watching as she pulled clothes from suitcases like a magician pulling silk hankies from a sleeve.

'You sound like Felicity when she said she hated her course,' Marion said with a laugh.

Lana wasn't listening.

'Alex is all garden-y and natural, whereas I seem to have a fascination with white, silver and synthetic fabrics,' she said, throwing some sort of beaded kaftan thing onto the bed. 'I can't wear any of this to dinner with him.' She stood up and paced the room. 'You know, I've just realised. I wore what Denny liked. He should have worn it if he liked it so much,' she huffed.

'That's good to recognise,' said Marion, 'but you also can't run the risk of dressing according to Alex's taste and what you think he would like you in. You have to wear what you like, what makes you feel good.'

Lana looked at her. 'I don't think I know what I like any more. I don't want to feel all sorry for myself, but it seems like all I've done is please everyone else. I was just starting to know myself when Mum left and I had to take over looking after Evie. Then I met Denny at a point I craved stability. I did whatever I could to make sure I was what he wanted. I wore what he liked, I went where he went, I even stopped listening to my music and switched to his taste. I mean, who does that?' She shook her head at the memories.

'Someone trying to survive,' Marion answered.

'Well, it now means I have no idea what I'm going to wear.'

'Let's go shopping,' said Marion, standing up.

'Where? I don't have money to spend on new outfits.'

'Trust me. You are coming?'

Lana stood up and stretched. 'OK, but only because you asked.'

Felicity came upstairs as Lana was shutting her door.

'Where are you off to?' she asked.

'Marion is taking me on a secret trip to find something to wear for dinner with Alex.'

'You can borrow my bonnet,' quipped Felicity.

'No, thanks. Dress code said strictly no bonnets,' said Lana. 'Wanna come?'

Felicity shook her head. 'No, I owe someone some chapters,' she said, and Lana clapped her hands.

'You do. You'd better get to it. I'll slide some crêpes under the door for your dinner. You're not allowed out until you're done.'

She went downstairs to where Marion was waiting.

'OK, fairy godmother, where are we off to?'

'Follow me,' said Marion.

'I've never waked as much as I do now I live here,' Lana said. 'All of my clothes are looser and I feel fitter – it's good.'

'I love walking. I think I will curl up and die when I can't walk any more,' Marion said.

Lana glanced at Marion, who was wearing a chic navy quilted jacket, and then she saw her trousers.

'You're wearing jeans!' she exclaimed. 'Why didn't I see that before?'

Marion gave a little giggle. 'I saw them at a shop I want to take you to. I thought maybe I was too old for jeans, but the girls there told me there's no age limit when it comes to style, so I bought them. They're very comfortable. I haven't worn jeans since the seventies and now I'm in my seventies wearing them all over again.'

'They look great. I hope I can be as cool as you when I'm in my seventies.'

'I'm not cool,' Marion snorted. 'But you and Felicity have certainly made me feel younger, and why should I dress like an old fuddy-duddy when I don't feel like that?'

'I agree.'

Lana slipped her arm through Marion's and they walked at a comfortable pace through the streets, down some backstreets and then down an alley. They stopped at a red door, above which was a small sign with the words 'Second Act'.

'What's this?' Lana asked as Marion opened the door.

'This is the best-kept secret in Bath,' whispered Marion. 'A recycled clothing store from the good and great of Bath. You'll find something lovely here for a fraction of the retail price. They buy clothes from people and sell them, earning an income from things that might otherwise have gone to charity.'

The interior was simple and elegant, with clean white walls and polished hardwood floors serving as a blank canvas for the vibrant array of high-end fashion that adorned the racks. The space was expertly designed to showcase the clothing in the best possible light, with soft, warm spotlights illuminating the room, casting a gentle and flattering glow over everything. The racks themselves were a sleek, modern black, doing nothing to detract from the clothes. The shop respected both fashion and the designers who made them.

Above each section, gold-and-white signs directed shoppers to the various categories of clothing on offer. 'Evening Wear' boasted a dazzling collection of gowns and cocktail dresses, their luxurious fabrics and intricate embellishments catching the light. The 'Outdoor Jackets' featured stylish coats and jackets, from classic trench coats to leather bombers, outdoor rambling coats, gilets and rain jackets, each carefully selected for its quality and timeless appeal.

The 'Cocktail Wear' section was a sea of jewel tones and sparkling embellishments, with dresses and separates perfect for any semi-formal occasion. The 'Casual' racks were filled with designer jeans, tailored blouses and cosy knits, all in pristine condition and ready to be given a second life in a lucky shopper's wardrobe.

As Lana browsed the 'Semi-Formal' section, she touched the exquisite selection of dresses, suits and separates, each bearing the label of a prestigious designer who had never graced her wardrobe. Denny loved luxury labels, but he didn't want to pay the prices, so everything he wore was a knock-off. Denny was a human knock-off, she thought as she picked up a Prada blazer. He would never understand the difference between price and value.

The 'Skirts and Bottoms' sections was a denim lover's dream, with styles ranging from classic straight-leg cuts to trendy wide-leg and distressed options. Skirts was a kaleidoscope of colours and patterns, from flowing maxis to sleek pencil skirts, all carefully arranged by size and style.

Throughout the store, plush black velvet ottomans invited shoppers to sit and try on shoes or take a break from the bargains, while large, ornate gilt mirrors allowed them to admire their reflections from every angle.

It was more than just a place to buy second-hand clothing – it was a treasure trove of opportunity, a place where fashion dreams could come true. As Lana and Marion began to explore the racks, chatting and laughing together, Lana had that funny feeling again that something grand was coming.

'God, this is like heaven,' said Lana.

'Now, what do you think? Where are you going for dinner?' Marion asked.

Lana shrugged. 'I don't know. I mean, he offered me a packet of custard tarts, so I don't think he's very posh.'

'I love custard tarts. You can't judge anyone by their dessert weakness,' Marion said as she picked up a pink lace dress. 'Too formal?'

'More like I'm too old. I don't think I can wear that style any more.'

'You can wear whatever you want. You know, my mother was a wise woman and she said, always choose an outfit by the fabric. Go by touch and then get a few things. You said you didn't want anything synthetic, so choose things like silk, cotton, cashmere or fine wool.'

Lana walked along the shirts, her fingers drifting over the clothing, and pulled out a silk one in a beautiful pistachio colour.

'That's lovely,' said Marion. 'Gorgeous colour on you.'

Lana kept walking and picked up another but in a print this time, a soft cotton T-shirt that was more formal than a normal top and a pale rose-coloured cotton peasant top.

Marion approached holding an armful of clothes.

'This is what I would wear if I was as gorgeous and as young as you,' she said.

'Marion, I will be here all afternoon trying them on.'

'Humour an old lady – I'll be gone soon.'

Marion put on a sad face and Lana giggled.

'You're mad, I tell you, but I love it.'

Lana took the clothes from Marion and went into the changing room.

'You have to show me – I have a chair. I'm all ready for the fashion show,' Marion said as Lana pulled on a nice pair of trousers with the silk shirt over the top.

She opened the curtain and saw Marion perched and ready.

'Lovely but slightly too corporate. Maybe good for court with your ex,' said Marion.

Lana turned and looked in the mirror. 'Yes, it's a bit too Lana from HR, isn't it?'

She closed the curtains again and took off the outfit.

'You know, I always wanted to do this with my mum, but she wasn't really available when I was a kid,' Lana said. 'This is nice. Sort of healing, in a way.' She pulled on the pink peasant top and a pair of washed jeans, and opened the curtains,

Marion nodded. 'That's perfect for dinner. You need some shoes. Perhaps a nice sandal with a heel.'

Lana looked back at her reflection and pulled her hair up into a ponytail.

'I don't look like I'm about to go and milk cows, do I? It's very … what's the word? Farmy.'

'I don't think that is a word and no, I don't think it looks like you're about to milk the cows.'

Lana waved her arms around, the fabric swinging. 'I like the way it flows.'

'If you like how it feels, you will like wearing it and you'll feel more confident and happier. Now try the rest on.'

Lana made a face. 'Really?'

'Really. I'm being a mum now. Try it all on. You never know, it might work.'

Lana poked her tongue out at Marion and closed the curtains.

'Were you having a teenage moment?' Marion asked, pretending to be shocked.

Lana popped her head out from behind the curtain. 'Yes, it was part of the healing journey.'

The two of them burst into peals of laughter.

30

Lana

Lana was wearing her pink top and jeans and a pair of wedge-heeled espadrilles that she had bought to wear to dinner with Denny once. He'd told her he hated them, so they had gone to the back of the closet, but it was time to reclaim them. When she opened the door at Temple Terrace, she wondered what Alex saw when he looked at her now.

'Gosh, you look wonderful, lovely,' he said, and she noticed he blushed, or perhaps she was hoping he was blushing.

'So do you.'

He looked smart, in jeans and a lovely pale blue shirt with nice shoes, but she preferred him in his gardening gear she thought, as she walked him through the house. Marion and Felicity were in the kitchen making dinner, both pretending not to be interested in who Lana was bringing inside.

She introduced them then said, 'Um, come and see the garden,' leading the way past the laundry room, where the mop handle was poking out.

Probably trying to get a look at my new bloke, Lana thought as she pushed the mop back against the wall.

'Here it is,' she said, stepping outside.

'A classic Georgian,' he said, wandering around.

'Yes, I went to one nearby. Marion showed me.' She felt awkward, seeing her pots all lined up like a child would do, regretting the half-hearted weeding she had done.

'Did you like it?' he asked, pausing to sniff the climbing rose and popping his head into the small shed.

Lana thought for a moment. If she was going to find out who she was and what she liked, then she needed to be honest.

'Not really. I thought it was really plain. I like my gardens fuller, busier, more ...' She tried to think of the word.

'Abundant,' they said in unison.

'Yes,' she said and smiled.

'I do, too. I can respect why we need to see what gardens once were, but we also need to evolve things, ideas, ourselves.'

Lana nodded. God, she had such a big crush on him. She saw Felicity and Marion at the kitchen window, pretending to wash dishes, shoulder to shoulder, when they had a dishwasher under the worktop.

When she turned back, Alex was examining the soil. He took a small plastic bag from his pocket and crouched, using the nearby trowel to dig deeper.

Lana made a face at the women through the window, surprised the mop wasn't there also, trying to gawk at them both.

'I'll take a sample, then I can show you how to test it and what it all means,' he said, standing up, sealing the bag and putting it back in his pocket.

'Is it weird walking around with a bag of dirt in your pocket?' she laughed.

'It's better than being a dirty bag,' he said, and she shook her head at him.

'Terrible – a dad joke.'

'Shall we go?'

'Yes, let's.'

Soon they were off, Lana sitting next to this hunk of a man. He had even put a towel over the passenger seat.

'I tend to have dirty cars. Comes with the territory, I'm afraid. Lucky you're not wearing white. I've chosen a nice little bistro I like and I hope you will, too. It's Italian.'

'Sounds perfect.'

And it was, it was all perfect. The restaurant was charming, the food delicious. She and Alex moved through the evening easily, trading stories and gaining little glimpses into each other's pasts and their hopes for the future. It was a perfect first date.

'Dessert?' Alex asked. 'They do an amazing tiramisu here. We could share?'

Lana beamed. 'That sounds lovely.'

The sound of Alex's phone ringing interrupted them.

'Sorry, I need to take this. It's Jess, Rosie's mum.'

Lana nodded, looking away to give him some privacy.

'Hey,' he said and listened.

Lana glanced at him and saw his face clouding.

'All right, I'm leaving now. I'll call when I've got her.' He put his phone into his pocket. 'I'm so sorry, Lana, but we will have to finish for tonight. Rosie's got drunk at a party and is vomiting. Her mum, Jess, is away this weekend and has asked me to fetch her. Rosie told her mum she was with me, but she's clearly not. The mum whose kid is having the party called Jess.'

'Oh no,' said Lana, and she stood up and pushed back her chair. 'Well, we'd better go and get her, then.'

'You don't have to come,' he said, gesturing to the waiter for the bill.

'I know, but I am, because drunk teenage girls can be hard work. I used to be one, and I looked after a sister who went through this.'

Alex swiped his bank card and they were soon out of the door and in his car.

'Why would she lie to Jess and me about this? It's ridiculous,' he said as he drove.

'Because she's a teenager who is pushing the fence posts to see how far she can go.'

'Throwing up and being incoherent and lying about where she was going to be this weekend is really pushing on those fence posts,' he said grimly. 'It's not like Jess and I don't talk – we don't have a bad relationship – and Rosie is our priority, so why is she trying to act out at us?'

'No, it's not that. She's tried it and she messed up. But I will give you one piece of advice ...'

'What's that?' he asked as he turned a corner.

'You don't say anything now. Her welfare is the main concern right now. You can save the lecture for tomorrow when she can actually take it in and everything isn't so fraught.'

Alex was silent for a moment. 'You're right. Thank you.'

He stopped outside a house. The front door was open and there were flashing party lights hanging haphazardly from a tree, music thumping from inside.

'Wait here – I'll be back with the drunkard.'

He half ran inside and Lana turned and checked the back seat was clear for Rosie. When she looked back at the house, she saw Alex carrying his daughter out of the front door. Lana jumped from the car and opened the door for him to put her in the back seat.

'Who are you?' said the teenager, slurring and looking at Lana with squinted eyes, eyeliner smudged down her cheek.

'I'm Lana, a friend of your dad's.'

'Good, he needs more friends. He's a loser,' said Rosie, and she leaned forwards to turn up the music on the stereo and started to sing, very out of tune and very loudly.

'Rosie!' Alex turned the music down.

'Dad, I love that song. It's my favourite song ever.'

'Don't say I'm a loser,' he said huffily.

'But you are. You do absolutely nothing You go nowhere but work and then you annoy me about my life. It's about time you started getting friends. Can she be your girlfriend?' Rosie peered at Lana. 'You're pretty, probably too pretty for Dad. He wears thermals, you know. It's so weird. I like your top.'

'Thank you,' Lana said as she watched Rosie burp a few times, remembering looking after Evie in the same state. 'Step back or lose your shoes,' she yelled at Alex, and as she moved out of the way, she turned to open the door of the car.

Alex moved just before Rosie projectile vomited across her friend's lawn.

'There she blows,' said Lana.

'How did you know she was about to do that?' asked Alex, looking at Lana with wonder.

'The burp – always a sign. I have a much younger sister. If we can get her home now, we might make it in time before the next one that's bound to come.'

Lana got into the car while Alex stepped around the vomit and buckled Rosie into her seat before jumping into the car.

'OK, sorry, this is not what I had in mind,' he said as he drove.

'It's life. It's messy and funny and fun. Besides, you're a thermal-wearing loser with no friends, so this must be super exciting for you,' she teased.

'God, she's so out of line,' he said, and Lana laughed. 'It gets cold when I'm gardening – I like to stay warm. Thermals are good.'

They turned into a driveway and he switched off the ignition.

'I'll get her into bed and then drive you home,' he said.

'No, I can sleep on the sofa. You can't leave her. We will need to check on her through the night. We can take it in turns,' Lana said firmly.

'Are you sure?'

'Yes.'

'OK. Could you open the door?' Alex handed her the keys.

Lana opened the front door as Alex carried Rosie inside and up the stairs. She took off her shoes and wandered through the house, noticing the warm interiors and lived-in feel of the home. There were lots of plants, naturally, and art and books and comfortable sofas. Plus a television – a normal one, not one strapped to the wall like a hospital or one that came up from a hidden area in a cabinet. Oh, and a dog, she noticed. A fat blonde Labrador was snoring in a dog bed in the corner near the heater.

Lana walked into the kitchen, which was clean and organised, and lifted the kettle to check for water before turning it on.

'She's in bed,' she heard Alex say and she turned to him.

'Is she on her side?' she asked, opening a cupboard and looking for mugs.

'Top right,' he said. 'Yes, on her side, with a towel under her head and a bucket for good measure.'

'It's optimistic of you to think that she'd use it.' Lana laughed.

Alex opened a tin and took out some teabags.

'I know, but it's hard to know what else she would need – besides being grounded for the rest of her life.'

'How old were you the first time you got drunk?' she asked, stepping back and letting him take over the tea-making.

'Fourteen.'

'And what did you drink?'

'Kestrel Super brew. Never been able to drink it again since.'

'Ouch.'

'What about you?'

Lana thought for a moment.

'Fifteen, neat gin.'

'Wow, that's brutal.'

'I know, but I still like a gin and tonic – I just didn't know you had to mix it with anything. I nicked it from my mum, and she was mad at me for weeks.'

'Young and stupid,' he said.

'Just like your girl upstairs.'

Alex steeped the teabags. 'I'm really grateful you came with me tonight.'

'That's OK. Been there, done that.'

'Oh no,' he said, putting his hand on his head.

'What?'

'I've made you tea and you like coffee. So thoughtless of me. Let me get some coffee. I have a cafetière somewhere,' he said, opening a cupboard.

Lana reached out and touched his arm.

'It's fine, Alex, I can drink tea. I do drink tea.'

She left her hand there.

He leaned down and kissed her mouth gently, and she returned his kiss. It was all perfect and Lana wrapped her arms around him as they kissed like teenagers.

'You're lovely,' she said.

'So are you.'

Just as he leaned down to kiss her again, she heard a voice call.

'Dad? I've been sick.'

Alex rolled his eyes and looked at Lana.

'I'll be back. Go and sit down. Nana, the dog, will keep you company, although she does snore and fart in her sleep. Then again, so do I.'

Lana laughed and took her tea over to the sofa. Nana opened one eye, no doubt assessing her new company, and then closed it again. Lana sat in peace, sipping her tea and listening to murmurings upstairs and footsteps she presumed to be Alex's walking around.

She finished her tea and rearranged herself on the sofa, which was very comfortable, adjusting a pillow under her head, her eyes becoming heavy, Nana's snoring as her lullaby.

31

Felicity

Felicity left the house after Lana and Alex had left for dinner, leaving Marion with her latest instalment to read and a copy for Lana on her bed. She checked the address that Gabe had given her. He'd told her to meet him out front and that she should just text him on arrival.

She flagged a passing taxi – she didn't have the energy to find her way by public transport tonight – and soon she was driving through the streets. She wondered what Gabe was wearing. Who were his friends? How would he introduce her? Did he think about her as much as she did him?

The taxi pulled up outside the front of a house. She paid the driver and texted Gabe as instructed. Within seconds, he came out and waved at her before pulling her into a huge hug.

'You came! I'm so pleased,' he said. He grabbed her hand and pulled her towards the house, where loud music was playing from inside. He leaned over to speak closely in her ear. 'I read that monologue – it's bloody brilliant. I'm going to do it.' He kissed her cheek. 'Thank you, Felicity, you're amazing.'

She felt herself turning pink, saying nothing as they made their way past partygoers chatting, drinking and dancing in the living room.

'Come and meet some other people I love,' he said, and Felicity's heart skipped.

A group of people were standing in the kitchen, laughing and drinking as Gabe half dragged her towards them.

'Everyone, this is my friend, Felicity. She's the one I've been talking about non-stop.'

They turned to Felicity and smiled. One of the young men stepped forwards. He was wearing a red bucket hat, a bright pink suit jacket, ripped jeans and trainers, with nothing under the jacket.

'Oh, hello, darling, I'm Oscar,' he said. 'I'm so pleased to meet you finally. Gabe won't stop rattling on about you, will you, darling?'

Gabe leaned over and kissed Oscar on the lips playfully.

'How do you know Gabe?' Felicity asked, confused.

'Darling, I'm Oscar – didn't Gabe mention me?'

She looked at Gabe, who smiled happily at the two of them. 'This is Oscar, my boyfriend.'

A few hours later, Felicity was surrounded by people she didn't know chanting at her.

'Shot, shot, shot,' cried the voices as she lifted the egg cup of tequila to her lips.

She closed her eyes and took the shot. The shots had been Oscar's idea and since he didn't have shot glasses, egg cups were the vessel of choice.

'Do it, babe. Lick the salt and suck the lime,' he encouraged.

Felicity did as asked. What else did she have to do? Yes, she could have gone home and been sad about Gabriel. But then she realised that he had never actually said he wasn't gay. Nor had he said he was straight. He had simply been her friend, and a supportive one at that. Someone who'd wanted nothing in return, who celebrated her and her knowledge for who she was.

It was kind of a relief to know that Gabriel wasn't interested in her romantically, because now she could go back to dreaming – a place where she felt safest. But right now, Oscar wasn't letting her do anything but shots and dance.

'You're amazing,' he said, placing his hat on her head and dancing around her.

'I'm really not,' she said as he handed her another shot.

She was getting used to the warm feeling it was giving her and it was certainly taking away her shyness.

'You are so. Gabe told me about the monologue and how good you are with all your literary knowledge. It's such a vibe! I love it.' He put his hands in the air and danced with his eyes closed.

Felicity followed his lead. It felt liberating as she did so and though she bumped into a few people, they didn't seem to mind.

She moved to Oscar's side. 'I thought I was in love with Gabe,' she admitted, shocked at her own honesty.

'Oh, you probably are, darling, everyone loves Gabriel. He's a true angel, I think,' Oscar answered as he pulled her to him and put his arms around her waist.

'I've never been in love before,' she said.

'It's a lot of work. Stay single and kiss lots of frogs for as long as you can.'

He laughed and Felicity laughed with him.

'Like the fairy tale,' she said.

'Exactly.'

'I'm writing a book.' She swayed out of time to the music.

'Are you?' Oscar gasped. 'What sort of book?'

'A romance.'

'Is it about Gabriel?' Oscar poked his tongue out at her.

'Sort of, but also not. It's a love story but historical.'

'Oh, dreamy. I bet it's fantastic. How far are you into it?'

'Just over halfway.'

'Send it to me – I want to read it,' he said as Gabriel came up to them, a joint in his hand.

He handed it to Oscar, who took a drag and then passed it to Felicity. She looked at it and then held it to her mouth, taking a drag, coughing excessively as the smoke went into her lungs.

Gabe took the joint from her. 'Come outside. Someone is skateboarding.'

He took Felicity's hand and she grabbed Oscar's. Together, they ran outside and watched someone she didn't know perform tricks, people cheering. The speakers were outside now and people were dancing both in the front garden and on the street. Felicity closed her eyes and danced and danced, feeling her body loosen, her mind free and her heart happy.

So this is what her grandmother said was for people with low IQs and too much time on their hands. If this was what it was, then Felicity was happy to be a part of it all.

32

Felicity

The bus ride home from the party was awful. With every turn, Felicity wondered if she might be sick, and every time people took their time getting on and off at each stop, Felicity wanted to yell at them to hurry up. Didn't they know she had her first hangover and thought she might die?

Her phone was out of charge and she couldn't find a spare charger anywhere at Oscar and Gabriel's house, where she ended up staying. She had slept top and tail with them in their bed, only waking when Oscar was cuddling her feet. She had crept out of bed and looked at the time on Oscar's phone. It was after eleven in the morning – she never slept this late.

In the bathroom, she used someone's hairbrush to smooth her bird's nest hair and ran some toothpaste over her teeth with her finger. After grabbing her bag, she had quietly left the house.

It was a cute house – old, but not as old as Marion's. It was cosy and fun, with posters everywhere and mismatched dishes and a cat named Meryl Streep, who seemed friendly compared to others she had been introduced to in the past. They lived with a third-year acting student called Helen, who hadn't come to the party because she was in Bristol auditioning for something. She was great fun, apparently.

Right now, Felicity wished she had magic powers to be transported into her shower and then into bed with some paracetamol. How she wished for a sleep that would last until her liver was cleansed…

Finally, the bus arrived at the end of the crescent and Felicity climbed down the stairs and walked towards Temple Terrace. Every step felt like she was walking through tar and she wondered if this hangover business was worth it.

She pulled her keys out and opened the door just as Marion did.

'Oh, you're home,' she said, looking flustered.

'I got drunk for the first time in my life, like very drunk, and then I smoked some weed, which made me cough. Then I danced in the street and I slept in a bed with two men,' she said proudly. 'I would say I am now a proper functioning adult with a new range of experiences to write about. Because how can I be a writer if I only write about what I've known? It's very limited at best, so now I can add hangover to my life experiences.' She laughed but then noticed Marion's mouth going up and down but no words coming out. 'Have I lost my hearing? Am I deaf?' Felicity looked around, panicked. 'Your mouth is moving but you're not saying anything.'

Marion pointed at the sitting room, the door open.

'Your grandmother is here,' she whispered, 'and your mother.'

Felicity stopped and stood very still. Perhaps this was just a hallucination from the joint she had, or from the tequila.

'Felicity, is that you?'

Oh, God, she thought, and she walked into the sitting room, where her grandmother was sitting in Marion's chair and her mother on the sofa.

'Sit down,' her grandmother commanded. 'What *have* you been doing?'

Felicity stayed standing.

'Living my life,' she said evenly.

She looked at her mother, whose hands were in her lap, her head down, avoiding her daughter's gaze. Her mother was paler than ever and she was wearing a black overcoat that was done up to her neck.

'Hello, Mum, how are you?' she asked gently.

She had always known her mum was different from the other mums. Quiet and timid, unable to cope with too much emotion or responsibility, her grandmother always said. But now Felicity wondered if in fact her mother was ever given the chance to cope after her father left them. She couldn't imagine that he would want to stay if her grandmother was always in their life.

'You need to come home,' Gran said, her walking stick upright, her bony hand clutching the top of it.

Gran had dressed to show Felicity she meant business, wearing her best cashmere twinset and pearls with a tweed wool skirt and her lace-up brogues. She could have been from the 1950s, Felicity thought, as she noticed her grand-mother was thinner than ever.

'I am home. I live here,' she said, surprised at her courage, yet it felt natural.

She believed her own words for the first time in front of her grandmother. She remained where she stood, in the centre of the room. Marion had gone, leaving her alone with them. She didn't blame Marion – she wished she could leave, too – but she knew this had to happen.

'You need to come home. You're out of control. You've given up your degree, you're working God knows what sort of jobs and now you're on drugs *and* an alcoholic.'

Felicity laughed, surprising herself and, judging by the look on her face, her grandmother, too.

'Don't be so impertinent,' she hissed at Felicity, but this only fuelled Felicity's inner fire.

'Stop acting as though you have any control over me at all. I'm here, safe, happy, independent and doing something I love. Be happy for me.'

Her mother looked up at Felicity and Felicity was sure she saw a flicker of a smile.

'If you don't return home with us, I will never speak to you again,' Gran said.

'Do you feel that way, too, Mum?'

'Of course she does,' her grandmother said, lifting her stick and banging it down on the floor.

Felicity glared at the old woman. 'Can you not speak for her for once? Mum, is that what you want?'

Her mother raised her eyes to Felicity and shook her head so imperceptibly that her grandmother didn't notice. But Felicity did and for a moment, she wished her mother could be free, but today wasn't that day.

'You might have control of Mum, but you don't have any over me,' said Felicity. 'You've wasted your time coming here – I'm not leaving. I'm busy and I'm happy. Mum, I'll call you and we can make a time to catch up – without *her*...' She glared at her grandmother and moved to the doorway. 'You can leave now. I have things to do.'

Her grandmother stood up, her cane by her side.

'You are a selfish, heartless child who has no idea the sacrifices your mother and I have made so you can pursue your education. We clothed you, fed you, put a roof over your head.'

Felicity had had enough. She turned to her grandmother.

'I owe you *nothing*. I won that scholarship to the private

school I attended. I have always had a part-time job since I was fourteen. I tended to you both hand and foot and gave up normal experiences both as a child and a teenager because you told me I was better than them. All those people – the ones who had friends and boyfriends and girlfriends and who went overseas and to parties and did God knows what else I wasn't allowed to do.'

Her grandmother's mouth dropped open in shock.

'You' – she pointed at her grandmother – 'have made me feel less than throughout my whole life. Every time I shone at something, you would remind me I was a bit shit, not pretty enough, too tall, too plain, too everything – but never enough. You did it to my mother until she became a shell and you nearly did it to me also. But this house, the people in it and the friends I have made in Bath, have reminded me I am worth something.'

Felicity turned to her mother.

'And you, Mum, you deserve so much more than her. You deserve to be loved, not controlled. So when you're ready to come out from under her crazy command, please let me know and we can start our relationship as equals.'

Felicity opened the front door.

'Please leave now,' she said to her grandmother, who marched out without so much as a glance at Felicity.

Her mother came past and touched Felicity's cheek. Felicity leaned down and kissed her mother.

'I will come and get you, I promise,' her mum whispered in her ear, and then they were gone.

Felicity shut the door and leaned against it. Marion and Lana's faces poked out from around the wall at the end of the hallway.

'You OK, darling?' asked Lana.

Felicity slid down the door and burst into tears.

33

Lana

Lana tried to concentrate as she tested the soil in Alex's shed, but he was so distracting what with his forearms and his slight stubble and his hip pressing against hers.

'You need to stop being so close,' said Lana, as she leaned in slightly and kissed his neck.

'Is that right?' Alex asked, turning his head and kissing her back.

'The staff will see you,' she said as she felt his hands around her waist, pulling her to him.

'And? What will they say? That we're being dirty in the office?'

'God, that's a terrible joke,' she said as her phone rang from the table, where she'd left it. 'It's my sister. I need to take it. Evie,' she said and heard crying down the phone. 'What's happened?' she asked, but she knew what it would be.

'Denny fired Petey,' she said.

'Oh, I'm sorry, love. Did he give a reason?' She sat on the armchair as Alex dropped some liquid from a bottle onto the soil.

'He said that Petey was shite and didn't sell enough. Petey tried to tell him that people were buying things cheaper online now and they were coming to the store expecting price matching. But Denny wouldn't listen.'

She knew Denny when he was like this, and she knew Bill Gates himself could come and tell him he was charging too much and Denny would tell him to sod off.

'So what will Petey do now? He can get another job, can't he?'

Petey was lazy at the best of times and had been unemployed for five months before Denny took him on. The problem with Petey was he didn't know what he wanted to do and so he did nothing instead. But she couldn't argue with his thinking about online prices versus Denny's exorbitant ones.

'The problem is...' Evie took a deep breath. 'Is that I'm having a baby. I'm pregnant.'

'Oh,' said Lana, stumped.

'Say something nice,' Evie cried. 'Don't just say "oh" – that's mean. I know you don't like Petey, but I love him. You don't see him like I do. He's very nurturing.'

Lana made a face down the phone. 'If you're happy with Petey and happy to have a baby, then I'm happy for you. Congratulations.'

'Thank you,' Evie said, sniffing. 'Denny is awful, isn't he?'

'Yep. Did you tell him where I was living? Or about the gardening course?'

Alex left the office and closed the door behind him, leaving Lana alone.

'No, I didn't, I promise,' said Evie.

Lana could tell Evie was telling the truth. She always gave a little cough at the start of a lie.

'He turned up at the nursery where I am doing my course last week and harassed me,' Lana said.

'Oh, jeesh, what a knob.'

'I don't think he will do it again. The guy running the course came out and gave him the old heave-ho.'

'Did he now? Is he handsome? Your own knight in wellingtons?'

Lana couldn't help but laugh. Evie always made her giggle. 'He's all right,' she said carefully.

'I won't ask any more, because I want you to tell me when you're ready. I won't say anything to Denny or Petey, even though none of us are speaking right now.'

'When's the baby due?'

'January, poor thing. Hope it's not born on New Year's Eve. That's a shite birthday.'

'Have you told work yet?'

Evie paused. 'No, they just gave me a promotion, so they won't be happy. I was moved up to head of Year Two and I think they are looking at me to be the head teacher in a few years.'

Lana smiled with pride. 'And you will be a wonderful head, Evie, I just know it. Anyway, don't worry about Petey. You can always go back to work and he can be a stay-at-home dad. You earn more than him anyway.'

Evie gasped. 'You know, you're right, I do, and he could. I'm going to talk to him now. Thanks, Lans, you always know the right answer.'

The phone went silent and Lana looked at the screen, wondering if Evie realised she was joking. She caught herself. She was being sexist, presumptuous. Of course Petey could look after the baby. Evie loved her job and could trust Petey with the baby's life if she went back to work.

The door opened and Alex popped his head around it.

'I'm going to be an auntie!' she said.

'Congratulations,' he smiled. 'Rosie's here.'

Lana felt her nerves rise. She hadn't seen Rosie since the night Alex had taken Rosie upstairs and put his daughter to bed. When Lana woke at seven the next morning, Alex had laid a thick bedspread over her on the sofa. It was Nana's snoring in her face with an occasional lick when she stirred that woke her up.

Lana had texted Alex that she would get an Uber taxi and then sneaked out of the house, shoes in hand, and headed home. This was only the second time she had seen him since that night. The last time she had been in class, they had studiously ignored each other until one of the women asked if they had had a fight. Alex had found this hilarious when she told him on the phone. She wondered if Rosie even remembered her.

Rosie came into the office, threw her school bag on the floor and sat in Alex's chair. She spun towards Lana.

'You were in the car when I vommed,' she stated baldly.

'I was.'

'You came home with us but weren't there in the morning. Why not?'

'I slept on the sofa and when your dog woke me all with licks and snorts and smells, I left.' She smiled. 'I'm Lana.'

'I know, Dad talks about you,' said Rosie in a way that gave Lana nothing to work with.

No insight whatsoever. But then Lana remembered that at fourteen, nothing matters to you except yourself.

'How was school?' asked Alex, leaning against the door frame.

'Shite, stupid, and I hate English and history. I'm failing. They said I will have to leave if I fail any more.'

'I don't think there are levels of failing, there's just failing,' said Alex. 'You need a tutor.'

'I don't want some crusty old person with dandruff and leather patches on their elbows to tell me about the olden days.' Rosie did another spin for effect.

'I know someone who might be able to tutor you,' said Lana. 'She's not old and she doesn't wear patches on her elbows and she has a very clean scalp.'

Rosie spun the other way and stopped on Alex. 'I might meet her, then.'

'Tell Lana, not me,' he said, and Rosie turned to Lana.

'Can I meet her?'

'Sure,' said Lana. 'Although she's pretty busy and might be booked up, so I can ask, but no promises.'

The threat of missing out was bigger than anything else at this age and Rosie responded just as Lana presumed.

'No. She has to take me. I'm failing,' she said dramatically.

Lana looked at Alex, who was stifling a smile.

'OK, well, give me your number and I can get her to text you if she's interested.'

Lana passed her phone to Rosie, who typed it in quickly.

'Are we going home soon?' she asked Alex, who nodded.

'Yes, I just have to talk to Lana about the soil type at her house.'

'That's just weird.' Rosie made a face and stood up. 'I'm going to find some custard tarts.'

Rosie left the office and Lana shook her head.

'She's a whirlwind.'

'More like a cyclone,' said Alex as he looked at the soil on the testing plate. 'Clay and loam,' he said. 'The soil, I mean. So the roses like it, which is why they are doing so well, but it means you have to choose plants that like that soil, otherwise you will have to treat it, which will take time and additives.'

Lana shook her head. 'No, I will work with what I have.'

'Great, let me make a list of things I think would work and I will send you the names. That way, you can look them up and work out where they can best be placed according to their needs. Maybe you can do a little drawing, or there are free online sketch programs you can use.'

'Is this homework, Mr Hayes?' she asked, biting her lip.

'Yes, and I expect that you will do it properly and on time, or we will have to discuss after class.'

He leaned down to kiss her, when they heard a sound of disgust from the doorway.

'Ew, gross, get a room. You're also too old for that!'

And there was Rosie, a cheeky look in her eye and mouthful of custard tart.

34

Lana

Lana wasn't sure she had ever felt about someone the way she did about Alex. She certainly hadn't about Denny, at least not as far as she could remember. With Alex, it was special, and it was more so because she knew he felt the same way.

She sat at his kitchen table now, showing him the drawing she had done on her iPad of Marion's garden.

'This is lovely, really, so clever,' he said. 'You have all these hydrangeas against the wall, which is perfect really, because they will be protected and will give a lovely show. And you want them blue, which is gorgeous against the pale pink roses. And I love the hostas against that other wall. They are criminally overlooked.'

'You don't think it's too amateur?' She wasn't used to getting good feedback, waiting for the 'but' to come.

'No, I don't. I love these choices, because you have chosen what you love, not what people think is in fashion. It's a garden made with love.'

Nana walked up to Lana and put her head on her lap.

'Hello, you,' she said to the dog, whose velvety nose was nudging her hand.

'She wants food,' Alex said, going over to the worktop, where he started to get Nana's dinner together.

'I should go,' said Lana, looking at her phone.

'Why? Stay here and we can order Thai. Rosie is at her mum's.'

His voice was casual, but Lana felt the energy shift. She hadn't been with anyone since Denny and she wondered if she even knew what to do any more. She felt like a 38-year-old virgin again.

'OK, sure,' she said, matching his casualness. 'That sounds great.'

'You know, I can get all those plants wholesale for you,' he said as he put Nana's bowl down.

Nana tucked in as though she had been starved for weeks.

'I don't really have much money at the moment.' Lana had promised to be honest both with herself and with others and she wouldn't lie to Alex about the state of things. 'I can't seem to get a job,' she said, meeting his gaze. 'I don't really have any experience in anything. Denny didn't want me to work, so I didn't, but it meant I fell behind.'

Alex nodded. 'OK, that's hard.'

'I am waiting on my divorce settlement. Until then, I enrolled on the course because I didn't know what else to do and I like being in the garden. I don't know if I can do it as a job, but it's nice to have hope for something, you know?'

He came and sat down at the table again.

'So what money I have I spend on rent at Marion's and the course.' She smiled. 'But thank you for the offer. As soon as I'm flush, I will order from you, my favourite nurseryman.'

He leaned forwards and took her hands in his. 'Thank you for telling me, Lana, truly.'

She smiled and felt her eyes prick. 'Thank you for understanding.'

Alex opened a lovely bottle of wine for them, nice enough even for Clair, Lana thought wickedly. They ordered Thai, eating and drinking and watching TV until finally, the chat show they were watching finished. Alex switched off the television with the remote and turned to Lana.

'Bedtime?' he asked, and she paused.

'You can stay in Rosie's room – I didn't mean to presume,' he said quickly.

She leaned forwards and kissed him. 'No, I want to go to bed with you, but ...'

He waited for her to speak.

'I haven't been naked in front of a man for many years. I don't even know what I look like any more.'

Alex laughed gently. 'Oh, Lana, here's the thing women don't understand. When we see a naked woman in our bedroom, we don't think anything else other than, woo-hoo there's a naked woman in my bedroom. All that self-judgement, that's on you. We aren't thinking that, trust me. And besides, you're the sexiest, funniest, most gorgeous woman I have ever had the pleasure to kiss.'

Lana stood up and pulled him to his feet.

'OK, now you have wooed me, take me to bed or lose me forever.'

Later, when Lana lay with her head on his chest, she felt a tear fall and she wiped it away quickly, trying not to let Alex see she was emotional.

'You all right?' he asked.

'Fine, that was lovely,' she said, trying not to let her voice crack.

He moved so they were facing each other. 'Lovely?' he echoed and put his nose against hers. 'That was incredible, Lana, truly. I nearly cried out.'

She laughed. 'I did cry, but in a good way.'

He kissed her and pulled her on top of him. 'Let's see if we can cry together this time, then,' he said.

Was this the third time? Lana wondered.

'I bought a coffee percolator,' Alex said when Lana came downstairs the next morning. 'And coffee from the roaster's in town. The man said this has hints of caramel, vanilla and chocolate.' He opened the bag of coffee and took a sniff.

Lana came over. 'Mmm, that does smell good.'

'Let me make it for you.'

'I'm just going to pop out to my car and get my phone cable and laptop charger.'

Lana had parked behind Alex. As she walked towards it, she noticed her front tyre was flat.

'Bugger,' she said, and then she looked at the back tyre, which was also flat. She walked around the car and saw all four were down. Then she looked at Alex's car and his were down, too.

'Shit, shit, shit,' she said.

She headed out onto the street and looked up and down to see if she could see Denny's BMW. This had to be his work. She marched back inside, picked up her phone and dialled a number.

'Police, please,' she said as Alex came over to her, gesturing, a look of confusion on his face. 'Yes, hello, my ex-husband has been to my boyfriend's house and has let down the tyres on both of our cars. I'd like to file a report, please.'

Alex walked outside.

Lana listened to the operator.

'No, I don't have any proof it was him at all, but I know it was him,' Lana said.

She listened to the operator and then hung up the phone as Alex walked back inside.

'I'm so sorry,' she said. 'I'm so embarrassed.'

'You don't know it was him.'

'I do. It's him all right. He's a petty little bitch,' she said, dialling a number on her phone again.

'Who are you calling now?'

'A company to come and replace the tyres,' she said. 'I will pay for this – this isn't your fault.'

'No, Lana, it's fine. I will pay for it, and yours,' he said, but Lana shook her head.

'I don't think I can see you until this divorce is over, Alex. If he does this and you have Rosie and there is an accident, I will never forgive myself.'

Alex pulled her to him. 'Don't talk nonsense. It's fine. It's probably kids being idiots.'

But Lana pulled away. 'Then why isn't the whole street out looking at their deflated tyres?'

She picked up her bag and put her laptop inside. 'I'm going to wait outside for recovery to arrive and see if he drives past. I can't trust him not to do something else unhinged.'

'What did the police say?'

'They said they can't send anyone unless there is more proof or more damage.'

That was Denny all over, doing just enough to muck up your life but not enough to ruin it.

Lana went outside and sat on Alex's fence, waiting for the truck to come. She didn't have any proof, but she knew it was Denny, and she couldn't risk Alex and Rosie being exposed to this bullshit.

Alex came and sat next to her. 'You don't mean that about us not seeing each other until after the divorce, do you?'

Lana couldn't look at him, because she knew she would cry. Instead, she straightened her shoulders. She was used to giving up what she wanted. She had done it for her mother, for Evie and for Denny. One more wouldn't hurt her, she thought. But deep down, she knew this one would hurt the most.

'Yes, I'm sorry. I need you and Rosie to be safe.'

And that was it. Denny had got his way once more.

35

Felicity

Since the confrontation with her grandmother, Felicity had lost her nerve after standing up for herself. Perhaps she should go back and finish her degree. Maybe she had been cruel and unfeeling. Her grandmother always managed to find new and verbose ways to tell Felicity she was a bitch, which is what all those harsh words meant.

As Felicity paced her bedroom, she felt more alone than she ever had in her life, which was quite a feat considering she grew up reading Shakespeare for fun and eating her lunch in the toilet throughout her school years. Lana and Marion had been lovely and kind after her grandmother and mother left, but she couldn't seem to settle and she couldn't seem to write.

She put her keys into her pocket and headed downstairs and out of the front door. The wisteria was in full bloom and today there was no one at the front of the house. She stood back to admire it, watching the bees around it, and the way the waterfall of flowers waved slightly in the breeze. It was a lovely day, but Felicity couldn't enjoy it, not when things were so uncertain with her family.

It was usual that Felicity would always go and make amends, and she would be punished for it for a time. Shamed for having a differing opinion to her grandmother, ignored for a few days and spoken about to her mother as though she weren't in the room. And then it would change again and she would be included. And for a time the sun would be out again in Felicity's world.

She was walking along the street, wondering where she could go, when her phone sounded with a text. She pulled it from her pocket, afraid but also hopeful it would be her grandmother. It was Oscar:

Come to the pub, we miss you.

Accompanying the text was a photo of Gabe and Oscar holding up drinks to the camera.

She smiled, tears stinging her eyes at the idea of being thought of. She texted back:

Which pub?

Rose and Crown on the corner.

It wasn't far from where she was and she walked briskly. If only her younger self could see her now. All those lonely nights as a child and now she was now heading to a pub to meet friends. And she had stood up to her grandmother. Life was full of surprises.

Oscar stood and waved. 'Hoo-roo!'

She approached the table. He was wearing an orange denim jacket, orange trousers and an orange bucket hat.

'Gabe said I looked like a carrot. Do you think I look like a carrot?' he asked.

She looked him up and down. 'No, you look like my favourite highlighter.'

'I'm happy with that. Better than being a carrot.'

'What are you smiling to yourself about?' Gabe asked Felicity.

'I was just thinking about Lizzie Bennet and if she would ever have gone to the pub if she lived in these times.'

'The pub? Lizzie would have been at the club – her and Charlotte Lucas on the floor getting down – while Jane herself would be trying to chat up the club owner and Lydia would be out with the smokers,' Oscar claimed loudly.

'Oh, for sure she would be with the smokers, talking to the promoter, acting like he's going to get her in free everywhere, forever,' Gabe added.

'Oh, Lydia, those drink cards don't pay for themselves. You will have to pay him back one way or another.' Oscar laughed and Felicity couldn't help but laugh along.

'I've never been to a club,' she admitted as she took off her bag and put it on her lap.

'Jesus, girl, were you raised in a cult?' asked Oscar, his eyes wide.

Felicity paused. 'No, just a pretty strict grandmother, and my mum has mental health issues.'

Gabe took her hand. 'I'm sorry, that's shit.'

Felicity nodded and the need to talk came over her like a wave.

'My gran and mum came over after the party and my gran was pretty awful to me,' she said.

'What did she say?' asked Oscar.

'You don't have to talk about it if you don't feel comfortable,' said Gabe, shooting Oscar a look, who ignored him and leaned into Felicity.

'You do, and you want to. Get it out and we can counsel you. I give excellent advice – solicited and unsolicited.'

Gabe nodded. 'He does, actually, even if you don't want to hear it.'

Felicity paused as though trying to remember, but she knew it by heart – it had replayed over and over in her mind since her family had left Temple Terrace.

'She said I was on drugs and an alcoholic. Said I needed to come home to Bristol with her.'

'Ha! If that's what she thinks, she should meet me,' said Oscar.

'And she said I am a selfish, heartless child who has no idea of the sacrifices that she and my mum made so I could pursue my education. She said that she gave me food, clothes and a roof over my head.' Just repeating the words made her feel ill.

Oscar snorted and made a face. 'So she did what you're supposed to do while raising a child?'

'What do you mean?'

'Feeding them, sending them to school, giving them a place to live that's not a cardboard box – that's not special. That's what a caregiver does. She doesn't need a celebration for doing the bare minimum.'

Gabe nodded. 'He's right. Do you want a drink?'

'A lemon squash, please.'

Gabe went to the bar and Oscar looked at her.

'You know I'm studying psychology, don't you?'

Felicity shook her head. 'I thought you were on the acting course with Gabe?'

'No, darling. I mean I could – I was a terrific Puck in high school, ask anyone.' He winked at Felicity, who laughed. 'So I am not at all qualified to give you this advice, but I will. It's never stopped me before.' He paused and then spoke. 'I don't have to be Freud to tell you that what your gran said is emotionally abusive.'

Felicity swallowed and looked down at the table.

'And I don't know you at all, really. But we had one great party together and I want to be friends with you the way Gabe is. He adores you.'

She glanced at Gabe at the bar, who was paying for her squash.

'But when I look at you,' Oscar continued, 'I can see how unworthy you feel, how you doubt yourself. And I think, and correct me if I'm wrong, that you think you're difficult and unloveable.'

Felicity nodded, looking up at him, her eyes stinging again.

'You feel invisible, don't you? And you also feel anxious and worried that nobody likes you, yet you wonder if you like anyone yourself, anyway.'

Felicity gasped. 'How do you know this?'

Oscar shrugged. 'I'm learning about this stuff, plus I watched a lot of Dr Phil and Oprah as a child. This is emotional abuse from your nasty nan.'

'Oh, great.' Felicity sighed.

'But you're changing, aren't you?' Oscar said.

Felicity looked him in the eye and nodded.

'Moving to Bath was an excuse,' she said. 'I never even wanted to do the master's. I just wanted to be away from her. And being here for six months before moving to Temple Terrace gave me space.'

'How so?' asked Gabe, joining them.

She thought for a moment.

'I began to find out what I liked and didn't like, and I found I didn't like where I was very much. And you know, I've always lived in my head,' she said. 'As a child I had this thing where I could play entire lives out in my head. Especially when I was anxious. I would go to my room and write stories about people with no problems and fabulous lives. I mean, all their problems were solvable.' She laughed.

'So moving to Temple Terrace and knowing I wasn't doing well in my course,' she continued, 'well, that was what made me want to write again, and I couldn't stop. I could see everything I was writing. It was like I was one of those psychic people. The ones who talk to spirits.'

'Channelling,' said Oscar. 'Spooky, I love it. Go on.'

Felicity paused. 'You think I'm crazy.'

But the men shook their heads.

'No, I think you're brilliant,' said Gabe.

'Who else has read your book so far?' asked Oscar.

'Just the women I live with,' she answered.

'And do they like it?'

She shrugged. 'They say they do. They ask for more chapters.'

'And do they have any reason to lie to you?'

Felicity shook her head. 'No. Unless they're just being polite.'

'I doubt they would ask for more chapters if it was only manners in question.'

Felicity hadn't thought of that, and she did think Lana and Marion were impeccably honest, both with themselves and others.

'So what did you say to your grandmother after she had a go at you?' asked Gabe.

She looked at him. 'I can recite it word for word, if you like. I can't stop replaying it in my head.' She took a breath as though she were about to recite a monologue and repeated everything she'd said.

Oscar and Gabe were hooked.

'And that's when her face was shocked, like proper shocked,' she said. 'I told her how she had made me feel less than my whole life. And that she did it to my mother until she became a shell and she nearly did it to me too but

232

Temple Terrace, the people in it and the friends I have made in Bath,' – she gestured to Oscar and Gabe – 'have reminded me I *am* worth something.'

Oscar stood up and applauded. 'That deserves a standing ovation,' he said, ignoring the looks people were giving him until Gabe pulled him down into his seat by the corner of his jacket. 'Now, send me this book, because if you write the way you speak, I think I'm going to like this story of yours.'

36

Lana

Lana came into the kitchen and threw a wad of cash on the worktop.

'What's that for?' Marion asked, wiping her hands on the tea towel where she was peeling potatoes at the sink.

'Well, I went to Second Act and sold everything I hate from my life with Denny. All the designer bags and tizzy clothes... I can't believe I ever wore that stuff. But they said it would sell well, so I sold it,' Lana said proudly. 'No point hanging on to things that no longer reflect who you are.'

'What a clever idea, and well done you. That's a nice little earner there,' said Marion.

'I'm going to pop it away for a rainy day,' said Lana. 'It feels nice to have a little cash. Like I can relax a little.'

The sound of the doorbell rang through the house.

'I'll go,' Lana said. 'Oh! Hey, Soph,' she said to Sophie, noticing her for the first time as she turned to go to the door.

Sophie was sitting at the kitchen table painting her nails.

'Hey,' answered Sophie, concentrating on a perfect application of neon yellow to her middle finger.

Lana went up the hallway and opened the door, and there were Alex and Rosie, both holding boxes of plants.

'Hello,' she said, surprised to see them.

She had only seen Alex at the nursery on the course since they last met. It was difficult not to take back everything she had said about waiting to see him until after the divorce as she didn't trust Denny.

'What are you two doing here?' she asked, keeping her voice light as she gestured for them to come inside.

'We bought you some plants for your garden,' said Rosie. 'Dad said you needed them.'

'You didn't need to do that. But it is lovely of you. Come through.' She led them down to the kitchen. 'Marion, you know Alex, and this is his daughter, Rosie. Rosie, this is my friend, Marion, who I live with, and her granddaughter, Sophie.'

Lana watched how the teenage girls looked at each other, the elevator stare of the other's school uniforms.

'You go to Castle College?' Sophie asked Rosie.

'Yeah,' she said carefully.

Lana wondered if she was waiting for something rude to be said. She was sure that Sophie's school was far posher than Rosie's, from what Marion had mentioned about Clair and Paul's need for status.

'Do you know Tamsin Willis?' asked Sophie.

'Yeah, she's one of my besties,' Rosie challenged.

'I met her at rowing. She does it for the club in Bath. She's so funny. I had such a good time with her last year.'

Rosie put the box of plants on the worktop. 'Right? She's hilarious, like so funny. She could be a comedian.'

'She did this thing on the river…' Sophie started to laugh hysterically before she could finish the story.

Lana looked at Alex.

'Shall we take these outside and leave these three to it?'

Outside, she put the box down on the ground and looked inside.

'Hydrangeas,' she said.

'Yes, the blue ones, and I have some extra blueing powder here,' he said, putting his box down. 'I also have some tube stock of things I think will work, the hostas, some campanulas and some lovely petunias to add some colour.'

Lana looked inside the box. 'You're so kind, Alex. You didn't need to do this.'

'I know, but I wanted to. And I wanted to tell you I miss you. I've been so miserable that even Rosie said she would come over and help me deliver them so I could stop being such a mope.'

Lana looked down at the plants, afraid of what she would do if she looked at him for too long.

'Have you heard from Denny?' he asked.

She shook her head. 'No, I've told my solicitor about it, though, and I am being careful and checking before I go anywhere.'

'That's not a way to live.'

'It is for now, and hopefully the solicitors can push this through.'

They looked at each other and Lana swallowed.

'I miss you, too,' she said.

'The gardening course is finishing next week and then I won't see you.'

She nodded. 'I know.'

Rosie came outside with Sophie. 'Hey, Dad, we have heaps of mutuals on Facebook, isn't that so weird?'

'So weird,' said Alex, turning away from Lana.

'You should come to my school,' said Rosie to Sophie. 'You know all of my friends already.'

Lana saw something cross Sophie's face, a look of something that was a cross between helplessness and hope.

'I wish, but my mum thinks I need to go to where she went to school.'

'Tell her mine is cheaper,' laughed Rosie.

They went inside and Lana put on the kettle. It was so nice to see Alex in her world for a moment. As she watched Sophie and Rosie paint each other's nails and talk to Marion about nothing and everything, she wished it could be different, but Denny was an unknown at present.

'Let's have a cup of tea and some of this cake that I got from the bakery,' said Lana, taking it out of the bag. 'Lemon poppyseed! But we have to let each other know if we have – and we probably will have – poppyseeds in our teeth.'

Everyone laughed and she looked up to see Alex next to her.

'Let me help,' he said.

It was hell, having him so close and not touching him.

'OK,' she said quietly, and they moved in sync to get the tea, milk, sugar, plates and forks for afternoon tea.

'Hello, are you having a party I wasn't invited to?' Lana heard Felicity ask.

Lana laughed and waved a mug at her. 'Already have a cup ready for you.'

Felicity was in her Austen costume and the girls looked at her, their eyes wide and mouths open in awe.

'You look amazing,' said Sophie.

'Awesome,' Rosie added. 'Do a twirl.'

'Felicity, this is Rosie. Rosie, I think you were going to text her about tutoring?'

Rosie made a sorry face. 'Soz, yes, I know I need to. Can we talk about it now?'

Felicity nodded. 'Of course. Let me go upstairs and take this off.' She lifted her skirts a little and Lana saw her work boots on under her dress.

'I didn't think Doc Martens were a part of the Regency dress code?'

Felicity stretched a foot out in front of her. 'They're not, but there are parts of the tour that are slippery and I am not going over like Denise did.'

'And fair enough, too,' said Marion. 'You go and get changed, then we can have some cake and you and Rosie can talk about tutoring.'

Lana poured the hot water over the tea and looked out of the window at the plants Alex had brought. She needed this settlement to happen sooner rather than later.

'You OK?' she heard Alex ask in her ear.

'I just want things to move forwards. I'm not a patient person.'

'It will, I just know it,' he said, and he leaned down and kissed her neck. 'That's a promise.'

Lana thought about Alex last thing at night and first thing in the morning, and today was no different. She was lying in bed wondering if he was doing the same, when she heard a knock at her bedroom door.

'Come in,' she said.

She thought it might be Felicity looking for more hairpins, but it was Marion, frowning.

'What's wrong?' Lana got out of bed and pulled on her robe around her pyjamas.

'Something has happened outside in the garden,' she said.

'What?'

Lana followed Marion downstairs and out into the back garden. All of the plants were pulled from their pots and hacked into little pieces.

'What happened?' she asked, nausea rising.

She looked around and saw the secateurs on the ground.

'So this wasn't a fox, then,' she said and turned to Marion. 'Call the police.'

'The police?'

'Yes, I know who did this and I know he used the secateurs.'

Lana went to the small door at the back of the shed that led to the alleyway behind the house. Just as she suspected, the lock was broken.

She came back to the pots, where she could hear Marion asking for the police to come and then she finished the call.

'He broke through the back gate,' said Lana, her nausea turning to fury.

'Who? Who broke in?' Marion asked.

'My ex, Denny. I'm so sorry, Marion. I should move out to keep you safe.' She couldn't believe this was happening.

Marion put her hand on Lana's shoulder. 'You will do no such thing. This is your safe place.'

'Clair will freak, though,' said Lana, tears welling. 'She will want me to leave for your safety.'

'Well, Clair isn't here and she doesn't get to make decisions for me, as much as she thinks she might. So, let's go and have some tea and toast and wait for the police, then we can decide what to do after that.'

And that's exactly what they did.

37

Marion

Marion had the feeling that things weren't yet sorted out and tied up with ribbon, but she couldn't work out which issue she was thinking about.

Was it Felicity and her awful grandmother and weak mother?

Was it Denny and his very obvious stalking and harassment of Lana?

Or was it her own family, what with Sophie staying over again two nights before, when she'd asked Marion if she was open to Sophie living there part-time? And what about Clair, who wasn't returning calls, and the stories that came into her hearing of Tom and Paul fighting at every turn?

Being a grandmother was hard. It broke Marion's heart to see Clair struggle and Sophie so clearly afraid of what was happening at home that she needed to find refuge at Temple Terrace. But Marion also knew she couldn't fix anything. This was adult business and more than anything, it wasn't her place to fix anything unless she was asked – and Clair never asked.

When Clair was little, she used to ask Marion if she could stroke her hair until she went to sleep, but as she became older, those habits disappeared and when Andy died, Clair became brittle, cold and distant. Even trying to hug Clair was awkward and Clair always pulled away first.

Lana was right about what Clair's reaction would be to the news that they had been broken into by Denny. She would have a fit, and have both Lana and Felicity packed and out on the street within an afternoon.

If Marion was honest, she would admit she was afraid of her own daughter, not because of violence but because her mercurial moods and sharp tongue seemed to have worsened since Geoffrey died. The money had been a particular trigger for Clair, and she had been furious with Marion for not keeping track of it and where he was sending it.

Marion hadn't known what to say, because the demise of Geoffrey's mind and health had been slow. At first it was tiny little things that people would blame on age, or not having had a coffee in the morning, or simple forgetfulness. She couldn't forgive even herself for not noticing sooner, but what would it have changed? she wondered. The money was gone by then and then the tumour was inoperable. Then Geoffrey disappeared altogether – just a body, sleeping mostly, until one day he was gone.

'I'm going to get changed and then we can go,' said Lana, coming into the kitchen still in her robe.

'Are you sure?' asked Marion, already dressed.

'Surer than sure.'

Soon they were on their way, Marion driving them in her car. They drove past Alex's nursery, and Marion glanced at it and then at Lana.

'Don't, I can't even think about him or I will cry,' said Lana. 'And today I need to be brave.'

'You can cry and still be brave.'

'I know, but not today.' Lana pointed ahead. 'Park behind that van.'

They pulled up and Marion manoeuvred the car.

'OK, give me a pep talk.' She turned to Marion.

'You need to do this! You have the upper hand. You are powerful, you are strong, you are Lana Rolls!' Marion cried.

Lana looked at her in surprise. 'I like that. I am bloody Lana Rolls. Although I think I might go back to my maiden name when this is over.'

'What's that?' Marion asked, intrigued.

'Smith – boring but reliable.'

'Nothing wrong with that.'

Lana pulled down the mirror on the sun visor and checked her face.

'I haven't had my hair dyed since I moved into your place and I hardly wear any make-up now. He won't recognise me.' She turned and opened the door. 'OK, you all right to stay here?'

'I feel like I'm the getaway driver. It's exciting. Now, go and be Lana Rolls, née Smith, soon to be Smith again.'

Lana stepped out of the car and with every step she took, she became taller and her posture straighter. Marion watched a woman transform into someone she was destined to be.

38

Lana

The store was busy when Lana walked through the door. The cool interior was in stark contrast to the warm day outside, with its sleek minimalist design dominated by whites and chromes. Bright LED lights illuminated the space, creating an almost clinical ambiance, reflecting Denny's need for control. The walls were lined with large flat-screen displays showcasing the latest smart home systems, each one playing a loop of high-definition videos of animals in the wild and exotic tropical birds in lush green jungles, demonstrating their cutting-edge features.

In the centre of the store, islands with gleaming white worktops displayed an array of the latest smartphones, tablets and laptops. Each device was meticulously arranged, their screens glowing with enticing demos and colourful apps.

Towards the back, a 'Smart Home' section featured mock-up rooms of a living area, kitchen and bedroom – all almost identical to the home they once shared, each out-fitted with the most advanced home automation technology. Motion sensors triggered lights and appliances as customers walked by, while voice-activated assistants cheerfully re-sponded to preprogrammed queries. It was spooky and weird and Lana was glad to be away from that world.

Lana couldn't imagine Marion in a house like this. Here, everything was new, polished, perfect – much like the façade she and Denny had maintained in their marriage for years. Whereas Temple Terrace embraced its own imperfections and became more charming and interesting with every year it survived.

As she looked around, she realised that Temple Terrace was the home she had always craved as child. It wasn't all mod cons. Instead, it had shown her what a home could truly be: warm, accepting, alive with both history and love.

'Welcome to Future World. May I help you with anything?' asked a solicitous salesman she didn't know as she approached the back office.

Petey's replacement, she thought as she said a prayer to the universe for getting Petey away from Denny. You couldn't have a worse role model, she had told Evie once, and she stood firmly by her opinion.

'No, thank you,' she said politely as she passed him.

'That's the office,' he said. 'There's nothing in there for you.'

'Oh, darlin' I know. Oh, how I know,' she said and she opened the door to see Denny sitting at his desk wearing the biggest pair of headphones she had ever seen.

His tracksuit was emblazoned with a luxury brand's logo all over it and he had a tan so deep it was completely unnatural. She couldn't understand how they could ever have been a couple, let alone a married.

'Lana,' he said, surprised.

'Mickey Mouse,' she answered, and she closed the door behind her as he took the ludicrous sound items off his head.

'What the *fuck* are you wearing?' he asked, looking at her peasant blouse, jeans and sandals. 'You in a revival of *Mamma Mia*?' He laughed at his own joke.

'Fuck off, Denny. Better than looking like a chav and speaking like a fake cockney. We all know you went to Badminton College and your parents are accountants. I'm more working class than you, so knock it off.'

Denny rolled his eyes and Lana looked around the office.

'Done some decorating, have you?'

The office was extreme, even for Denny's tastes.

The walls were painted a stark white, providing a clinical backdrop for the numerous framed posters featuring luxury cars and movies like *Fight Club*, *American Psycho* and *Scarface*. He was such a cliché, she thought as she looked at how the posters were haphazardly hung, as if Denny had simply slapped them up wherever he wanted on the day.

Denny sat at his massive overly ornate desk, its polished black surface reflecting the harsh fluorescent lights overhead. The desk was cluttered with the latest gadgets, all emblazoned with premium brand logos. A huge, ultra-wide monitor dominated the desk, displaying a dizzying array of stock market charts and real-time data feeds. He was the king of his little empire, she thought.

The office seating area was no less pretentious. A pair of white leather couches faced each other, their surfaces adorned with gaudy gold-embroidered scatter cushions featuring a designer logo. Between them was a garish chrome-and-glass coffee table, its surface cluttered with high-end car magazines and technology trade publications. In one corner, a sleek modern bar was stocked with expensive bottles of whiskey and cognac.

'You don't even drink this,' Lana said as she walked over and picked up a bottle of Japanese whiskey.

'It's for invited guests,' Denny snarled.

'Is Royce's mum the new decorator?'

From his expression, she knew the answer was a yes. She wondered if the baby and its mother were living in their former home now. Gee, her bed wasn't even cold, she thought as she picked up a cushion from the sofa, looked at it and then put it down again.

Even the office lighting seemed to be an attempt at making a statement. Instead of traditional lamps or overhead fixtures, it was illuminated by a series of colour-changing LED light strips, which pulsed and shifted in time with the fluctuations of the stock market. The effect was both dizzying and disorienting – no wonder he was acting strange.

As Lana took in the entirety of Denny's office, it was with a sense of pity, but mostly frustration and anger, at how he still didn't get it. The room was a desperate attempt to project an image of success and sophistication, but it was all wrong. Every element, from the mishmash of brand logos to the frenetic technology, seemed to be screaming for attention and validation. The office was a reflection of Denny himself – a man so consumed by the pursuit of status and the trappings of wealth that he had lost sight of what truly mattered.

'If you're here to get Petey his job back, you're too late – I've replaced him. He's an idiot and he's mouthy. Told me I didn't know anything about pricing,' he snapped.

'I'm not here about Petey,' she said, but she was pleased to hear that Petey had given Denny a bit of his own back.

She sat down in the chair opposite him.

'I didn't invite you to sit down,' he said, his small eyes squinting at her in the everchanging lighting.

'I don't need an invitation, Denny. I'm here on official business.'

She paused for a moment, enjoying the confusion on his face.

'You did a spot of pruning at my place last night,' she said.
'What do you mean?'

He sat back in his chair and put his fingertips together as though he were some sort of villain in a movie. She knew this pose – it was from some stupid power posing course he did last year.

'Oi, Darth Vader, stop with the power poses. You look like an idiot.'

Denny lowered his hands. 'You've changed, Lana.'

'I should bloody hope so. Now, why did you break into the house where I am living with two other women and julienne my plants like Gordon Ramsay on a bender?'

'I don't know what you're talking about.'

God, he was a good liar, but Lana was on to him.

'You do know, Denny, you know a lot more than you let on. I reckon you or whatever person you have watching me saw Alex come over to mine. Out of spite, you then got them or someone else to break into my property and destroy all the plants he gave me and my landlord for the garden.'

'No face, no case, lovely,' he sneered.

Lana leaned forwards. 'You did, didn't you. Well, the police have been round and they have the secateurs. They are dusting them for fingerprints right now. So will it be yours or one of your idiots who work in the warehouse? It will be easy enough to trace.'

'They can't trace me. I won't give them my fingerprints,' Denny said, leaning back in his giant office chair and rocking back and forth.

So it was him, she thought.

'You forget, Denny. We gave our fingerprints when we were first married and your first shop was broken into in Bristol so they could take ours out of the mix. Our digits are on file.' She leaned back in her chair and crossed her legs.

Denny ran his tongue around his lips, always a nervous tic of his when he was flying too close to the sun, or sunbed in his case.

'I don't know why you're doing this, Denny. You don't want me back, but you don't want to pay me out or to be happy. What *do* you want, Denny? My demise? Me living in some sort of squat in squalor, would that make you happy?'

Denny said nothing.

'Because we were not happy and I'm not asking for the moon – I'm asking for what I'm worth in terms of me helping you to build this business in the first place.'

'You did nothing,' Denny snarled. 'You were nothing when you met me – you and your slutty sister and her dumb-arse boyfriend. God, I had to put up with all of you and your sad fucking existence. You sucked my teats for years.'

'Eww, gross. And for the record, I would rather be nothing than be you.' She spat her words at him and then remembered not to lower herself to his level. 'Anyway, I don't think a court will see it as such. All those years I worked with you to help build it up, the research I did for new locations, the nights you had dinner on the table ready for you. You never had to so much as wash a shirt, let alone iron it. I did it all, Denny. I was the one who allowed you to be able to do this to the level you have.' She gestured around the room. 'And you know what? You should be proud of it all, cos you've done well. *I'm* proud of you. You worked hard, but so did I.'

She paused.

'You can hate me for leaving you, but I don't know why. You don't go and have a baby with someone else if you're happily married. You chose to sleep with someone else and then you denied both her and the kids the truth, like you did me. You need to be truthful to yourself, Denny. You don't want me any more than I want you.'

Denny said nothing.

'But to come into my home and damage other people's property, to let the tyres down on both my car and the man I'm seeing, that's just sad and dangerous.'

Denny seemed to sink in the chair, deflated, all fight and power pose gone, as Lana continued.

'So, you have a choice. You let me go, give me what I'm asking for in the divorce —which is fair and equitable — and we both move on. Or I get you charged, give an interview about domestic abuse and stalking to the media, and your whole empire comes crashing down. No woman is going to want to buy the latest hairdryer or washing machine from an abuser and a stalker.'

'That isn't domestic abuse or stalking,' said Denny indignantly.

'Yes, it is,' said Lana, her voice rising in frustration.

She was incredulous at both his ignorance and denial. She pulled her phone from her bag and opened it, reading aloud the passage she had saved earlier. She had a feeling she would have to explain what his behaviour was to him.

'Stalking includes malicious communication, damaging property and physical or sexual assault. If the behaviour is persistent and clearly unwanted, causing someone to feel fear, distress or anxiety, then it is classed as stalking.'

She looked at him. 'You have made me feel unsafe, you have made me worry for the safety of those around me. It stops now, Denny, or I will bring this all down and you will be selling hairdryers and laptops out of the back of your car in a pub car park before the end of the year.'

Lana stood up and moved to the door.

'I expect my solicitor to hear from yours by close of business today with the offer or I will be moving forwards with my plans tomorrow.'

She held her head up as she walked through the store, aware that people were looking at her. Some knew exactly who she was. She could imagine the gossip in the staffroom. Let them gossip, she thought, joining Marion in the car.

'How did it go?' Marion asked, but Lana said nothing.

As Marion turned the ignition, Lana knew Denny would be watching through his office window. She put on her sunglasses, turned up the radio and held her breath until she was out of sight from the store. Only then did she ask Marion to pull over, her eyes shining with tears.

'That was so scary,' she said. 'But I did it.'

'Did what?' asked Marion, looking confused.

'I told him that the police had his fingerprints from the secateurs and that I would expose him unless he left me alone and he gave me the settlement.'

'But the police haven't even been to the house yet, they said it wasn't a priority.'

'He doesn't know that, though,' said Lana, and she sat back in her seat, grabbing Marion's hand. 'I don't think I could have done this without you, Marion. You make me feel brave.'

'You are brave. You left him, didn't you, and without my assistance or input. You raised Evie without me. You have been brave your whole life, Lana, never forget that.'

Lana felt a few tears fall, more from relief that it was all done than anything else.

She and Marion sat for a moment and as she gathered herself, her phone rang. Lana took it from her bag and looked at the number.

'My solicitor,' she said.

'So quickly?' Marion shook her head in disbelief.

'Hello, Lana speaking. Yes, no problem, I will be there at three.' She put the phone down and looked at Marion. 'He wants to settle,' she said, and she started to laugh. 'After all that rubbish, he wants to settle.' Lana burst into tears, Marion rubbing her back, letting her get all the pain and fear out.

When Lana had cried herself out, Marion handed her a fresh tissue.

'Now, you need to take me home, freshen up, then go and see the local nurseryman about some fresh plants before you visit your solicitor.'

Lana blew her nose. 'I might go after I see the solicitor. I need things to be squared away once and for all.'

'Good idea,' said Marion.

39

Marion

Before class, Marion and Arthur sat in her study reviewing their latest assignment from Meera. Arthur glanced up at the photos in a silver frame on the desk.

'Is that your Geoffrey?' he asked, nodding towards a picture of a Marion and Geoffrey from thirty years ago.

Before Andy died, before everything changed, she thought.

She nodded, a familiar pang of loss mingling with fond memories. 'Yes, that's him. Taken on our last trip to Cornwall.'

Arthur smiled softly. 'He looks like he was a good man. Ethel and I loved Cornwall, too, you know. Perhaps ... perhaps sometime we could take a day trip down there. As friends, of course. To remember the good times.'

Marion felt a rush of affection for her new friend. 'I'd like that very much, Arthur. Very much indeed.'

Her phone rang and she saw Clair's number flash on the screen.

'Hello, darling,' she said. 'How's things?'

The words down the line were strangled by a sob.

'Clair, what is it?'

'It's Paul,' said Clair, sounding hysterical. 'He's missing.'

'What do you mean, missing?'

'He's gone. He-he-he's not at work, he's not at his office and I c-can't track him on his phone. He left me a very

255

odd voicemail saying he was s-sorry for everything and that I shouldn't come l-looking for him,' she sniffed. 'I'm so w-worried.'

'Have you called the police?' Marion was already walking upstairs to pack a bag.

'No, should I?' Clair always knew what to do, except now.

'Yes, call them. I'm on my way over.'

Marion looked at Arthur. 'That was my daughter. Her husband is missing,' she said as though trying to make sense of what she had just heard.

'Has she called the police?'

Marion shook her head. 'I don't know. I need to go there. Can you tell Meera I can't come tonight?'

Arthur stood up. 'Of course, what else can I do?'

'Nothing. I'm sorry, can you see your own way out?'

Arthur was writing on her notebook. 'This is my home number and my mobile. Call me for anything. My son is a detective over near Worcester, so I might be able to speak to him if you still can't find him.'

Marion only half listened, her mind on other things. Lana's bedroom door was open, so she knocked to get her attention.

'I have to go to Clair's for a bit. Something's happened with Paul.'

Lana was moisturising her face. 'Is he OK?'

'I don't know yet. He's missing. I'll let you keep the home fires burning back here,' she said. 'Let Felicity know.'

'Of course, don't worry about anything. Let me know as soon as you find anything out.'

Marion heard the front door click as Arthur left.

Marion grabbed whatever she could remember and drove to Clair and Paul's house. They lived outside of Bath, on a country estate in an old Georgian house. It was a grand house – too grand, Marion always thought – but Clair had set her sights on it the moment she had seen it and Paul had bought it for her. The house was fine, a little too *Country Life* magazine for Marion's tastes, but Clair had always wanted to live well and Marion couldn't fault that.

The gardens were spectacular, south-facing, with a mostly flat lawn that they all used to play croquet on with the twins when they were little. As she drove towards the house, she could see the nearby church in the background. It looked like a picture postcard, except no one wanted to be in this destination where she was heading.

Part of her was cross with Clair for not talking to her before things got to where they were now. She'd known Paul wasn't well, and then there was Sophie, who had been over more frequently, yet neither Clair nor Paul had thought to ask where she was, seemingly not missing her.

Marion parked the car and made her way past the beautiful swimming pool that wasn't used much any more, past the fruit cages with peaches and apricots and apples, towards the back door. She opened it to see Clair on the phone, pacing the kitchen.

'Yes, he's six foot, brown hair, brown eyes. No, his phone is off. OK, I'll wait.' She turned to Marion, her eyes swollen. 'I'm talking to Missing Persons. They said the voice message is concerning.'

Marion nodded. 'Of course.'

Clair turned her attention back to the phone. 'OK, I'll wait. Yes, I'm his wife. No, the children are at school. Oh, OK.' She put her hand over the phone. 'I need to fetch the children home.'

'I'll call the school and go and get them.'

Clair put out her hand and grabbed her mother's arms. 'Thank you,' she said sincerely.

'Of course, darling.' Marion went into the other room to call the school.

As she stood in Paul's study on hold on the phone, she looked around to see if she could see anything that would give a hint as to his state of mind, but it looked to her as though Paul had left everything in order. The papers were neatly stacked in one corner, the pens put away, the laptop closed.

Marion left shortly after, Clair remaining behind in case he came back. She noticed Clair's eyes seemed to dart around the room, as though looking for him in every shadow. As she drove, she tried to think what to tell the twins.

'Gran, what's wrong?' Sophie asked.

Marion noticed Tom didn't speak, throwing his bag into the back and sitting in the front seat before Sophie could claim it.

'It's your dad,' Marion said, twisting in her seat to face them.

'Is he sick?' asked Sophie.

'Or dead?' Tom added, and Marion was taken aback at his tone.

'He's missing. The police are coming to the house now and they will need to talk to you both.'

Sophie sat back and chewed a fingernail as Marion drove, Tom fiddling with the radio, trying to find a station he liked. In the end, he gave up. It was the best decision, she thought, because whatever song he'd played would be associated with this day forever, whatever the outcome.

A police car and another car blocked the expansive driveway as Marion pulled in. The twins left their school bags in the car. Marion could see a police officer speaking to Clair in the front sitting room. She had her hands over her eyes and was nodding. Marion paused, taking a deep breath, and she walked inside.

'Where are the twins?' Clair asked.

'In the kitchen,' said Marion. She looked at the police officer and the man who she presumed to be the detective from Missing Persons. 'Any news?'

'Hello, I'm Detective Mark McIntyre from the Serious Fraud team.'

'Fraud?' Marion said, looking at Clair.

Clair started to cry. 'Tell her,' she said to the detective.

He cleared his throat and spoke. 'Paul was actually arrested yesterday.'

Marion gasped.

'There is a large amount of money missing from his client accounts. We spoke to him yesterday and he admitted everything. He was more than compliant, ready to hand himself in. Said he wanted to tell his family himself.'

'Except he didn't come home,' said Clair. 'He left that voice message.'

'We released him pending further inquiries. Since you rang in, we have been trying to track his phone and his licence plate,' said the detective. 'But I wonder if the children know anything.'

'They wouldn't,' Clair said, but Marion frowned.

'Sophie doesn't, but I think Tom knows something.'

'Really?' Clair's head snapped up. 'He needs to tell me, now. Tom!' she shouted, her voice high-pitched and angry. 'He should have told me earlier.'

'Let me talk to him,' said Marion gently. 'You look for a nice photo of Paul for the police.'

'OK,' said Clair, scrolling through her phone as though her life depended on it.

Tom was in the kitchen looking in the refrigerator.

'Find anything worth eating?' she asked.

He shook his head. 'We never have anything worth eating. Dad's such a health nut. It's an eating disorder, I reckon. All he does is say "food is fuel",' he said, impersonating Paul

Marion smiled. 'That's a pretty spot-on impression.' She perched at the kitchen island on one of the wooden stools. 'Have you noticed anything about your dad lately?'

'Nothing,' he shrugged. 'He's just been on my case a lot. Like, I don't want to row, but he basically said he will disown me if I don't row.'

'I'm sure he doesn't mean it.'

'I reckon he's so fucking mental at the moment, he does. I mean, he's missing and he left Mum that sad message. I heard her playing it, and I found the letter…' His voice trailed off.

'What letter?'

Tom stood very still and then reached into the inside pocket of his blazer. He handed Marion a note.

'I found it two days ago.'

She started to read it and then closed it. 'Did you show anyone this?'

He shook his head.

'Did your dad know you read it? Took it?'

Tom's face crumpled and he started to cry. 'I thought that if I kept the letter, he wouldn't do it. I thought he would forget it and make everything OK again.'

Marion went to him and held him. Even though he was taller than her, he was still her beloved grandson.

'I need to show the letter to your mum, OK? You're not in trouble, I promise.'

Marion held his hand and led him into the sitting room. She handed the letter to Clair, who started to read it and gasped.

The detective moved forwards, but she waved at him to stay away.

Marion looked at the detective. 'It's from Paul admitting his involvement. It says that he kept trying to plug a leak he couldn't fix. Every time he did so, it just became worse.'

The detective nodded and Clair finally handed it to him. 'I'll be back,' he said, leaving the room with the other police officer.

Sophie came in and sat next to Clair. 'What's happening?'

'Dad stole money from clients and now can't pay it back,' Tom said.

Marion sighed. 'I don't think he stole. I think things just got a bit out of control and he didn't know how to fix it. People panic under stress.'

Tom collapsed into an armchair. 'Do you think he will try to kill himself?'

'Tom!' Sophie cried.

'Well that's the fact of the matter, isn't it?'

Marion sat in the other chair. 'Don't be angry at him, Tom. He is in pain and making bad choices to try to get away from the shame he feels. Being angry won't help him or you.'

'Thank you, Mum,' said an exhausted-looking Clair.

'Dad told you to sell the house and you said over your dead body. Maybe it will be over his dead body now,' Tom shot at his mother.

'Wow,' said Sophie, her mouth open.

'Tom, stop it. Don't be cruel,' Clair said.

'It's true, Mum,' Tom said. 'Why am I the only one who is saying what the truth is here?' He glared at Sophie. 'You keep running away to Gran's house, but I'm the one here who had to listen to the fighting.'

Sophie looked down at her hands and Marion felt guilt wash over her.

'I should have been here for you,' Marion said to Clair.

Clair ran her hands through her hair. 'You had your own issues, Mum. You didn't need mine on top of them.'

Marion saw Sophie wipe tears from her cheeks with her hands.

'I should have sold the house when he said,' said Clair, almost to herself. 'It's just a house.'

The detective came back into the room.

'I have sent the picture over to Missing Persons and the police will remain outside in case he returns, but be reassured – there are people out there looking for him.'

Marion gave him a grateful smile.

'He might turn his phone back on, so if you want to send him a message to say everything will be OK, sometimes that works,' he said.

Clair grabbed her phone. 'OK, let's do that. Kids – you, too.'

Marion escorted the detective to the door.

'The silly thing is that it isn't a huge amount of money,' he said to Marion. 'Nothing that he couldn't solve if he sold the house and changed his lifestyle, but him running makes it worse than it is. I mean, there's very little in life that can't be managed, I've come to learn. There's a solution to every problem, just some people forget it when they need to hang on to it.'

40

Felicity

Oscar was already sitting inside the café when Felicity arrived.

'You're early,' she said, adding teasingly, 'You're never early, you OK?' Her friendship with Oscar was becoming as important as hers with Gabe.

'I am sooo excited,' he said as she put her bag down on the seat.

'Do you want a coffee?'

'Oat latte, please. Oh, and a slice of banana bread.'

Felicity placed their order with Gabe and returned to the table.

'So, what are you so excited about?' she asked.

'Well, there are two things.' Oscar opened his tote bag and pulled out Felicity's manuscript. 'This' – Oscar tapped the pages with a pink varnished nail – 'is fantastic. It's fast-paced, it's fun, it's sexy and it's modern, yet set in the 1800s. You're so talented to be able to pull this off.'

'Oh, you read it?' gasped Felicity.

It wasn't finished yet, but it wasn't far off. She had been writing during every spare moment, which was proving to be less time than normal, since she was now tutoring Rosie. Then there were the four tours a week she was running plus two shifts at the bookstore. She had never been happier.

'No, darling, I didn't read it,' Oscar said easily. 'I haven't read a book since I was twelve. But I sent it to my aunt, who's a literary agent. Those are her words I just quoted.' He leaned forwards across the table. 'She wants to see the rest, so when can you finish it?'

'An agent?' Felicity wasn't sure what this meant.

'Yes, they are like your manager. She will help you to secure a publishing deal – she knows everyone. She's also a massive bitch, which I love, so if she thought it was a pile of poo, she would have said so.'

'I don't know what to say. I mean, why would you do this for me? You didn't have to.'

'I know, but I think you're so clever and when you said you were writing a historical romance, I knew it wouldn't be like all the others, that it would be grounded in intellect and it would be fun.'

Gabe approached carrying their coffees and banana bread, placing them on the table.

'Have you asked her yet?' he said to Oscar.

'Asked me what?' she said, trying to gauge what it was they wanted from her.

Oscar spooned some sugar into his coffee and stirred. 'Well, Helen is moving to Bristol. She's got a job in a touring show of some musical, I can't remember what.'

'*Chitty Chitty Bang Bang*,' added Gabe.

'And that means—' Oscar started.

'We have a spare room,' finished Gabe.

Felicity's head moved from one to the other.

'I'm getting whiplash. Can one of you do the talking?'

Oscar nodded. 'Yes, I can.'

Gabe leaned forwards. 'So we're wondering if you wanted to move in with us?'

'Hey, you stole my line,' Oscar said.

'You want me to live with you?' asked Felicity.

'Yes, we do. We still have two more years on this course and we want to live with someone easy-going, cool and sensible.'

'Me?' Felicity asked again.

'Yes. I mean it's probably cheaper than where you are now and it's not as posh, but it will be fun. And we have Meryl Streep,' Oscar said.

Felicity had taken a liking to Meryl Streep, the cat, bringing her toys and fancy treats whenever she went over.

'Can I think about it?' she asked. 'I don't want to leave Marion in the lurch – she needs the income.'

'Of course. Helen's not moving out for another month, so take a few weeks,' said Gabe.

'And then say yes,' said Oscar.

Felicity smiled.

'I didn't think I would ever have friends like you two,' she said. 'Actually, I never imagined I would ever have friends at all.' She laughed.

Oscar made a sad face. 'That's pathetic. Snap out of it.'

Felicity burst into laughter. 'God, you are all business, aren't you?'

'And a little bit of showbiz,' Oscar added.

'I have to get back to work,' said Gabe. 'Come over tonight?'

'I can't. I have a book to finish!' said Felicity.

'Yes, don't annoy her,' said Oscar. 'She needs to finish this – she has an agent waiting.'

That afternoon, Felicity went home and found the house empty. Marion was still at Clair's, she assumed, wondering what had happened with Paul. She wouldn't pry, but she figured it was bad since it had been two days since Marion left.

But a quiet house was good house for writing, she thought as she set up her laptop at the kitchen table and turned on the kettle. As she took off her boots, she heard her phone ring. Picking it up, she saw her mother's name flash on screen and took a deep breath. It was never her on the line – it was always Gran.

'Hi, Gran,' she said.

'No, Felicity, it's Mum,' came her mother's voice.

'Is everything all right?' she asked, but her instinct told her it wasn't.

'It's Gran. She's had a stroke,' her mum said.

Felicity paused. 'A real stroke? Not one of Gran's attempts to bring me back to her?'

She could list on two hands the number of times her grandmother had weaponised her health to bring Felicity back into the fold. A heart flutter, a headache that could be a tumour, a sore back that was an indicator of some rare degenerative disease. They never amounted to anything, because Gran was so toxic she would probably live for ever, like lead or radioactive polonium.

'No, a real one, Felicity. She's in the stroke ward in Bristol. They said there isn't anything more they can do and I should prepare you for the worst so you can say goodbye.'

Felicity looked at her boots on the floor. 'She already said goodbye to me, Mum.'

Her mother said nothing.

'Do you want me to come?' Felicity asked.

'Yes,' came the reply.

'I'll leave now. I'll get the train.'

Felicity pulled her boots back on and picked up her bag. It was only a short train trip to Bristol, but she had the feeling it would feel like a lifetime.

★

The hospital smelled like antiseptic and Brussels sprouts, Felicity decided as she waited for her mum in the foyer. Not an ideal pairing on the best of days, today was not one of them.

Her mother emerged from the elevator and walked towards Felicity. She was paler than usual and thin, very thin. Felicity wasn't sure she had ever seen her mother look so dreadful and a wave of guilt washed over her for leaving her alone with Gran.

'Hello,' her mother said without any emotion. 'You'd better come up.'

Felicity was still undecided whether or not she believed about the severity of her grandmother's illness, but she walked through the hallways and past the other wards. Surely this was too much for her to pull off even by her grandmother's standards, she thought, looking at the other patients.

Her mother stopped outside a closed door. 'It's not easy to see her like this,' she said, preparing her.

Felicity nodded and her mother opened the door.

Her grandmother was lying on her back, oxygen clips on her nose and a monitor taking her vital signs. She was paler than the white sheets and her hair was spread across the pillow. This had to be real, because Gran would never let herself be seen like this.

Felicity leaned down and whispered in her ear.

'I forgive you,' she said, and she saw a tear fall from her grandmother's eye, but Felicity felt nothing.

Was it a sign she was a cruel person? Why didn't she feel anything?

She turned to her mother. 'OK, I'm going home.'

'Felicity!' her mother gasped.

And then Felicity remembered all the times she had cried in her room as a child after her grandmother had been so cruel to them both. Remembered how much she wished that her grandmother would love her mother. She would have given up the little love her grandmother showed her if her mother could have had it, believing perhaps the love would make her mother brave, brave enough to stand up for herself.

'I don't have anything left for her, Mum, I don't. And I can't pretend. I'm not good at pretending unless it's on the page.' She leaned forwards and kissed her mother's cheek. 'For what it's worth, I forgive you, too, for not standing up for me. But most of all, I forgive you for not standing up for yourself.'

'Why are you like this now, Felicity? At this time?' her mother whispered.

'Because I know what it's like to be free, Mum, and I hope, when Gran goes, you will, too. And when you do, you call me. But I'm telling you now – I won't come to the funeral and I won't pretend any more, not even for you.' She walked to the door. 'I love you, Mum. When you're ready to start your new chapter, I'll be there. But for now, I need to live mine.'

With that, Felicity stepped out of the room, her footsteps echoing down the sterile hospital corridor. Each step felt like a declaration of independence, a statement of who she was becoming. She was finally becoming the main character in her own life.

41

Marion

Clair sat on the sofa with a twin either side of her.

'We sent Dad a text saying we love him and everything will be OK,' Sophie said as Marion came into the room. 'He will read it and come home, I'm sure.'

Marion sat down and faced the three of them.

'I think it's bigger than that, darling,' she said gently.

'What do you mean? That's everything, isn't it – the love, I mean?' Clair snapped.

'It is everything. But then there are practicalities. The policeman told me that it wasn't a huge amount of money – well, it is – but it's not like he took the money and ran off to Barbados with it.'

Clair stared at her.

Marion took a deep breath and braced herself for what was coming.

'Things may very well change and be OK. But only if you all tell him you're prepared to change your lifestyle and make some changes. For example, sell the house.' She looked at Clair. Then the twins. 'And maybe change to a less expensive school,' she added, watching Sophie's face relax a little and Tom's eyes narrow in interest. 'And you, Clair, maybe you can get a job and give him some breathing room.'

Clair was silent for a moment. '*You* never had a job,' she said accusingly.

'I know, and I regret it every day, which is why I'm renting my bedrooms out to strangers. But I'm changing things. I am now taking a course in finance, and I have already found ways to save and have more control over my future. You can't keep your head in the sand, darling. The only way out of this is work, and being honest with yourself and others.'

Clair fell back on the sofa and closed her eyes.

'I haven't made it easy for him,' she said. 'I kept telling him all the things we needed, like holidays and new skis and the pool re-tiled, and now I don't care about any of it. It was just things to fill my days with.'

Marion was silent, letting Clair process aloud.

'I think after Dad lost your money, I was so desperate to hang on to ours that I forgot what it was that mattered. This is my fault.'

'No, I shouldn't have stopped rowing. He loved coming to see me row,' said Tom.

'That's OK. I think the rowing was something he could focus on,' Clair said.

'I should have been at home more,' Sophie added.

'No regrets, only forward movement,' said Marion. 'Now, text Paul as well and tell him you have a plan and all will be OK. Tell him he needs to come home. If he opens his phone, which he might well do, he will see it's not all so hopeless, because that's what he's feeling right now.'

Clair started to type as Sophie and Tom looked over her shoulder and added in their bits.

'And tell him I want to go to Castle College. I've already looked up the fees – just one term at Bath Grammar is the price of a whole year at Castle College, and Tom can go, too.

There are boys and they do sports and stuff there. Maybe not rowing, but they play tennis and lacrosse.'

Clair typed as though her life depended on it. In this case, perhaps Paul's did.

Marion held up her hand to the bickering twins.

'This is getting too complicated. He just needs to know we have this in hand and he doesn't need to worry. How's this?' she asked and started to read:

Paul, please come home. We have had a talk as a family. We can sell the house and then pay the money back. The kids want to change schools and I will get a job. We need to rethink our lives and as long as the four of us are together, then nothing else matters. We can solve anything, Paul, please know that. This is all fixable. Trust in us to make this better.

Marion looked around. 'Thoughts?'

'Send,' everyone said, and she did.

'And now we just have to hope he opens his phone,' Clair said.

Later that night, when Marion was lying in bed in Clair's spare room, she wondered why she hadn't pushed Clair more about Paul. Was this why they wanted Marion to sell Temple Terrace? Did Clair know?

As though reading her mind, Clair knocked softly at the door and entered, her thin frame backlit by the hall light.

'Hello, sweetie, any news?'

'No,' she said and paused. 'Can I hop in with you?'

Her voice reminded Marion of when Clair was seven and had had a bad dream.

'Yes, of course. Come and snuggle,' said Marion, and she pulled back the covers on the empty side of the bed.

Clair climbed in and started to cry.

'It will be OK, Clair. We can solve this whatever happens.' Marion stroked her daughter's hair as she spoke.

'It's not just that,' said Clair.

'You can tell me anything, Clair, you know that.'

Clair wept a little harder. 'I've been so awful, so judgemental about you.'

Marion continued stroking Clair's hair.

'And I think I was angry because you knew what to do. I could see something was wrong with Paul and the money, but I didn't know how to fix it.'

'It's OK,' said Marion, because it was OK. It was all solvable.

'I don't like change. Change scares the shit out of me,' said Clair. 'Change is things like Andy dying and Dad getting sick. Change is never anything good.'

'It can be, though. Having people living in my house has been an enormous change, but a good one. I have been revived and I have laughed and I have seen bravery and ingenuity.'

'I was jealous of them,' Clair said into Marion's shoulder.

'Why, darling?'

'Because you're the most capable person I know and you were giving it all to them and not to me.'

'I always have capable suggestions for you, Clair, you know that.'

'I know, I was being a child, an angry, bitchy child, and I need to apologise,' Clair said resolutely. 'I'm sorry, Mum.'

'That's OK and I'm sorry I wasn't more available.' She kissed her daughter's head.

'God, I hope Paul looks at his phone.'

'Me, too, darling,' she said to her girl. 'Try to sleep. Things will be better tomorrow if you've had some sleep.'

'Can you keep playing with my hair? It helps me relax,' she pleaded.

Marion smiled into the darkness.

'I will play with your hair all night if I have to, my lovely girl. Now close your eyes. It will be all right, whatever happens. I will be here.'

42

Lana

Lana parked outside the house and walked to the front door, nerves rising. She wondered if it was too soon.

Before she could let her nerves carry her back to her car, the front door opened and there was Alex. She held out a bunch of flowers and a bottle of wine.

'What's this?' he asked.

'I am wondering if you'd like to take me on a date?' she heard herself ask.

'What about Denny?' he asked, looking behind her. 'Is he planning on cutting down my box hedge or deflating my tyres – and with it, my love life?'

Lana burst into laughter. 'Denny is done. And I got my settlement offer from him. So I am now a happy little divorcee.'

'Oh, Lana, that's amazing! How?' he asked, pulling her into the house and kissing her.

'Well, let's just say I will need to replace those plants you got me for Temple Terrace.'

'Lana?'

She heard Rosie at the top of the stairs.

'You're back!' Rosie yelled.

'I am.' She smiled up at the girl.

'For good this time?'

'For as long as you'll have me,' she said to both of them.

Without another word, Alex pulled her into his arms and kissed her on her mouth.

'Eww, gross, get a room,' said Rosie, and then she was back in her room.

'So, what will you do now you have your settlement?' asked Alex. 'Travel the world, find a younger lover, buy a sports car?'

'I think that's Denny's plan,' she laughed. 'No, I think I might just stick around town and see what's on offer. And don't forget, I'm going to be an aunt! I have aunty duties.'

'Is aunty a word?'

'It is now.'

She sat on the sofa and Nana came and put her head on her lap for pats.

'I think I might buy somewhere to live. A little place somewhere.'

'You can live here.'

'Too soon. As much as I appreciate it, I would like my own place. I've always lived with someone. Be nice to get to know myself.'

Alex sat next to her. 'I think that's a great idea.'

'I'll have to tell Marion, though. She will be sad, but I am sure she will find someone to move in. It's a wonderful home.' She put her head on Alex's shoulder. 'I missed you.'

'And I you.' He kissed the top of her head.

'I've been thinking. I might actually enrol at Wiltshire College on the landscape design course.'

Alex grabbed her hand. 'I think that sounds amazing.'

'Yes, I did this course with this very sexy gardener who really helped me to understand what I wanted.'

'Oh, did he?'

'Yes, he did, so I figured I might as well go all the way.'

They both burst into laughter and he kissed her again, sliding down on the sofa until they were lying face to face.

'I love you, Lana Rolls.'

'And I love you, my gorgeous Alex.'

43

Marion

Marion's phone rang from a number she didn't recognise.

'Hello?' she said.

'Marion?'

'Paul, where are you?'

'I don't know. I remembered your number, though. I borrowed someone's phone.'

He started to cry, so Marion waved at Clair to catch her attention.

'It's Paul,' she mouthed, her hand over the phone. 'He doesn't know where he is. He's very upset.'

Clair took the phone and held it to her ear.

'Hello, darling. Everything is fine, I promise. We have to come and get you, though. Mum and I can come together, can't we, Mum? Where are you, darling?'

Marion admired her for being so calm and gentle. Paul was clearly having some sort of breakdown.

'I don't know,' he sobbed.

'Darling, put me through to the person whose phone this is, OK?'

'Hello?' came an elderly man's voice.

'Hi, that's my husband there. He's unwell and I need to come and get him. Can you tell me where you are?'

'We're in Worcester,' said the man.

'OK, I need you to stay with him or call the police, please. He's a danger to himself.'

The man paused. 'I was on my way to the library. I can meet you there.'

'The Hive?' asked Clair.

'That's the one.'

'Leaving now. Call this number if you have any problems.' Clair turned to Marion. 'Let's go.'

'Five minutes,' Marion said, and she picked up her phone and pressed a number. 'Arthur?'

'Marion, how are things? I've been worried.'

'We have found him, but he's in Worcester. It will take us a while to get there. Do you think you could ask your son to go and be with him until we arrive? I don't want any old bobby in a uniform upsetting him.'

'Where is he?'

'At The Hive. The man who found him is staying with him until I get there. I'll send you a picture of Paul in the meantime.'

'Thanks, leave it with me,' said Arthur.

Within moments, she had forwarded the photo and was on her way to Worcester in Clair's car.

'He's lucky that man was someone nice,' said Clair. 'But where is his car and phone?'

'Don't worry about that yet. Let's just get him home safely.'

'I think he will need to be admitted.'

They drove in silence for a bit.

'Who is this Arthur?' Clair asked finally.

'A friend. I met him in the financial class I'm taking. Lovely man, but we're just friends. He's a good sort – your dad would have liked him a lot.'

Clair glanced at her mother. 'I'm glad, Mum, really. You seem...' She paused. 'More confident lately.'

'I feel more confident. Knowing what is happening in your life gives you a tremendous sense of peace.'

Clair sighed. 'I have forgotten what that feels like.'

'We will find it again, I promise.'

Clair reached over and grabbed her mother's hand. 'I wish I had come to you sooner. You are always so good in a crisis. You have a way of making me feel things will turn out OK.'

'Because they will.'

'You think so?'

'I do. Even if they don't go the way you want, things work out eventually. I never thought I would survive after Andy died, but I did. And life was different, but there were still good things, like the twins. They're a beautiful part of my life now.'

Clair nodded. 'I know, I forget that sometimes. I feel like I've ruined everything.'

'Shh, that's not helpful to anyone to think that way and if you were to blame, I would tell you, you do know that?'

Clair gave a little laugh. 'I know you would.'

As they entered Worcester, Marion gave directions from the map on her phone.

'You're a whizz on that phone, Mum. I don't know anyone your age who can manage maps, apps and so on like you can.'

'You can thank the twins for my technology evolution. They refuse to have a grandparent who won't stay up to date.'

'Good for them,' said Clair as they arrived outside the library.

Clair parked in a 'no parking' spot and jumped from the car.

'You'll get a ticket,' Marion said.

'I'd rather a ticket than no husband,' said Clair, and she ran into the library.

Marion couldn't argue with that and she followed her inside. The library was designed to resemble a beehive.

Clair was looking for Paul, when Marion spotted him sitting with an elderly man in a raincoat and newsboy cap and a man in a suit, who she presumed to be Arthur's son.

'Clair, over here,' Marion called.

Paul was chewing on a sandwich. He was unshaven and was wearing a T-shirt and some trousers but no shoes. He was filthy and looked so tired that Marion privately thought hospital would be the right place for him.

'Hello, darling,' said Clair, crouching at his feet. 'How about you finish your sandwich and then come home with me and Mum?'

Paul didn't look at her but continued to chew slowly.

'He's had a rough time, hey?' said the older man.

Clair nodded. 'Yes, he has.'

'I seen blokes like him after the war. He needs to see someone.'

She nodded. 'Yes, we will take him to see someone now.'

Marion smiled at the man in the suit.

'Hi, I'm Dave, Arthur's son,' he said, and he shook Marion's hand. 'Paul's not in good shape. There's a warrant out for him, but I pretended I didn't see it. He needs a full psych eval first. I think going to a police station would make things worse right now.'

Marion sighed. 'Thank you, Dave, really, we are so grateful.'

Dave nodded. 'It's fine. Dad speaks very highly of you. I'm really glad he has a friend. Since Mum died, he's been very lonely.'

'Yes, he's a lovely man. We're both on the financial course for seniors at the library, did he mention that?'

Dave frowned. 'The financial course? No. Why is he doing that? He was a chartered accountant before he retired. Can spin straw into gold, to be honest. Financially, he's very savvy.'

Marion shook her head. 'I don't know, to be honest, but I have to think about Paul now.' She approached Paul and realised he needed a firm hand. 'Come on then, Paul. Finish that and say goodbye to the nice man. We have to head off,' she said gently.

Paul stood like a meek lamb, handed the man the crust and nodded. He took Marion's hand and let her lead him to the car, with Clair following, thanking the older gentleman.

Marion put him in the back seat of the car and then walked around to the driver's side.

'I'll drive. You call some places and see if you can get him in. He can't go home like this.'

Clair threw her the keys while Marion took a moment. This was the biggest car she had ever driven, but she was a confident driver and as she slowly pulled out of the parking spot, the thought occurred that it had plenty of airbags just in case.

As they drove the hour and a bit back to Bath, Marion saw that Paul was asleep, his head lolling back and forth.

'They can take him at Woodside,' Clair said eventually, after numerous calls to the GP and various clinics. 'It's in Bathwick.'

'OK, just give me the directions.'

'We'll drop him off and then I'll go and fetch a bag of things for him. Hopefully after some sleep and medication he'll be all right in a few days.'

Marion nodded but said nothing, because she didn't think Paul would be all right in a few days. Whatever had

283

happened had changed him, changed their whole family, but whatever that change was, she didn't think it was going to be all bad.

And this was change, she wanted to remind Clair. It wasn't death or endings, it was just change.

She also needed to find out what Arthur had been playing at.

44

Felicity

Crowds of people flocked around Felicity and Gabriel as they booked them onto the tour. Felicity even had her photo taken with some tourists, posing with a parasol in her new white dress that Denise had made her for summer. The tour was becoming so popular that Felicity was being mentioned in online reviews, including an iconic one that read:

> The guide, who could have come directly out of an Austen book, brought to life hilarious trivia and insight into past cultural norms in equal measure. You will be left appreciating how far you have come beyond the social structure of eons past.

'If that's the review you got as a tour guide, imagine what you'll get as an author,' Oscar said.

Felicity had sent him the book but he still hadn't had time to read it yet, so she'd stopped asking.

'Dress looks good,' said Gabriel, about to conduct another tour.

'Yes, Denise outdid herself,' Felicity said and looked down at her favourite dress.

It was made of fine, lightweight muslin, which draped beautifully and allowed for a gentle breeze from the River

Avon to keep Felicity cool. With its high empire waistline just below the bust, fitted bodice and sweet square neckline, it suited her well. The pretty lace around the neckline and pale blue satin ribbon around her waist added a touch of refined detail to the otherwise simple design.

The best part of the costume was the delicate parasol that Denise had found in a car boot sale. Easy to carry and light-weight, it had ivory-coloured silk stretched over a wooden frame. She could even use it as a pointer. Denise had added the same detail from the dress onto the edges of the parasol, its handle intricately carved with a floral design that made Felicity happy just to look at it.

Since she had been at Temple Terrace, she had started wearing less black and wool. Marion had taken her to the shop selling second-hand clothes, where Felicity had bought some jeans and a few pretty tops. She still wore her boots, but she was feeling less like she wanted to be invisible from the world.

'You ready to start?' asked Gabe. 'Or do you want me to, and you get their surnames?'

'You can start,' said Felicity, taking the iPad from Gabe.

They were a well-oiled machine now, knowing exactly what the other person was doing.

Felicity checked in some tourists from China and America and then turned towards a woman. It was her mother.

'Ruth,' she said. 'Ruth Booth.'

'Mum,' said Felicity. 'What are you doing here?'

Her mother looked better than Felicity had ever seen. She had had her hair cut shorter and she was wearing a little mascara and a denim jacket.

'You look amazing,' said Felicity.

'So do you. I love this on you.' Her mother touched Felicity's dress.

'Thank you, it is gorgeous. I'd better get to work, though. Can we get a coffee afterwards?'

Her mum nodded. 'I would like that very much.'

As Felicity went through the machinations of the tour, she might have given a little extra to the spiel theatrically, pausing a little longer when it came to using urine as a mouthwash for extra impact. She was pleased to see her mother engaged, laughing and even chatting to a few of the others.

Finally it was over and Felicity approached her mother with Gabriel in tow.

'Mum, this is my friend, Gabe. He and his boyfriend, Oscar, have been wonderful to me. Gabe was the one who got me the job here on the tour.'

Felicity waited to see what her mother would say, but she merely smiled at Gabe.

'Thank you for being such a great friend to Felicity,' she said.

'It's pretty easy when she's so amazing,' said Gabriel, his smile hesitant. 'I'm heading off,' he said to Felicity. 'I'll take the iPad with me.'

Felicity kissed his cheek. 'I'll call you later.'

Gabe made a face at Felicity behind her mother's back and mouthed WTF at her.

They made their way inside the Assembly Rooms, Felicity conscious of her Regency finest dress.

'You find us a table and I'll get the drinks in. Tea?' she asked.

Her mother always had tea, weak with a dash of milk.

Ruth squinted and looked at the drinks menu above the counter.

'I'll have an iced coffee, actually, with a scoop of ice cream.'

Felicity looked at her mother. 'Who are you and what have you done with my mother?'

Her mother gave a little laugh. 'Get our drinks and I'll tell you what happened.'

Felicity smoothed out her dress, leaning her parasol against her leg shortly after.

'I knew you wouldn't come to the funeral, so I didn't bother asking. Thought I'd save us both a lot of energy that could be used elsewhere,' said her mother in her small voice.

Felicity nodded. 'Good decision.'

Their drinks arrived and her mother pushed the ice cream down with her straw as Felicity watched it bounce up and down in the coffee.

'When Mother died,' her mother said, 'I thought I should have been sad — and I was in my own way. But then I saw the letters—'

'What letters?'

'When your father left us, he went on a work trip to South America. It was remote work, isolated. He was a civil engineer and he was clever, like you. He spoke Spanish, French and Italian and had his master's degree at twenty-five.'

Felicity had asked about her father her whole life, but her mother had never said anything and her grandmother refused to speak about him unless it included venomous bile, so Felicity had learned to stop asking.

'OK,' said Felicity carefully.

'Well, I found the letters he sent to me, asking for us to come to him, to join him in South America.'

'What do you mean, you found them? Gran told me he left us for another woman and moved to a foreign country. You know, for years I thought "Foreign Country" was a place and would look it up in the atlas. That's why I thought she said anything foreign was bad.'

Her mother sighed and nodded. 'I know. It was all such a mess. When I had you, I had terrible postnatal depression. Nothing you did – just my hormones. I was very unwell. Then your father went to South America. It was only supposed to be for a few weeks, but it ended up being months. Something to do with political unrest, where he couldn't leave for a while.'

'I never knew that,' Felicity said, trying to take it all in.

'And then I got a letter from him saying he was staying for ever. He said he had met someone else and she was pregnant. So I had a complete breakdown and ended up in hospital. Gran looked after you for months.'

'Oh, God, that's awful,' Felicity said, trying to decide which part was worse.

'When I came out, Mum had packed us up and moved us into hers. I was so frail and vulnerable, I let her take over.' She paused. 'My thinking at the time was that if my husband – your father – didn't want me, then I shouldn't have any say in my life, because I was surely worthless.'

She dunked her ice cream again and looked at Felicity.

'And then Mum died. She obviously didn't expect to die of a stroke and so quickly, because her affairs weren't in order.'

'How so?' Felicity poured the tea.

'It was a lie, all of it. She wrote him a letter allegedly from me stating that I didn't want him any more and that I had met someone else. He sent a return letter begging me to reconsider, which she never gave to me. Instead, she rewrote his letter, signing it on his behalf, put it back in the envelope, resealed it and pretended it was from him.'

'How do you know it wasn't from him?' Felicity asked.

'Because it was typed and everything else was handwritten, but I didn't pick it up at the time because I was so unwell.'

Her mother's face looked so pained that Felicity silently cursed her grandmother.

'But when I went through the house, I found all of his letters going back years. It seemed she had taken out a PO Box address and he had been sending them there. She had read them all, storing them in shoe boxes all this time. They were even in date order.'

Felicity gasped. 'What?'

Her mother nodded. 'I don't think she expected I would ever find them.'

Felicity shook her head. 'No, she knew you would find them when she died. She did that deliberately.'

Her mother looked up at her. 'You are most likely right. We both know only too well the strange cruelties of that woman. But right now, as I sit here across from my beautiful, clever, funny and brilliant daughter, I want to apologise to you. I should have done better as a parent. And I shouldn't have given up so easily.'

Felicity sat with her hands in her lap, thankful for the pungent scent of peppermint tea to remind her this was really happening and she wasn't in one of her daydreams.

'Jesus, Mum, that's fucking insane,' she said, clasping her hand over her mouth, waiting for the reprimand that didn't come.

'It is fucking insane,' said her mother. 'You wouldn't believe it if you read it in a book.'

Felicity shook her head, trying to make sense of it.

'Want to hear the even more dramatic ending?' Her mother paused for effect. 'Your dad is very much alive and is living in Argentina! I'm flying out to see him next month.'

'Are you serious?'

'Yes, I am. I'm selling Mum's house and I'm hoping you'll join me. Build some sort of reconnection with David.'

'Can I have some time to process this, please?'

'Of course. I'm not saying we will all be one happy family again, but neither David nor I have been with anyone else. He told me he's been following you on social media. He's so proud of you.'

That was the final straw for Felicity and she started to cry.

'Why didn't he call me? Or message me on social media or send an email?'

Tears fell from her mother's eyes. 'Because Gran was so awful. Her very marrow was poisoned. Anyone who came into contact with her was either infected or they stayed as far away as possible.'

'Her marrow was poisoned,' said Felicity. 'That's a perfect way to describe her. But you know, I don't want to talk about her. She has taken enough from us, not including time,' Felicity said.

'I agree.'

'I want to tell you all about my new life now, Mum. Because for the first time, I'm really proud of both it and myself.'

Her mother leaned forwards. 'Tell me everything, my beautiful girl.'

45

Marion

Marion stood at the kitchen sink, her hands submerged in soapy water as she washed up after their study session. The late-afternoon sun cast long shadows across the lemon-yellow walls, highlighting the worn edges of the kitchen. They had been studying for the course and Marion still hadn't confronted Arthur about him pretending he was financially illiterate. Arthur was drying the mismatched china alongside her, carefully placing each piece back on the crowded pine dresser.

'Arthur?' Marion began, her voice steady but with an undercurrent of accusation. 'I was chatting with Dave when I picked up Paul that day and he mentioned something rather interesting about you.'

Arthur's hand paused mid-air, a delicate teacup suspended between the tea towel and the dresser shelf.

'Oh?' he said, his tone carefully neutral.

Marion turned to face him, wiping her hands on her apron. 'He said you used to be an accountant. A rather successful one at that.'

The teacup clinked softly as Arthur set it down, his shoulders sagging slightly. 'Ah, yes. I suppose the cat's out of the bag, then.'

'Why didn't you tell me?' Marion asked, leaning against

the sink. 'All this time, I've been struggling with compound interest and tax deductions, and you've known it all along?'

Arthur turned to her, his expression a mixture of sheepishness and sincerity. 'I didn't mean to deceive you, Marion. It's just … well, it's been a lonely few years since Carol passed. When I saw the advert for Meera's class, I thought it might be a good way to meet people. To make friends.'

Marion's expression softened, but she pressed on. 'But why pretend to struggle with the material? Why let me explain things that you already knew?'

Arthur smiled gently, picking up another teacup to dry. 'Because watching you learn, seeing your confidence grow week by week – it's been a joy, Marion. Your enthusiasm is infectious. And, well, I found I rather liked being your study partner.'

Marion felt her irritation ebbing, replaced by a warmth that had nothing to do with the gentle heat emanating from the Aga. She moved to the table, sinking into one of the chairs.

'You could have just asked to be friends, you know,' she said, a hint of amusement creeping into her voice.

Arthur chuckled, hanging the tea towel on its hook. 'At our age? Feels a bit like being back in school, doesn't it? "Will you be my friend?" It's not that simple any more. To make a friend, someone has to be brave and I think I forgot how to do that at my age, so it felt easier just to ease myself into a place where the stakes weren't so high. In enrolling, I thought at least I might meet a few people to go for coffee and so on, but with you, I found genuine friendship.'

Marion considered this, her eyes wandering over the familiar kitchen: the lemon-shaped tea cosy, the vase of roses from the garden on the windowsill, the faded script on the kitchen island. This room had seen so many changes, so many new beginnings.

'Well,' she said finally, a smile tugging at her lips, 'I suppose I can forgive you. On one condition.'

Arthur raised an eyebrow. 'And what's that?'

'You help my daughter, Clair, and her husband, Paul, with their money troubles. Things are pretty terrible, from what I can gather. She needs someone impartial to look at the situation and help her to find a way out, deal with the money he took and so on.'

Arthur nodded, suddenly seemingly aware of the enormity of what she had just asked him. 'It would be my pleasure, Marion. Worrying about money and your children is terrible, so let me help Clair until she can help herself.'

Marion felt her eyes sting and she felt a surge of affection for her new friend. Yes, he had deceived her, but his heart had been in the right place. And really, wasn't that what friendship was all about? Accepting each other, flaws and all?

'Thank you, Arthur. I mean that with every fibre of my being. Thank you.'

That evening, Marion told Lana and Felicity the depths of the situation.

'Oh, Marion, what a terrible time,' said Lana as she poured the three of them a glass of wine each.

Lana had laid out a lovely spread of picky bits to eat, including cheeses and dips and olives and all their favourite things. Picky dinners had become an easy favourite for the ladies of Temple Terrace and since they hadn't seen each other for over a week, this was the perfect catch-up.

'It was terrible,' said Marion. 'But also grounding. Arthur is going to help them with their banking and the finances. I'm taking him to her house tomorrow and then to Paul's office to see the extent of things. She needs to understand it and Arthur is a good teacher, despite his fibs to me.'

Lana laughed. 'Men are so dumb sometimes, even old ones. They underestimate women and overestimate themselves. How did he possibly think you wouldn't find out?'

Marion shrugged. 'I think he's just insecure. I told him that friendships require one person to be brave and that telling porky pies wouldn't help to create good connections – or something along those lines.'

Lana shuddered. 'Porky pies? I thought Denny was here for a moment.'

'Sorry,' Marion said and put her hand on Lana's arm. 'Lies. Porky pies was an old Geoffrey saying. Don't worry, I won't use rhyming slang again.'

'No, it's fine. I'm just still sensitive to him and his rubbish.'

'How long will Paul be in there?' asked Felicity, popping an olive into her mouth.

'No idea. As long as it takes. But Clair is putting the house on the market next week.'

'That's quick,' said Felicity.

'It will take a while to sell. It's a big, fancy house and only those with big, fancy money can afford it. There aren't as many of them as one would think.' Marion turned to Felicity. 'And how are you? What's happening with you? Anything new?'

Felicity thought for a moment. 'Not much,' she shrugged.

Marion ate a piece of cheese.

'Oh, except Oscar, Gabe's boyfriend, sent my manuscript to his aunt who is an agent. Apparently, she likes it and wants to work on it with me to get it ready for submission.'

'Oh my God, Felicity, you never said a thing!' exclaimed Lana.

'I haven't seen you.' She laughed. 'Oh, and my gran died

and I found out my dad is still around. Seems my grandmother blocked him out of our lives and lied to us all these years.'

'Oh my God!' It was Marion's turn to exclaim. She put her glass down. 'When?'

'Which part?' Felicity asked.

'All of it,' Lana said.

'Gran died two weeks ago,' she said.

'How?' Lana asked, shaking her head.

'A stroke. Probably blamed it on me as it was happening.' Felicity sighed.

'Did you say goodbye to her?' asked Lana.

'Sort of,' said Felicity. 'I went and saw her and told her I forgive her.'

'Ouch,' said Marion. 'I don't know whether to be impressed, terrified of you or to tell you off.'

Felicity took a sip of her wine. 'Be none of them. That woman hated me and she hated my mum, because we weren't completely controllable. She didn't want to be a mother and she reminded Mum of it every moment of her life until she broke her.'

Lana and Marion were silent.

'So I don't owe Gran anything and I told Mum I wouldn't go to Gran's funeral. I don't think she ended up having one for her. No one would have gone anyway. She was truly the most unlikeable woman.'

'I must say, I didn't warm to her,' Marion admitted. 'She asked me why I had so many foreign things in the sitting room.'

'Because of the rug?' Lana asked.

'No, the mugs with the squiggles on them. I did tell her they were from John Lewis, but she refused to believe me. Said they were Egyptian.'

Felicity gave a hollow laugh.

'So, it seems my dad is alive and in South America. Mum is selling Gran's house and going out there to meet him.'

'Are you going?' asked Lana.

Felicity shook her head. 'No, I will meet him later. Right now, he and Mum have to work things out – there's a lot of pain there. I hope she finds her way through this.'

'She will,' said Marion. 'She asked me if you were OK and happy that time she came over with your grandmother. She seemed worried, but I told her you were fabulous and clever and independent. She said she was glad you were here but not to tell you she asked after you as she didn't want it getting back to your grandmother.'

'I'm so happy to hear that,' said Felicity. 'I think she will be OK, too. She just needs to get out from the being controlled mindset.'

'You're so right,' said Lana. 'It was the same for me.' She paused and she looked between them. 'Actually, I've decided I'm going to buy myself a little place when my settlement comes in. So ...' She paused. 'So I'll be moving out in the next few months.' She burst into tears. 'I don't want to but I do. And I wanted to say thank you to you both for being such wonderful housemates and friends. I couldn't have wished for better than this.'

Marion felt her eyes prick and she blinked furiously. 'You girls have made me young again. You made me brave and strong and capable. I forgot how for a while. But I couldn't have handled what's happened with Paul without the backing of you girls.'

'What about me?' cried Felicity. 'I left my course, wrote a book, got a job as a tour guide and a tutor ... *and*, I have actual real friends. Well, I haven't quite finished the book yet, but it's close.'

'Yes, hurry up and finish,' said Lana. 'I'm dying to read it.'

'Speaking of friends,' said Felicity, 'And I don't want you to think everyone is leaving you, Marion, because I love living here, but Oscar and Gabe have asked me to move in with them. Their housemate is moving out and I really like the house they're living in. Then there's their cat Meryl Streep – I adore her.'

Marion grabbed Felicity's hand. 'Go with God, my darling. I want this for you. This whole fun youth thing, do it, have a ball.'

'Well, it won't be for a month or so, as Helen has to move out first, but she's going after she's organised.'

The women sat in silence for a moment.

'So I guess you'll have to find new room-mates, Marion,' Lana said.

Marion sighed. 'I think I might just know who might want to move in.'

46

Marion

The pristine white kitchen of Clair and Paul's home felt cold and sterile, a stark contrast to the warm, lived-in charm of Temple Terrace, Marion thought as she sat at the sleek granite island, her hands wrapped around a mug of tea, long gone cold. Across from her, Clair perched on the edge of a bar stool, her face etched with worry. Arthur occupied the third stool, a spread of papers and Paul's work laptop before him on the worktop, his brow furrowed in concentration.

Clair broke the tense silence.

'So, Arthur, now that you've gone through everything, can you tell me exactly how bad it is?'

Arthur looked up, removing his reading glasses with a sigh. 'Well, Clair, I'm afraid it's as serious as you feared. The amount Paul misappropriated from his clients, plus the legal fees, comes to just over £500,000.'

Marion reached out to take her daughter's hand. Clair squeezed it, her grip tight.

'Right,' Clair said, her voice steadier than Marion anticipated. 'So, selling the house is definitely our only option?'

Arthur nodded gravely. 'I'm afraid so. But the good news is, in this market, the sale should cover both the debt and the legal fees, with perhaps a small amount left over.'

Clair took a deep breath. 'How much do I need to earn to support the family and start rebuilding our finances?'

Arthur shuffled some papers. 'Yes, I've run the numbers. Your mother said you were interested in becoming an estate agent? If you can secure a position in that, and earn around £50,000 a year with commission, and adhere to a strict budgeting plan, you could be back on your feet in five to seven years.'

Marion watched her daughter carefully. There was a determined set to Clair's jaw that she hadn't seen in years.

'Five to seven years,' Clair repeated softly. Then she straightened her shoulders. 'Well, it's not ideal, but it's doable. I've already started looking into getting my licence.'

Marion felt a surge of pride. 'That's wonderful, darling. You've always had an eye for property.'

Arthur nodded approvingly. 'It's a smart move. The real estate market in Bath is robust. With your local knowledge and connections, you could do quite well. You will have to rent somewhere less expensive once the house sells.'

'And the children?' Marion asked gently.

Clair's face fell slightly. 'I've told them we'll be moving and that they'll be changing schools. They're … adjusting to the idea. Sophie's taking it better than Tom, but they're both being braver than I could have hoped.'

As if on cue, they heard the front door open and the twins' voices drifting down the hall. Moments later, Sophie and Tom appeared in the kitchen doorway.

'Hi, Mum. Hi, Gran,' Sophie said, her eyes darting between the adults. 'Is everything OK?'

Clair managed a small smile. 'We're just working out some details with Gran's friend, Arthur, who is very clever with money. Why don't you and Tom grab a snack and start on your homework? I'll be up to chat more in a bit.'

As the twins rummaged in the fridge, Marion marvelled at her daughter's composure. This was a side of Clair she hadn't seen in a long time: resilient, practical, determined.

Once the children had gone upstairs, Arthur began gathering his papers.

'I'll draw up a detailed financial plan for you, Clair. It won't be easy, but based on what I've seen today, I believe you're up for the challenge.'

Clair nodded, a glimmer of determination in her eyes. 'Thank you, Arthur. For everything.'

As Arthur packed his briefcase, Marion stood and wrapped her arms around her daughter.

'I'm so proud of you, darling,' she whispered. 'We'll get through this together, one day at a time.'

Clair returned the hug fiercely. 'One day at a time,' she repeated, her voice stronger now.

As they pulled apart, Marion saw a new resolve in her daughter's eyes. Yes, there were hard times ahead, but for the first time in years, she felt truly hopeful about Clair's future. This crisis, painful as it was, might just be the making of her daughter.

A week later, Clair was making meatballs in the kitchen when Marion arrived.

'Come in,' Claire said. 'Do me a favour and pull up my sleeve. I'm getting mince everywhere.'

Marion obliged as Sophie came in to show off her new uniform.

'Gee, that was quick,' she said to Clair, referring to the new school. 'You got her in right away?'

'Yes, and under the circumstances, the grammar isn't charging us the early termination fee, so we can start afresh with no monies owed.'

'How is Tom about it?' asked Marion.

'Tom is fine,' said Tom as he walked into the kitchen and hugged Marion. 'Hello, Gran. You seem shorter.'

'It's because I'm crumbling under the weight of being responsible for you.'

He laughed and cut a slice of Parmesan cheese from the block on the worktop.

'Don't pick at it, grate it,' Clair said. 'Well, the house is on the market. I just have to hope it sells. And I'll have to find us somewhere to rent for a while. I don't think we will get back onto the housing market again,' Clair continued, her tone more accepting than disappointed. 'Arthur put me in touch with an old client of his who owns the biggest estate agents in Bath. He said he can help me to find a place to rent and I can start as a property manager with them while studying for my licence.'

Tom started to grate the cheese as Sophie filled a pan with water for the pasta.

'That's fantastic,' said Marion. ' But what about, instead of renting a place ...' She paused as three sets of eyes locked on her. 'What if you all move into Temple Terrace?'

Nobody moved.

'Lana and Felicity are moving out and the house is far too big for me now. And I was thinking, I could even move into the library – turn that into my bedroom. And there is that small bathroom downstairs for me to use. That's all I need. I don't like the stairs anyway.

'Then you three can have the upstairs floor and when Paul gets out of hospital, he has a safe place to be. Plus, he won't be alone if you're out working, Clair. And it's close to the school.'

'Mum—' said Clair, putting her hands in the meatball mix, sleeves and all.

'I know you probably don't want to live with your mother, but you wouldn't have to pay rent and we can split the bills. We can be a big family again.'

Clair started to cry. 'You know what? I really want to do this,' she said to the twins, who were jumping up and down. 'Are you sure?' she asked her mother.

Marion laughed. 'I can't think of anything I want more. That house will be yours one day and it deserves a family, so come home and let's look after it and each other for as long as we can.'

Clair took her hands out of the meatball mix and washed them in the sink, crying and laughing at the same time. When her hands were finally clean, she embraced her mum tightly.

'I love you, Mum,' she whispered in her ear.

'I love you, too, darling.'

After dinner, which was a very loud sort of meal, with ideas being thrown out about which bedrooms the twins would have, it was decided they would have the rooms where Lana and Felicity were staying, and Clair and Paul would have Marion's room.

'But there are so many books to go through if we're going to get the library ready to be a bedroom,' said Clair.

'I know! I will have to go through them and get an antiquarian bookseller to assess their value. You never know, there might be some money in those shelves.'

Clair laughed. 'Dad's taste was pretty broad. Surely there can't be many who want books about the ancient fossils of Kenya or the gardens of Babylon?'

'You never know,' said Marion. 'He was a man of mystery and delighted in unusual topics.'

The children helped to clear up before going upstairs.

Marion looked at Clair. 'How is Paul?

He had been in the clinic for a few weeks and Clair still hadn't seen him, but she spoke to his doctor every day. They kept saying he wasn't ready yet.

'He's doing better, they said. He's on new medication, but apparently he is talking more. He can now recognise that something happened, but he can't quite put all the pieces together yet.'

Marion sighed. 'Such a tough illness to navigate. Anyway, changing the subject, you will have to work out what you want to bring with you from here.'

She looked around at all the lovely furniture and art. Clair had made it into a show home. It was as good as any decorator could have managed.

'This stuff?' Clair looked around. 'I'm selling it.'

'Selling it?'

'Yes, we don't need any of it now, especially if we move in with you. I mean, I'll keep my bed and linens and so on – practical things – but all the rest? I'm putting it up for auction. I was going to downsize anyway, but now I can get rid of it all.'

'I am shocked,' said Marion. 'But also very proud of you.'

'You know,' said Clair, leaning forwards, 'the real estate agent asked me if I could make one of their houses look like this one. I thought I might take a few bits from here, perhaps move some furniture around and put some new paintings on the wall. They'll pay me.' She leaned back, looking proud.

'You would be fantastic at that.'

'Yes, they call it a home stylist,' Clair said, taking a sip of her wine. 'I can do it as a side hustle while I'm studying for my licence.'

'Well, you certainly have great taste,' said Marion.

'I do,' Clair said, smiling smugly as she raised her glass. 'I got it from my mother.'

47

Lana

'So, you want the books stacked according to topic on the table?' Lana checked as she stood at the top of the ladder.

Felicity was standing below her, ready to accept those that were about to be handed to her. The room had that musty scent that wafted from aged pages that some love and that makes others sneeze.

'That's right,' said Felicity. 'I have got a pile here on architecture and art, another for heraldry, with gardens of the world over here, but I can't reach the top on that ladder.'

Lana pulled out a book. 'Ancient cartography?' she said slowly.

'Old maps.'

'God, we have Google Maps now, people,' Lana said, handing the book to Felicity, who turned it upside down and ran her fingers through the pages like the strings on a harp. 'What are you doing?'

'Checking that nothing has been left in the pages. I see it all the time at the university bookstore with second-hand books. People leave notes, shopping lists, all sorts. Even a few pound notes sometimes.'

'A few pounds would be nice,' laughed Lana.

It was planned that Clair and the twins would move in in two months, which gave time for Marion to sort the library, have some cupboards built in and get some removal firms to bring her bedroom furniture downstairs. The bathroom was fairly piddly and if she'd had the funds, she could have opened up a wall and gone into the small storage room to create an ensuite, but she didn't have that sort of money. Lana had offered to lend it to her, but Marion said she was too old to start having debts. She would make do. As long as Clair and the family were safe then she didn't mind where she showered.

'Oared warships?' Lana read from the ladder.

'Military and navy,' said Marion.

Felicity put it in the pile as Lana read out, '*The Real Story of Kenya.*'

'African pile,' said Marion. 'It's hard to let go of those books. Geoffrey loved Kenya so much.'

Felicity took the book and opened the front cover, about to put it on the table. She went to run her hand through it, when something dropped out.

'Marion?' she said.

Marion looked up from the books she was sorting. 'Yes?'

'You need to see this.'

Marion moved some books that were blocking the view and looked at what Felicity was standing over.

Lana climbed down from the ladder and looked over Felicity's shoulder. 'Oh my God.'

Marion looked down at the book and saw the inside had been carefully cut out. Inside the hole in the middle of the pages were stacks of fifty-pound notes.

'What on earth?' Marion said.

Lana climbed up the ladder and grabbed another book. '*Kenyan Cooking,*' she said and opened it.

'Shit, more money.' She handed it to Felicity.

Lana started pulling all the books about Africa and Kenya

off the shelves, and there were a lot of them. They ran all along the top shelf that spanned two walls. And in every one was the same cut-out section with a large amount of notes.

As Lana took down the books, Felicity removed the cash and handed it to Marion, who had to sit down. Thousands of pounds littered the table and it was still coming. The notes were all new, as though Geoffrey had asked the bank for new notes. Perhaps he had, she thought, and she started to cry.

'Oh, Marion, it's a lot to get your head around,' said Felicity as she came and sat next to her at the table.

Marion shook her head. 'All this time I said he had sent his money to Africa, but he was actually hiding it here, in books on Africa. He said he always felt safest in Kenya and he wanted to go back there again. I suppose this was his way of trying to make sure the money was safe, in his muddled, broken brain.'

Lana was counting the money. 'There is about two hundred thousand pounds here, all in fifty-pound notes.'

Marion shook her head once more. 'I don't think I could ever have imagined he would have done this with the money. All this time, it was right here, in the library.'

She picked up her phone and texted Clair to come over when she could. Then she sat and stared at the pile of money.

'You know, I would still prefer Geoffrey to be here right now, well and happy,' she said.

'Of course you would,' said Lana. 'But he didn't leave you completely high and dry. I think he thought he was looking after you, in his own way.'

Marion nodded.

'Was there more than this that was missing?' asked Felicity.

'I don't know. I don't think so. He took out all the cash. He was planning on investing it before he became sick. We were never wealthy, but we were comfortable. We always had enough.'

Lana picked up a wad of notes. 'I think you will be very comfortable now, and you can get your bathroom.'

Marion made a cheeky face at Lana. 'You know, you're right. I *would* like a nice bathroom if I'm to live downstairs.'

'And you deserve it,' said Lana.

Felicity was going through the rest of the books, when the doorbell rang.

'That will be Clair,' said Marion, and she went to let her daughter in.

'You OK, Mum? I was going to see Paul when I got your message. They said I can see him today.' Clair leaned forwards and kissed her mother on the cheek.

'That's wonderful news, darling. Yes, I'm fine, but I need you to see something.' She led Clair into the library, to Felicity and Lana and the stacks of books.

'Hi,' Clair said to the women. 'I wanted to apologise for my behaviour the last time I saw you. I'm not usually such a monster. Although all evidence would prove to the contrary.'

Felicity and Lana smiled.

'Don't worry about it,' said Lana. 'We aren't always our best selves when under pressure.'

'Clair, I need you to listen to me for a moment, darling,' Marion said. 'You know how your father said he put the money from the savings account into Africa?'

Clair nodded, seemingly relieved at Lana's swift forgiveness.

'Well, we worked out today that he put it into African books, literally,' she said, and moved a stack out of the way, revealing all the money on the table.

Clair's jaw dropped. 'You are joking,' she said slowly, processing what was in front of her.

'Nope,' Felicity said. She opened a book and showed Clair

where Geoffrey had cut out one of the hiding places for the money.

'Mum, this is amazing – and also really sad,' said Clair, and she started to cry. 'Poor Dad. He must have been so confused, and yet, it's all here.' She put her arms around her mother. 'Well, it's all yours now, Mum, so what will you do with it?'

Marion sighed. 'I think I will talk to a very good retired accountant I know and see if I can afford to get a fabulous bathroom and wardrobes to match, if you can help me choose? As for the rest, I will live on it until I pop my clogs.'

'I couldn't think of anything I would like to help with more,' said Clair, hugging her mum. 'You know, you were right. It does all work out for the best. I've just heard we have a rich international family viewing the house tomorrow. They have asked if they can buy the place fully furnished, art, pot plants, the lot. Even the cutlery.'

Felicity looked at Lana. 'People with money are crazy, I've decided.'

'I know, they bloody are,' Lana laughed.

'OK, I have to run and see Paul. I'll come by with the kids later. We can do chippy tea, your treat,' said Clair, and then she was gone, the door clicking pleasantly behind her.

'The bloody nerve of her,' joked Marion. 'Does she think I just have cash lying around for fish and chip dinners?'

48

Marion

Three months later...

Marion swept the yellow wisteria leaves from the path every morning so people didn't slip. She was still first to rise in the house and she liked being outside in the morning. The twins would kiss her good morning on their way to school, shouting at each other as they went to catch the bus. Letting them take the bus had been a big step for Clair, but now she couldn't believe the freedom it gave her, especially since she was working full time.

After their house was sold – with everything in it – they moved into Temple Terrace in a flurry of suitcases and chaos. Paul had paid back his clients their money and wasn't charged thanks to Arthur, a good lawyer and some strong letters from his mental health team at the clinic. Marion's bedroom and bathroom were finished after Clair project-managed the whole process and Marion couldn't have been happier.

Clair emerged through the front door not long after the twins.

'Morning, Mum,' she said. 'I'm off to Bristol. Got a house there that needs my help. I tell you, people just don't understand how important staging is in a property.' She shook her head and pulled her coat around her.

'Lucky they have you, then,' said Marion.

Clair nodded. 'I know,' she laughed before giving a little wave and rushing off to her new sensible hatchback that used barely half the fuel of her old one.

Clair had taken on her lifestyle changes like an evangelist, even telling the children that they had to get part-time jobs, use the library instead of buying new, and to shop second-hand. She had sold more than half of her clothes to the Second Act shop and was reinventing herself again, in jeans and trendy trainers with fun jumpers.

Marion swept the final few leaves into the gutter and went back into the house. She put the broom away and looked outside. Paul was checking the plants Lana and Alex had given her that Paul had planted under Alex's guidance. He spent a lot of time outside now, gardening and walking the new puppy that Clair and Marion had got the twins. The sixteen-week Cavalier King Charles named Loki was a one-man dog. He loved Paul more than anyone else in the house. Paul pretended he didn't want Loki, but he always seemed to have him on his lap or chasing behind at his feet.

'You ready?' she called to Paul.

'Coming. I'll just put Loki's harness on him.'

Marion applied a little lipstick in her new bathroom and brushed her hair. She was letting it grow out a little and it felt nice having hair around her neck. Not to mention that Sophie and Rosie, who were now best friends, had told her it was cool to have longer grey hair.

Marion pulled on her walking coat and waited by the front door. Paul and Loki came soon after.

'Keys?' he asked.

She jangled them at him.

'Right, let's go,' he said, the door locking satisfyingly behind them. 'Long way or short way?'

'Long way,' she said, and they started their daily walk to the bakery.

They would chat about nothing and everything on these walks and Marion had begun to discover a man she hadn't known before. Paul was hurt, yes, but he wasn't broken now. His recovery was slow, but he took his time – it wasn't a race – taking comfortable walks with Marion to the bakery, where they would share a pastry and have a coffee each while Loki sniffed around the table for crumbs.

The slower life suited Paul. Marion thought it suited everyone, but sometimes people didn't understand how important it was until they were forced. Forced to be present, to take stock and see what really mattered. Paul had discovered that he liked to potter in the garden and he liked to cook – and he was good at it. He also liked to watch reality TV shows with Sophie and Marion, the three of them separating narcissists from sociopaths.

'Not everyone can be a narcissist,' Sophie reminded him.

'No, but not everyone wants to be on the telly, only narcissists.'

How they had laughed.

'If you don't slow down then your body will slow you down,' she remembered hearing. It had always stayed with her.

It didn't matter if Paul went back to work or not. He was safe and healing at Temple Terrace, and Marion was happy to have everyone under her roof.

'You home tonight?' asked Paul after a silence. 'I'm making a tagine. I saw the recipe in *BBC Good Food* – it looks good. It's got dried apricots in it.'

'Sounds lovely, but I'm having dinner with Lana and Felicity,' she said as they skirted a group of tourists.

'How are they?'

'Wonderful.'

She saw them every fortnight for dinner and it was always a new restaurant or at Lana's. She had her own place now, although she was always round at Alex's. Felicity was happy living with Gabe and Oscar, and she had nearly finished the book. Her mother had been round theirs a few times, even spending time with the boys and Meryl Streep.

Time was a healer, thought Marion, but honesty was even better. The more truthful everyone had been over the past six months, the more things had turned out in their favour. And it also applied to herself, she thought.

'How's Arthur?' he asked as they walked.

'He's well. We're heading off to Cornwell next month. Going to stay at a nice little B & B I found, do some Cornwall things. He's such a terrific friend.'

'He's been very helpful to me and Clair. I'm grateful to him.'

The two walked over the Avon river and into a little park, where they let Loki off his lead to chase some birds.

'This is nice, isn't it?' said Marion, more to herself than to Paul.

He put his arm around her shoulders and pulled her close.

'I don't think I would be here without you, Marion.'

She wasn't sure what to say. Paul had been complicit in coming to Temple Terrace and had gone along with all of Clair's plans. He had given up control at the clinic, realising that he had no control over anything except how he responded to things. He had spoken to Clair, but he had never expressly said anything like this to Marion before.

'Well, it wasn't just me. It was your wife and the kids, too,' she reminded him.

But he shook his head. 'No, it was you. You helped Clair to see what needed to be done. You looked after the twins, you looked after me and you have given us a home.' He stared ahead at Loki playing on the grass.

'We're family. We do what we must to keep each other going.'

'Not every family has that or wants that,' he said.

She knew he was speaking of his own family, who he didn't speak to often. She doubted they even knew of the troubles he'd faced.

Loki was racing around and Paul clapped for the dog's attention and he came running.

He turned to Marion. 'If you had said to me six months ago that I would be living in Temple Terrace, planning a chicken tagine for dinner after having a walk and coffee with my mother-in-law ... well, I would have told you that you were barking mad.

'You know what? These little outings of ours every morning, they're one of the things I look forward to when I wake each morning. Each morning, I wish that my children would be happier, that my wife loves her work. And that I have a silly puppy who follows me around and who I adore.'

At his words, Loki started to bark at them both.

'Oh, I am barking mad,' laughed Marion, speaking to the puppy.

'Why is that?' Paul asked as he clipped the lead onto Loki's harness.

'Because I truly believe – and I believe it because I've seen it – that things always turn out for the best if you just stop trying to control the outcome. Let it flow and allow life to work out for you the way it's meant to. Perhaps you were always meant to be cooking a tagine and walking the dog, it's just that you were told or you told yourself otherwise.'

They walked in silence for a while.

'When Andy died, Clair and I had just started seeing each other,' he said.

'Yes.' Marion nodded.

'And her pain, it was unbearable to witness, so I started to buy her things. I didn't know how to make it better, so I just bought her *things*, expensive things, and it seemed to take the sadness away for a while.'

Marion was silent.

'And then I came to believe that that's how I made things better, so I kept doing it, but the things became more expensive. I couldn't keep up.'

'Did she ask for those things, though?' asked Marion as the bakery came into sight.

Paul gave a rueful laugh. 'That's the thing. She never did. She thought I wanted them and I thought she wanted them. Then suddenly we had this life neither of us wanted.'

Marion sighed. 'It can happen,' she said, thinking of Lana.

'And I know she will be thrilled that I've made dinner tonight, when we'll sit chatting about the property she's working on. Tom and I will talk about him starting his photography course at school and Sophie will work on teaching Loki tricks with me. And all that, that's better than anything I could buy any of them.'

Marion put her hand on his arm. 'Yes, but it's also down to you. You're the glue in that whole scenario. Without you, none of it would happen, so you're the magic there, Paul.'

He stood outside the bakery and she could tell he was welling.

'Get us a seat and I'll order,' she said, and she went inside to look at the pastries.

'Morning, Nisha, one pain au chocolat and an almond croissant, please,' she said to the girl who served her most days. 'And two lattes.'

'Morning, Marion. I'll bring them out,' Nisha replied, so Marion went back and sat in the sunshine.

'This is the last of the sun, I think, before autumn really kicks in.'

Paul nodded. 'I think I might get a raised vegetable garden.'

'That sounds like a good idea.'

'You wouldn't mind? It's not really part of the sort of Georgian garden Geoffrey liked.'

Marion laughed. 'Well, Geoffrey is dead and I like veg, so plant away.'

'I'll pop over to Alex's nursery after this, then. He said he has one for me, a display one. Said he'll give it to me for nothing.'

'Wonderful,' said Marion as their coffees and pastries were brought out to them. 'It all sounds absolutely wonderful.'

49

Marion

One year later...

Marion laid out her favourite china on the kitchen table. A whole year had passed, a year full of challenges, triumphs, and the unbreakable bonds of friendship and love. Even the wisteria had buds on its vines again at the front of Temple Terrace. Everything was budding, it seemed.

Lana had now moved in with Rosie and Alex and Nana the dog, and she was in her first year studying landscape design at Wiltshire College. She loved it and she was good at it. It seemed she had a natural sense when it came to putting plant combinations together that she didn't know she had.

Felicity, too, had undergone a remarkable transformation. With her grandmother's passing and the revelation of her father's true fate, she was encouraged by Gabe and Oscar to meet him. It had been a turning point, as her father was a genuinely brilliant man who worked as a writer, engineer and translator and who owned a little café in Buenos Aires. What was supposed to be a two-week trip ended up being a month and she promised she would be back for six months the following year to write a new book. Oscar's aunt, the literary agent, was happy with the work Felicity had done on her first book and was ready to send it out to publishers.

And her mother? Well, let's just say she was busy in

Buenos Aires serving coffees and making up for lost time with David.

As for Marion, life had taken an unexpected but wonderful turn. With Clair, Paul and the twins now living at Temple Terrace, the house was once again filled with the laughter and the love of a family. She had a great friendship with Arthur and had reconnected with some old friends from when she was with Geoffrey. She even went to the theatre and out to lunch on occasion, but she always did her budgeting at the end of the week with Clair and they stuck to it religiously.

'Nothing you buy will feel as good as financial peace of mind,' Arthur once said. He was right. So much so that Clair had printed it out and stuck it on the fridge.

But perhaps the most remarkable change of all had been the one within Marion herself. Through the love and support of her housemates, family and the friends she'd met on her course, she had rediscovered a sense of purpose and joy that she thought she had lost forever. She was smart and good with money, something she never knew about herself, and she had learned to embrace change, to open her heart to new possibilities and people, and to cherish the precious moments that made life worth living.

As Marion sat in the kitchen waiting for her guests, she was excited at the prospect of seeing her old housemates. The house was quiet, as Paul and Clair and the twins had gone on holiday to Spain. Not a fancy Four Seasons holiday but a cheap and cheerful one – and by the looks of the photos coming back, it was a success.

Marion knew that the story of Temple Terrace was far from over. There would be new challenges to face, new joys to celebrate and new memories to cherish. But no matter what the future held, one thing was certain: the love and friendship that had been nurtured within these walls would always endure.

The sound of the doorbell made her jump.

'Hello, ladies! Come on down,' she said. 'I have champagne and the dinner of all dinners planned.' She gestured to the table, which was laden with an enormous grazing platter.

'Picky bits!' they both cried out in excitement.

She poured them all champagne in her best French crystal flutes and they raised them to the ceiling.

'To the ladies of Temple Terrace,' she said. 'And to the incredible journey that brought us all together.'

The three women clinked glasses, their laughter echoing through the hall of the grand old house and ringing out into the garden.

'Now, I have a favour to ask you both,' said Lana.

The other two leaned in and Lana extended her left hand.

'I'm getting cut and carried, and I want you two to be my bridesmaids.'

'Cut and carried?' Felicity asked.

Marion jumped up from her chair. 'She's getting married!' she cried and threw her arms around Lana.

Felicity cheered and the three women hugged.

'You used rhyming slang,' Felicity finally said.

'I know, but I'm so over Denny and it's a good saying. Seemed perfect for the moment.' Lana laughed.

'I love it,' Felicity said. 'Now, tell me, how did he propose? I do love a good love story.'

'I'm too old to be a bridesmaid,' said Marion.

'You're my matron of honour,' said Lana, and she kissed Marion on the cheek. 'You know how much I adore you, Marion, don't you?'

The women hugged again.

'And I you. You two have been the most wonderful lights

in a dark time and without you, I don't know where I would be,' said Marion.

Lana and Felicity looked at each other.

'And you to us, Marion. You are the safe harbour we needed. And this beautiful house ... well, it's the perfect place.'

Marion smiled, reaching out to take each of their hands.

'It's funny, isn't it?' she said. 'Bath has always been a place of healing. People have been coming here for centuries to "take the waters" and find restoration. And here we are, finding our own kind of healing right here in this old house.'

'It's like the house itself has healing powers,' Felicity mused.

Lana chuckled. 'Don't forget the garden. There's something about getting your hands in the soil that just ... sets things right in your soul.'

Marion squeezed their hands. 'You're both right. This house ... it's seen so much life, so much joy and sorrow. And now it's helping us to write our own stories of renewal.'

The three women fell silent for a moment, each lost in their own thoughts, the gentle tick of the kitchen clock the only sound.

Finally, Lana spoke up, her voice bright with emotion.

'Well, I propose a toast.' She reached for her champagne flute, raising it high. 'To Temple Terrace, our very own healing spring of friendship.'

Acknowledgements

Thank you to my editor, Rhea Kurien, for her North Star-like directions on the book; to Sanah Ahmed, for guiding the ship into harbour in much better shape than it started and to the Hachette crew, who have been super responsive, helpful and lovely to work with.

Thank you to my agent, Tara Wynne — always a rock, always fun to work with, always returns my calls. Thank you to the Curtis Brown Australia team, who keep things moving along for me.